FICTION
Lyons
Lyons, Andrew.

Darkness in him /

DARKNESS IN HIM

Darkness in Him

Andrew Lyons

ST. MARTIN'S PRESS   NEW YORK

www.stmartins.com

Library of Congress Cataloging-in-Publication Data

Lyons, Andrew.
    Darkness in him / Andrew Lyons.—1st ed.
        p. cm.
    ISBN 0-312-30146-4
        1. Saint Louis (Mo.)—Fiction. 2. College students—Fiction. 3. Accident victims—Fiction. 4. Pregnant women—Fiction. I. Title.

PS3612.Y57 D37 2003
813'.6—dc21
                                                                2002033283

First Edition: January 2003

10 9 8 7 6 5 4 3 2 1

To my parents, whose love and support helped me believe
my dreams could become reality

ACKNOWLEDGMENTS

I cannot appropriately thank everyone who played a role in the development of this book. But rest assured, all the people I mention here put themselves out in one way or another. In many cases they did so for no other reason than to help, with no expectation of anything in return. I am grateful to them all. Many thanks to those who helped me navigate the tricky waters of the publishing world: Joel Gotler, Noah Lukeman, Justin Manask, Jennifer Weis, Joanna Jacobs, George Witte, Sally Richardson, Peter Grossman, Sabrina Johnson, Jeff Davidson, Ron Weschler, Tony Ludwig, Alan Riche, and Patsy Nichols. Special thanks go to Danny Llewelyn and Megan Karasch, both of whom got the ball rolling.

Valuable research assistance came from Dale Eastman at Point to Point Travel, the staff of the North-American Inter-fraternity Conference, as well as Rob MacPhee. I am indebted to Alisha Lyons, Judi Sherman-Wolin, Eric Cohen, Kamy Wi-coff, Kristen Reardon, Ron Mills, Scott Mantz, the McMullens, Scott and Melanie Bomar, Melissa Pervel, and Kristy Paige.

Each provided encouragement and support when they were desperately needed. Danny Brassell, Danielle Zeitlen, and Celeste Kearsley offered the same, as well as valuable early feedback and constructive suggestions.

Finally, very special thanks to four people. Dr. Roger Lyons provided invaluable medical expertise. Barbara Lyons helped unearth crucial research information. They also conceived me, so thanks for that. Keith Ferguson served as a bottomless well of enthusiasm and a great sounding board during every stage of the process. And finally, to Jay Lyons, my little brother, the jack of all trades who served as an early editor, a legal resource, a human primer on publishing, and most of all, a good friend whose counsel I could always trust.

DARKNESS IN HIM

CHAPTER ONE

Do you ever stop for a moment to take stock of your life? You know, do you ever look at where you are and wonder about whether it's where you thought you'd be at that point? I have an older cousin who once told me when I was about five that I should spend all the time I could with him while I had the chance. He said that by the time I was a teenager he would be so rich and famous that he wouldn't have any time left for me. When I reached thirteen, he was a mechanic at a garage. Now I'm twenty-two years old and he's the assistant manager at an auto parts shop.

I know a guy at school who says he wants to be a millionaire by the time he hits thirty. An old girlfriend of mine once told me that she wanted to be married and pregnant with her second child by age twenty-five. We were sixteen when she made the announcement. My friend Rick told me that he wanted to know how to play every Eric Clapton song on guitar by the time we graduated from college. I think he may have actually achieved his goal.

I was born in 1978. So that meant that one of the most important milestones in my lifetime would be when the calendar switched from the year 1999 to the year 2000. When I was little, I figured out that I would be twenty-one when that happened, almost certainly a senior in college and probably well on my way to knowing where my life was headed. I would know what job I wanted, who I wanted to spend my life with, and what kind of person I was. That milestone came a few months ago. And as I look back on my childhood prediction, I'm amazed at how close I came to guessing right. That is, until recently.

The events that changed my life actually occurred before the calendar switched over. It was mid-December of last year and finals were finished. My fraternity at Jefferson University in St. Louis was throwing an end of the semester bash to ring in the new year and (some claimed) the new millennium. The theme of the party was "the future." It wasn't very original but it allowed everyone to wear goofy outfits and claim they were the styles of tomorrow. It also allowed a bunch of lazy frat boys to put tinfoil all over the walls and say they had given the house a futuristic look.

I was running late for the party. I knew I was going to get hammered so at the last second I decided to leave the car and walk the twenty minutes from my apartment in Delmar to the house on the row. I lived off campus in a place with my aforementioned buddy, Rick. He wasn't in the fraternity but I had known him since freshman year and I preferred living with him to having some one-bedroom bunk-bed hole in the frat house. The only downside to living in an off-campus apartment was that, while it was within walking distance of school, it was not in the best neighborhood, which became more obvious at night.

So I was a little nervous as I moved along the snow-covered sidewalks. I'd also done some preparty drinking with Rick, so

I had to walk slower than I liked to avoid slipping. More than once, coming home sloshed from a party, I had fallen on the icy walk and nearly cracked my head open. That combination of factors led me to arrive at the party just after ten, even though I had promised to make it by nine-thirty to help supervise the bar.

My fraternity house was on what was called fraternity row. There were eight houses on the row. Most had been built many years before and were starting to fall apart. My house, Kappa Omega, was the second one on the row. That is, it was the second closest to the academic buildings and intramural fields. When I arrived, the party was well under way. I could hear the music from a quarter mile away and by the time I stood outside the front door I felt like I was at a live concert.

The front courtyard (really just a cement square) was full of people milling about, pretending to talk about anything other than the fact that this was the last big party of the semester and how they wanted to get laid. I looked up to see people hanging out of several of the second- and third-floor bedroom windows. One of them screamed something unintelligible at me. I smiled and waved, as if I had a clue what he said.

One of the pledges stood at the front door, guarding it, preventing too many of the wrong element (any guy who wasn't a brother) from getting in. I was a senior brother who was well respected within the house, so he let me in immediately. He even seemed to bow slightly. I stepped inside and, despite my skepticism about my fellow Kappa Omegs' collective creativity, I had to admit I was impressed. The tinfoil looked very convincing. The addition of a strobe light, three hundred sweaty, dancing people in costumes, and general drunkenness made "the future" seem a little less ridiculous than it had in the abstract.

I pushed my way through the throng of overinebriated underclassmen to get to the keg. Two more freshman pledges saw me and immediately filled up two cups full of Schaefer Light (the beverage of champions), easy on the head. I took a sip from one. I was already under the influence of my preparty extravaganza back at the apartment so I felt no need to chug.

I looked around, hoping to spot my girlfriend, Jordan. We had agreed to hook up at ten and it was a little past that right now. After a few seconds I gave up. There were just too many people in a confined space for me to see much of anything. The main level of the house had been converted into one big dance floor with the bar in the back right corner. I decided to try to make my way to the stairwell in the back left corner of the room. It led to the basement as well as the second and third floors. I thought that Jordan might be looking for me on one of those levels at that very moment.

I tried to get to the stairs while causing as little trouble as possible, doing my best to avoid banging into the couples that were grinding to Seal's "Crazy." Right in the center of the room, I ran into Dan Curson. Dan was a brother. We were both seniors and although we weren't great friends, we were cordial. Dan was very drunk. He gave me a big hug, then asked if I'd seen his girlfriend, Kelly. I told him I hadn't. Apparently, the two of them had gotten into another of their seemingly countless fights. She had accused him of flirting with another girl, which he probably had. But since he was toasted, he was in self-righteous mode, going off on how there was nothing wrong with talking up another girl. The violation was fucking that other girl.

I considered debating that point, but decided against it. Dan wasn't the kind of guy to get into a philosophical discussion, not in class, not over late-night coffee, and certainly not at a raucous party. I let it go, told Dan I would let him know if I saw Kelly, then continued on the search for my own girlfriend. I finally reached the stairwell. It was so crowded that I had to wait at the bottom for a few minutes just to let things clear out. I finished my first beer and was halfway through the second when I realized that to get back to the keg and refill I would have to negotiate that mess of a dance floor all over again.

Unless . . . I remembered that one of the brothers, Kevin

(Kevie Poo to his friends, for reasons I can't remember), had a massive stash of liquor in a discreet place in his closet. That was my new destination. Finally, the stairs cleared out. I was halfway up to the second floor when I ran into Evan Grunier, still another brother, who was on the way down. He was also a senior. I was not a big fan. Evan was funny, a good student and very activities-oriented. He was also decent looking if you could ignore his squinty eyes. Just the kind of guy who would make a good brother, right?

Well, he was also an asshole. He had a real mean streak. His jokes were funny but almost always at someone's expense. It didn't surprise me that once he got into Kappa Omega he always managed to be the one who came up with the most unpleasant, cruel ways to torture the new pledges. He was an all-around jerk. Luckily, since I was very well liked, and could be a sarcastic bastard if I had to be, he didn't mess with me too much. He even seemed slightly intimidated by me, which I have to admit I kind of liked.

"Have you seen Jordan around?" I asked him.

"No, but I've been upstairs most of the night," he said.

"I'm gonna check the other floors. If you run into her, will you tell her I'm looking for her?"

"Sure, Jake. Of course, if I run into her, I may just have to steal her away from you. That is one damn fine woman you've got yourself. Why she ever decided you were good enough for her is beyond me."

"Thanks for the vote of confidence, Evan. You're a prince among pricks. I'm going upstairs now to look for that 'damn fine woman.' You behave yourself while I'm gone."

"I make no promises," Evan warned me with a wicked grin on his face. I just nodded, suddenly weary of him and his smirky quips.

I made my way up to the second floor. There were about ten bedrooms on that level, as well as the main bathroom. For parties, it served as the public restroom for guests. I poked my head in and called out to Jordan just in case she was in one of the stalls. There wasn't any answer but there was a stench so foul that I doubted any female guest would even consider using the facilities. That was another reason I was glad I didn't live in the house. I was not a clean freak by any measure, but this place was constantly enveloped in the unsettling aroma of refuse and unflushed toilets.

I caught a glimpse of myself in the mirror. Despite the smell, I couldn't help but give myself a quick once-over. I looked pretty good. Even through the alcohol haze, my blue eyes appeared alert. The windy trip over had messed up my dark brown hair a little but I left it alone. I liked it.

Despite my atrocious eating and drinking habits, I managed to keep in good shape. I was lucky to be tall and have fairly broad shoulders. But if it weren't for pickup basketball games and the obligatory weight-room trips, I would have gone to pot by now.

My second beer was now just a memory so I headed up to the third floor. It was possible that Jordan had gone in search of a clean bathroom up there. Even if I couldn't find her, that was where Kevie Poo's room, and more important, his stash, were. I knocked on his door to allow him to hide anything more hardcore than alcohol from view, then entered. Kevie and three girls I had seen around campus but did not know were sitting in a circle, sharing a bong. Apparently Kevie wasn't concerned about the authorities.

After introductions were made, I walked over to the closet and, without permission, proceeded to pull out a bottle of rum and a two-liter Coke. I filled up a big (probably thirty-two ounce) plastic cup. Kevie asked if I wanted to join him and the girls, but I passed. I had to find *my* girl. I stepped back out into the hall and tried to think.

The drinks I had downed back at the apartment with Rick had fully kicked in and the Schaefer was doing its job as well. The hallway began to sway slightly. It took me a moment to realize that it was actually me swaying. I tried to compose myself and come up with a plan of action. It was now ten-thirty.

Jordan had agreed to meet me at ten and she was rarely late. I decided to head back down to the main room.

As I rounded the corner, I discovered that I had a good view of the entire dance floor from my elevated spot. It didn't take me long to find her. She was standing near the door, talking to Evan. Her back was against the wall and Evan was uncomfortably close. She looked trapped. Every few seconds, she glanced around, as if she was in desperate need of an escape but didn't want to be outright rude and make a dash for it. I decided to help her out. I pushed my way through the crowd as quickly as I could without knocking people over. As I got closer, she glanced in my direction, saw me coming and betrayed a relieved smile.

I picked up the pace. I didn't want her to be uncomfortable for one second longer than was necessary. Despite her uneasiness, Jordan still looked great. Most people wouldn't have even picked up on how awkward she felt at that moment. We'd been going out for over a year and a half and I still sometimes had trouble telling when she was unhappy. She always looked so cool and collected.

Part of that was a result of her being almost unacceptably cute. She had shoulder-length hair that could best be described as somewhere between light red and strawberry blond. Her complexion was fairly pale and you could always tell when she'd been out in the sun because even if she protected herself against burning, she would freckle, especially on her nose.

She was of average height, about five-foot-six with an athletic build. She rarely wore revealing clothes so you wouldn't notice it at first glance, but she had an amazing, trim, sexy body. Tonight she had decided to share a bit of her perfection with the world. She was wearing a tight, black shoulder-baring dress that hugged every one of her magnificent curves. I usually found myself attracted to more voluptuous, full-bodied women than Jordan, but there was just something about the way everything fit together on her that made me lustful even after nineteen months together.

There was no question that she was an attractive girl, but there were lots of attractive girls at my school. A few other things set Jordan apart from all of them. First, there was her smile. She had one of those ear to ear, Julia Roberts–style grins that can light up small cities. Some people have said (for reasons beyond my comprehension) that they don't like Julia Roberts's smile. I have never heard anyone say they don't like Jordan's. When she breaks into a laugh, and you catch those pearly whites and know that you're the reason she's happy . . . well, there's not a better, warmer feeling in the world. And she has these incredibly friendly brown eyes that could make even the most hateful person consider starting a love-in.

And then you get to know her. Obviously none of the traits I mentioned above would have the same impact if the person who possessed them was cruel or self-involved. Amazingly, Jordan is one of the least cruel or self-involved people I have ever met. She's the kind of girl who makes even the most awkward, insecure, geeky person feel good when she's talking to them. She oozes goodwill.

Evan, the person she was currently forced to talk to, needed none of her qualities to help build up his confidence. There was nothing insecure about him. I wondered as I reached them if it was possible for her sweetness to rub off on him and wear away a little of *his* cruelty and self-involvement. I doubted it.

"Hey babe," I said, interrupting whatever Evan was saying as I put my arm around her shoulder, "I was getting a little worried about you. I thought we were gonna hook up at ten."

"We were," she agreed, "but Joanie started puking on the way over and we had to take her back to the suite. It was *very* unpleasant."

"Thank you for that vivid description. I see Evan's been taking care of you while I wandered the upstairs halls in my search for you. Ev, did you let her know I was looking for her?"

"I was about to get to that," Evan lied, "I was just telling Jordan about what a bitch our Con Law class was this semester."

"And I was just telling Evan that I hear you complain about it often enough that I don't need to hear it from him, too," Jordan said. She sounded pleasant but I knew that this did not bode well. My nervousness about my grade in Con Law (and in Business Law as well as Government Philosophies) had been a source of friction between us the last few weeks. The last thing I wanted to do at the final party of the semester was remind my girlfriend that she was annoyed with me.

"Yeah, let's not bore each other with talk of classes and grades," I said, trying to change the subject.

"And bitchy professors," Evan added, refusing to comply, "can you believe what a vindictive slut that Professor Sheridan is? I cannot stand her."

"That's nice talk," Jordan said.

"You know what, Ev? I think I'm gonna take my girl and get reacquainted if you don't mind. We can talk about Sheridan later, okay?"

Without waiting to hear his response, I grabbed Jordan by the hand and led her through the crowd to the stairs. We hurried down past the back exit to the basement. Most of that level was composed of the dining room (or slop room, as it was affectionately referred to). About twenty people were hanging out. There was a private brothers' keg down here and it was being used to full effect. I led Jordan into the adjoining pool room. It was even more crowded. I stopped for a second to let my brain catch up to my body. Jordan watched me with amusement.

"What's the plan, Fearless Leader?" she asked with something less than reverence in her voice.

I glanced around. Then I noticed the swinging doors that led from the slop room to the kitchen. I pushed them open. There was no one in there. I wandered around the corner and poked my head into the pantry. No one in there either. I waved for Jordan, who was still hovering by the swinging doors, to join me. She made her way toward me, acting as if she was humoring me by doing my bidding.

When she got close, I grabbed her and pulled her into the pantry. She pretended to be shocked by my aggressiveness. I pushed her against one of the shelves. I thought I was pretty careful but the force of her body hitting the wood caused a bag of flour to fall off the shelf and split open as it hit the ground. White powder rose up in a mist, covering my jeans and her black skirt.

"It looks like you'll have to change out of that thing," I told her, as I began to pull the dress up toward her waist.

"Fresh!" she said, feigning indignation, as she slapped my face teasingly.

"I'm sorry ma'am," I said as I took a sip of my rum and Coke, "but I can't help it. You make me feel very naughty."

"Put that thing down," she ordered, pointing at my plastic cup, "you might spill it and you smell like a distillery as it is."

I did as I was told. Then, I grabbed her and gave her the long deep kiss I'd been planning to plant on her since I saw her on the dance floor. That took a while. Afterward she pushed me away. I took a step back and watched as she began to pull her dress back up just as I had tried to do earlier. I moved to the pantry door and started to pull it shut.

"Leave it open," she said, "and come over here."

I did as I was told.

CHAPTER TWO

We lay on the floor of the pantry, using unexploded flour bags as pillows, listening to the throbbing bass of "Groove Is in the Heart," as it pulsated through the floorboards above us. For a futuristic party, we sure were playing a lot of older stuff. While I was still incredibly drunk, and now covered in flour, I was also lying next to the woman I loved. That made me a happy camper.

"I'm going to miss you over winter break," I told her, "I don't know if I can stand being away from you for a month."

"Absence makes the heart grow fonder."

"Not when we're talking about you. You should have an amendment to that rule—closeness makes the heart grow fonder." I knew I sounded cheesy but I didn't care.

"Then how come you don't want to be close to me during break? You could have come on this cruise with my family. They love you. They wanted you to come."

"I know, and I wanted to come, too. But I have that interview for the summer internship. If I don't get it, I'm screwed and this is the only time they would see me. I told you that."

"Jake, how come every time you want us to do something special, like go camping in the mountains or go to Texas for your parents' anniversary, I do it? But when I suggest something that requires a little sacrifice on your part, you can't do it."

"These interviews are important to my future."

"Yeah, well going to Paris for two weeks for that art history program was important to my future, but I decided that being there for your parents was important to *our* future."

"I didn't force you to come. You offered."

"Because I knew how much it meant to you. And I'm glad I went. It was wonderful to be there. But I'm always the one going here and there and doing this and that. I can't remember the last time you gave up doing anything law-related for something that was important to me."

"You're not being fair. You know that any time I pass something up, it means someone like Evan Grunier is a little closer to getting it."

"So what?"

"So what?" I repeated, "How can you ask so what? If you understand me at all, you know why so what."

"What terrible thing could possibly have happened if you went to my brother's first show instead of attending that seminar with old Professor What's-His-Ass?"

"Professor Millicent is the foremost authority in the United States on death penalty precedent."

"Yeah, and it was my brother's very first professional show. He sold four pieces. You'd think he'd be happy, but he kept asking where you were. You promised you would go, Jake. You lied."

"I didn't lie. The situation changed. It was Fred Millicent."

"He was giving another fucking death penalty seminar three weeks later. You could have gone then. My brother only had his first show once."

"My dad pulled strings to get me into the first one. I couldn't say no."

"You could have told him you had a prior commitment."

"Told my dad that?"

"Yes."

"You're kidding, right?"

"Listen to yourself, Jake. You are so intimidated by that man. I cannot tell you how sick I am of hearing how you have to get the right grade, the right LSAT score, the right internship. It never ends. Then there's the right law school, the right specialty, the right firm. You are never going to do enough things "right" to make him happy. Why don't you try to do a few things that make you happy?"

I didn't know what to say to that. As it turned out, I didn't have to say anything. She wasn't done.

"And while you're at it, maybe you could do a few things to try to make me happy. You turn up your nose every time I even mention one of my classes. I know art is not the most exciting thing in the world to you, but I love it, so don't you think you could at least express an interest?"

"I am interested," I said.

"No you're not. But that's not even the worst of it. You know what the worst thing is? It's the way you treat me when you're caught up in the goddamn law thing. You're so indifferent to me when you've got anything even slightly intense going on. Then, when your load is lighter, you're Mr. Affection. Like tonight, you couldn't wait to get me down here now that finals are over. But if you had a test tomorrow, it wouldn't matter if I was leaving for a year starting this evening, you wouldn't take me to the airport. I don't even know if you'd call to say good-bye. When it comes to us, you are so selfish."

She stopped talking and took a deep breath. Her eyes were brimming with tears. I was torn. Part of me wanted to take her and hold her in my arms and tell her how sorry I was. But another, more vocal part of me was pissed. For the last two minutes she had pretty much attacked everything that was important to me. And she had done it tonight, when we were supposed to be having a good time. This was not the night to throw all that shit at me. I was tired. I was confused. And I was seriously drunk. It wasn't like I was going to be able to have a meaningful discussion about our future together in my current condition.

But she didn't give a shit about any of that. All that mattered to her was that I was selfish and that I didn't love art. Of course that wasn't exactly what she said, but at the time, with my brain at half power, that's how it sounded to me. In retrospect, I should have kept my mouth shut or just left. But I didn't.

"If I'm so fucking terrible, then why the hell are you with me?" I demanded. "Why would you want to spend your time with someone who's all about selfishness and grades and trying to make his family proud? Why did you even come here tonight if that's how you felt?"

"I've been wondering that myself," she said, getting up from the flour-covered floor. "I guess I thought maybe you'd say something or do something to convince me that I should stay, that it's worth all the crap. But you don't seem interested in doing that."

"Do you want me to beg you to stay? Do you think I'm going to do that? You drop this bomb of bitterness on me out of nowhere and you expect me to take it in stride?"

"No, but I thought you'd at least acknowledge what I'm saying is true and be willing—wait, actually *want* to do something about it." She was standing at the pantry door now. I held up a hand for her to stop.

"Listen, Jordan. I love you. I want to be with you. I want to wake up with you every morning and go to sleep with you every night. You are everything to me." I paused for a minute to catch my breath. Jordan, thinking I was through, started to move toward me. But I wasn't finished.

"But if you think that I'm selfish and that I don't care about what's important to you, well then maybe you should find someone else, someone who won't challenge you, who'll just make it easy. Maybe we're just not right for each other. You seem to think we're not."

"You are being such an asshole right now," she said through her tears.

I couldn't stop. "Maybe your Mr. Right is upstairs at this moment, flipping through a textbook about Botticelli."

For a few seconds, she just stared at me like she didn't recognize me. I think she was stunned. She hadn't seen me this way before. I had never been this way before. After what seemed like an eternity, she spoke.

"Good luck with your interview. I hope you get the internship." Then she walked out. I could hear her heels on the linoleum floor as she left the kitchen. But soon the noise from the music above drowned her out. I lay back down on the pantry floor, not entirely sure what had just happened. After a few minutes in which my mind simply refused to operate, I managed to sit up. The plastic cup of rum and Coke stood patiently next to me. It was still half full. I picked it up and began to chug.

When I got back up to the main floor, the room was even rowdier than when Jordan and I had left. I made a token attempt to find her, but not surprisingly, she wasn't around. My cup was now empty and I stumbled to the keg in the back corner, in desperate need of a refill. I pushed my way past the freshman girls and the pledges who were trying to impress them with their now–improved social status. I tried to work the keg but kept coming up with a foamy concoction that wouldn't do at all. Eventually I told a pledge to do the honors and to go easy on the head or else.

He looked startled. My comment was unexpected because I was not one of those brothers who traditionally threatened pledges. I had a reputation for being pretty easygoing, the kind of guy who you could come to if you had a problem, not the kind of guy who would cause the problem. But I was a brother nonetheless. So the pledge poured me a beer and made sure that it had as little foam as possible. I hadn't intended to sound so menacing but I was in no mood to apologize.

I took my thirty-two ounce beer and wandered into the fray. It took me a second to realize that I didn't have any idea where I wanted to go. I wasn't looking for Jordan. My best friend in the house, Jeff, had flown home earlier in the afternoon and there was no one else among the hundreds of revelers at this party that I really wanted to talk to. As I stood in the middle of the dance floor, totally clueless as to my next move, Kevie bumped into me.

"You look about six sheets to the wind," he yelled at me, his own bloodshot eyes reflecting something less than the picture of sobriety.

"I'm a tad drunk," I screamed back over the propulsive beat of Sugar Ray's "Fly."

"Do you want to crash in my room?" he asked. "You look like you could use a little break."

"No, I'm cool," I said, giving him what I hoped was my most reassuring face. He nodded, more in ambivalence than acceptance, and disappeared into the multitude.

I took a moment to gather myself and decided to go outside for a minute to get a breath of fresh air. It took a while so that by the time I actually reached the realm of the outdoors, I had worked up quite a sweat. I stepped outside into the chilly St. Louis evening, which managed to dry my perspiration in seconds. I wandered over to a bench at the far end of the concrete courtyard and sat down.

The song changed. Len's "Steal My Sunshine" was now blasting into the Missouri evening. But there was something else mixed in. The sound was sobbing. It was not part of the song I realized, but a person, somewhere nearby. I looked around. Finally I saw her. Hiding in the shadows along the wall of the house was a girl, crying uncontrollably.

I got up and walked over to her. When I got close enough, I realized that it was Kelly Stone, the girlfriend of my fraternity brother, Dan Curson. She was also in Jordan's sorority, Delta Theta. She was covering her face, which was pointless since her sobbing was what had drawn me there in the first place.

"What's wrong, Kelly?" I asked.

"Nothing."

"You're standing outside of a raging party, in the freezing cold, bawling, and you're telling me nothing's wrong. Come on, just tell. You can trust me."

Kelly looked up at me. Her mascara had smeared so that long blue streaks ran down her face. She looked like she'd had a lot to drink, too. Even in that condition, Kelly Stone was one of the hotter girls on campus. She was a senior, planning to graduate with a degree in sociology. She was one of those rare girls at Jefferson University who could have posed for *Playboy* in one of their college pictorials.

She was a perfect example of the voluptuous type that I usually went for—brunette with a large chest and huge, full hips that looked like they could handle just about anything. She had piercing blue eyes that led you to believe there was a lot going on behind them. There wasn't. She was in my Baby Bio class this semester (with two hundred other science-challenged students) and I'd heard a few of her questions for the professor. If they were any indication of her intellect, she was lucky to be in college at all.

Dan had been going out with her since sophomore year and there had been talk around the house that he was going to ask her to marry him soon. Clearly, that plan had gone awry. I suspected that whatever had upset Kelly had something to do with Dan's inappropriate flirting.

"What did he do?" I asked.

"Who?"

"Come on, Kelly. You don't have to play games with me. You know who I'm talking about. Now what did he do?" Kelly gave up the charade.

"He's cheating on me," she wailed.

"How do you know?" I asked.

"How do I know? How do I fucking know? How's this? I

saw him making out with some girl and take her into his bed-room. Is that fucking sure enough for you?"

"Are you positive that it was Dan?" I asked, realizing the stupidity of the question too late.

"Of course I'm positive. You don't think I'd recognize the guy I've been dating for two years, especially when he's leading some slut into his room? It was him."

"I don't know what to tell you, Kelly. I'm sorry."

"That's it? I see my boyfriend cheating on me with some sophomore bitch and all you can say is 'I'm sorry'?"

"I wish I had something comforting to say, but the truth is Dan pretty much admitted he did this sort of shit when I talked to him earlier tonight. Besides, I'm not really in a consoling sort of mood. I think I just broke up with my girlfriend a few minutes ago."

"Are you serious?" Kelly asked, wiping away her tears. "You and Jordan? No way, it must be a mistake."

"I don't think so," I said, taking a big glug from my Schae-fer cup.

"But you guys were perfect together. You finished each other's sentences."

"What?"

"I've always said that if you could find someone who could finish your sentences, you had found 'the one.' I don't mean someone who interrupts you but a person who actually said what you were going to say before you said it. You and Jordan are like that."

"Well, apparently, I didn't take enough of an interest in art for her."

"God, art is so boring. I took an intro class this semester. I'll be lucky to get out of there with a C."

"To be honest, it was little more complicated than that. She's pissed because I spend so much time worrying about law school. She thinks I ignore her."

"Are you kidding, Jake? I have to tell you that of all the Kappa Omega boyfriends, you are definitely the sweetest. Most of them are fucking slime. She's lucky to have you, or she was. And as far as that law thing goes, I think she's way out of line. I spend half my time just trying to get Dan to graduate. You'd think she'd appreciate a guy who actually has goals."

"Amen, sister," I said, happy to hear myself praised.

"Listen," she continued, "I love Jordan. She's a sweetheart and I'd never say anything against her but . . ."

"But . . . ?" I pressed.

"But if the worst thing she can say about you is that you want to do something with your life, well then, I think you're doing okay. Of course I understand her wanting to spend more time with you. What girl wouldn't? You're a great guy. But to break up with you because you want to get into law school? That's just stupid."

"Well, maybe I'm not being fair. It's not quite that simple. I mean, it's not just the law school thing that she's pissed about . . ."

"Whatever. Don't defend her. You're way too understanding. There's no excuse for the way she's acting. You deserve better."

"Thanks."

We stood there for a moment, silent, by the side of the house. All of a sudden, without a word being spoken, the vibe changed. I don't know how to explain it. We both waited, neither of us speaking or moving. We watched our breath as it faded into the night air. A new song started. It was another one by Seal, this time, "Future Love Paradise."

I knew the words by heart and since the silence between us was suddenly awkward, I sang along. I did my best to keep up as he mused about kings and queens and future power people and finally asked, "Can I reach out for you if that feels good to me?" As I said this last line, I felt my hand reach out for Kelly's wrist and pull her toward me almost involuntarily. I repeated the words, "Can I reach out for you if that feels good to me?"

She nodded. Before I knew what was happening, we were

kissing. Not just a quick peck, but serious, hardcore, tongues-
on-the-prowl action. It lasted the length of the song and beyond. I didn't know how many songs later it was when Dave
Matthews demanded that his muse "hike up your skirt a little
more and show the world to me." I repeated the request to
Kelly. She was more than willing to comply. She was wearing
jeans that she quickly unbuttoned and slid down around her
knees. It was only as she pulled down her panties that my brain
started to kick into gear. I regret to admit that I did not say,
"We've got to stop," or "This is wrong." I believe my exact
words were: "Hold on. We can't do this here. Let's go back to
my place."

CHAPTER THREE

By the time I returned to school for the spring (and my last) semester at Jefferson University, it was mid-January and many of the problems I was facing back in December had been resolved. My internship interview had gone well. It was for a highly regarded New York firm, McHenry, Solis & Steiner. Like most major firms, they never hired college kids, only law students. But they had just started a brand-new pilot program that allowed a few top graduating seniors to work for them. It was considered very prestigious and acceptance could do wonders for a law school application. Since they had a satellite office in San Antonio, my hometown, I met with one of their people there. The guy told me I should expect a call to set up a follow-up interview in New York sometime in February.

My grades ended up being better than I expected, as well. I had managed to squeeze out an A– in Con Law. Business Law was an A, which I pretty much expected, as I did with the A I got in Government Philosophies. Baby Bio was an A+, as

was Women's Studies (a required elective). My GPA heading
into my final semester was a 3.87 and it was unlikely that up-
coming classes like Legal Ethics and Introduction to American
Literature would change that. Professor Sheridan of Con Law
was teaching Ethics but the word was that she wasn't nearly as
harsh in this class.

As long as I didn't totally slack over the course of the next
three and a half months, I was pretty safe. My LSATs worked
out well, too. I ended up getting a 169, which, along with my
other credentials, gave me a legitimate shot at getting into my
big three, Stanford, Yale, and especially Harvard.

And I managed to patch things up with Jordan as well.
Almost immediately after my slip up with Kelly, I started to
feel guilty. But I had a flight out of town the next day and
didn't get to talk to her. What I ultimately ended up doing was
calling her while she was on the cruise with her family. I left a
really long message that kept getting interrupted because the
machine would only let me talk for sixty seconds. So I ended
up leaving about six sixty-second messages in which I apologized profusely.

I told her that I had been drunk at the party and totally
insensitive. I told her that she was absolutely right—that I had
been selfish and more interested in my stuff than hers. I told
her that I wished I was with her on that cruise right now. I
told her that I would make every effort to be less obsessed with
law school and not let myself be controlled by what my dad
wanted for me. I didn't tell my dad this. I told her that I had
bought a book on art history (which was true) and planned to
finish it by the time we got back to school (which I did).
Finally, I told her that I was miserable without her and I would
do whatever it took to prove myself worthy of her. I said that
if that meant begging, then I would buy some kneepads and
get on a plane to Florida.

It worked. She called me the day she got back and we had
a three-hour talk in which we worked everything out. I met
her at the St. Louis airport when she got in (she arrived a day

after I did) and took her out for dinner at Tony's followed by a night at the Ritz-Carlton in Clayton where we made up multiple times. Of course, I didn't mention anything about my indiscretion. I was pretty sure Kelly wouldn't want our night together to get out either but I reminded myself to have a little chat with her when I got the chance.

So all in all, things were going well. Classes started up and I got back into my routine. The workload was the lightest I'd had since freshman year and I made sure that the extra free time was spent with Jordan. I also made time to play a few holes with Jeff and Kevie when I got the chance. Rick and I were planning a big "only three months till graduation" party for the end of January and it sounded like half the school was going to show up. I ran into Dan Curson, who told me that he and Kelly had broken up and gotten back together over winter break. I told him that Jordan and I did the same thing and we had a good laugh.

It was actually at our house party on the last Saturday of the month where things started to get complicated. The event itself was a great success. Everybody had a great time. But about halfway through the evening, Kelly cornered me. I knew that she and Dan were going to show up but this was the first time I had actually seen her since the mistake and there was a bit of awkwardness, which I tried my best to hide. We talked about classes for a little while. She was pumped that she had gotten her C in Bio. But after a few seconds she leaned in close to me and lowered her voice.

"I need to talk to you, privately."

"Do you really think that's such a great idea right now?" I asked, trying to keep the happy mask plastered to my face.

"Not right now. Let's meet for coffee tomorrow night. How about Meet & Eat at eleven?"

"We have a chapter meeting tomorrow night," I told her.

"I know, but those are always over by ten, ten-thirty at the latest. Jake, it's important. Please, be there."

"Okay, okay. I'll see you at Meet & Eat tomorrow at eleven. Happy now?"

She nodded and went off in search of Dan. I looked around. As far as I could tell, no one had paid any attention to us. I took a moment to let the tension seep out of my body, then headed to the living room where Jordan was waiting.

The chapter meeting on Sunday night got out early, around nine-thirty, so I had time to run home for a little while before I met with Kelly. I called my folks and my little brother, who was fighting his own version of senioritis, only the high school variety. When I finally hung up, it was 10:45. I would be late if I didn't hurry. It was extra cold that night, even more than usual for St. Louis in late January, so I made sure to put on my gloves, watchcap, and my heaviest jacket, which I rarely wore. I had taken out my contacts the second I got home because they dried out too much when it got this cold. With so little time, I decided not to put them back in. I'd just wear my glasses.

I hurried outside and hopped in the car. But when I turned the ignition, the thing wouldn't start. It made that awful clicking sound that indicated the battery was in dire shape. I looked over at Rick's black Ford Tempo in the next space. My roommate was at his fraternity meeting right now (he was in Beta Nu). His meetings often ran past midnight and most Sundays he just walked to them and slept at the house rather than return to our neighborhood at that hour. I ran back upstairs, grabbed his keys off the breakfast table, and hurried back down. I turned the key and was rewarded by the magical sound of a car that worked. I gave it about ten seconds to heat up, then headed out.

On the short drive over, I tried to figure out what Kelly wanted. Dan had already told me that they'd gotten back together and she knew that Jordan and I were back on, so I doubted she wanted to warn me to keep things quiet. She wasn't a genius but that unspoken understanding was a given. It was unlikely that Dan had found out. He was at last night's party and had acted completely normal. If he'd known, I would have known. It was possible that she had mentioned our night together to one of her friends, but I figured that if she had, we'd already have had a little chat.

There was, of course, the other. There was a slim chance that she might be pregnant or had a venereal disease she neglected to mention. We hadn't made protection a priority that evening. After we left the frat house and hurried back on the slick sidewalks to my apartment, there was only one thing we were focused on.

It was so cold out that night that once we got inside my place, we went straight to my bedroom and got under the covers without even taking our clothes off. Within seconds, we were unzipping and maneuvering just those items of clothing necessary to get the job done. We were both incredibly inebriated so the process took longer than it should have.

While we struggled, I did think briefly about the possibility of grabbing a condom, but I remembered that I was all out and that if I really wanted one, I would have to go into Rick's bedroom and feel around in his top dresser drawer. That was not going to happen. I didn't even know if he was home, but if he was, I didn't want to do any explaining about the situation.

So I let it go and got back to the task at hand. By now Kelly had pulled me out of my underwear and was leading me home. Apparently, foreplay wasn't a priority for her, which was good because I was ready to get down to business, too. It didn't take long. Two minutes later, we were lying at opposite ends of my queen bed. I was still drunk, but the realization of what I'd done was already starting to hit me. I looked over at Kelly. She didn't seem to be basking in the glow of our intimacy either.

"Here's what I'm thinking," I told her, "I'm too messed up

to take you home now. Why don't we sleep this off and I'll drive you back to your place early tomorrow morning?"

"Okay," she said.

I looked at my clock. It was about 12:30 in the morning. I set my alarm for five, rolled over and fell asleep immediately. When the alarm went off, it felt like I'd only closed my eyes a few seconds before. I hit the snooze button and pulled the covers tight around me. Then I heard the groan. That was all it took for the whole thing to flash through my brain. Images of exploding flour and making out by the frat house wall and clumsy, unsatisfying sex all crisscrossed through my synapses at once. I looked over at the clock again—5:02.

I felt sick. Jumping out of bed, I ran to the bathroom just in time to get the vomit in the toilet bowl. I leaned over it for a few minutes, waiting to see if there was more to come. Apparently not. I stood up very slowly, took a swig of some mouthwash, and gingerly made my way back into the bedroom. Kelly was still there. It hadn't been a dream. In the few minutes I was gone she had managed to commandeer all the covers and wrap them around her.

I sat at the end of the bed and silently castigated myself. My flight was leaving for San Antonio in about six hours. I had not packed, my apartment was a mess, my girlfriend had just broken up with me (or had I broken up with her?) and I had managed to sleep with a girl I didn't like that much less than an hour later. This was not the way to start winter break.

I shoved Kelly softly. She muttered something incoherent and clutched at the blankets. I shoved her again, a little harder this time.

"Fuck off," she said. That was coherent. I had run out of patience so I stood up and roughly shook her on the shoulder. That worked. She looked up at me, her eyes squinty. I could see the flood of recognition in her pretty, vacant blue eyes. She sat up without a word. After a moment, she reached down to put on her boots. It took a second to register that they were already on. She had never taken them off the night before.

Quietly, we snuck out of the apartment the back way and took the fire-escape stairs down to my car. I didn't even know where she lived so she had to guide me. I got nervous when I realized that she was directing me to the campus dorms. Rather than drop her off in front of her building and risk being seen by one of her nosy sorority sisters, I let her out on the street nearby and had her walk the rest of the way. She got out, grabbed her coat, shut the door, and walked toward her suite. She didn't say, "good-bye" or "I'll talk to you later," or even wave. I was glad.

When I got to Meet & Eat, it was 11:10. I could see through the window that Kelly had already arrived. She was seated at a booth in the corner, looking clearly uncomfortable even from this distance. I parked and walked in, peeling off my coat, gloves, and cap before I got into the overheated restaurant. The parking lot wasn't well paved and I had to maneuver carefully on the frozen gravel and ice surface. There were cracking pot-holes to negotiate and countless jagged chunks of asphalt littered throughout the lot, any of which could lead to a turned ankle. It was as bad as walking home from the frat house after a party.

I sat down across from her. The waitress, Dot, an older woman with glasses even thicker than my Coke bottles, asked me what I wanted. I wasn't very hungry so I just got some decaf coffee and soup. Kelly was drinking milk. I watched the lady try to write down my order with her badly arthritic hand. She had to be in her seventies and I wondered if she was still working because she needed the money or just to avoid bore-dom. After she left, Kelly and I sat there for a moment, not sure what to say. I noticed that her eyes were red and her nose was runny. She had been crying recently.

"So what is it, Kelly?" I asked, trying not to sound too worried.

"I'm pregnant."

I let the comment sink in. I was surprised that the first thing

I felt was relief. A disease would have meant concrete problems for years to come. Pregnancy was at least a manageable situation.

"Are you sure?" I asked.

She nodded.

"I took the test on Friday. Then I took it again on Saturday just to make certain."

I tried to be as delicate as possible but the next question had to be asked.

"Kelly, please don't take this the wrong way, but what makes you think I'm the father? We only did it the one time. Are you telling me that you and Dan weren't having sex any time around that night?"

She wasn't as upset as I thought she'd be. Obviously, she'd been thinking about the various scenarios in detail.

"It's possible that it's Dan's. I was so pissed at him after seeing him with that girl and I felt so guilty after you and I hooked up that nothing happened between me and him until about a week ago. But we were making love pretty regularly up until the night of your frat party. We usually used protection, but not always."

"So don't you think that you should be talking to him?" I asked.

"I'm going to, but I wanted to tell you first . . . in case."

"In case what?"

"In case it is yours. I've been doing a lot of thinking and here's what I've decided to do. I want to wait a few months. By then, the baby will be pretty far along. You can take a paternity test. If it's not yours, then everything's cool. I'll tell Dan that I only just found out. The two of us will make things work. If the test shows that the baby's yours, then you and I will have some more serious talking to do."

It seemed that Kelly had been doing quite a bit of thinking since she made her little discovery. I didn't know the science of paternity tests, but I had no intention of living months in limbo, wondering whether I was a father or not. Plus, her reference to "serious talking" made me very uncomfortable. While I let all this tumble around in my brain, little Kelly added the kicker.

"The thing is, Jake, I have a feeling. I know this baby is yours. I just *feel* it's not Dan's."

"I see," I said because I couldn't think of anything better. The old lady brought my coffee over.

"Your glasses are as thick as mine, boy," Dot noted. I nodded. What was I supposed to say to that? I had other shit on my mind. She waited for a response. When she realized none would be forthcoming, she walked off, clearly miffed at my refusal to banter.

"What are you thinking?" Kelly asked.

"How do you know it's going to take that long for a paternity test? Can't we do one right now?"

"I just figured it would take a while. You know, until the baby's more developed."

"Don't you think we should check into that before we agree for you to walk around campus for two months, pregnant? By then, you might be showing."

"It just made sense to me to wait," she said defensively.

"Yeah, well maybe we shouldn't let the person who barely passed Introduction to Biology make the science decisions in this situation." After I said it, I realized just how unpleasant that must have sounded. I'm not sure from where exactly in me it bubbled up. Before I could even apologize, the tears started to well up in her eyes. I tried to reach for her hand but she pulled it away. Just then, Dot returned with my soup.

"You want any more milk, miss?" she asked Kelly, who kept her eyes down and shook her head no. Dot walked off, clearly not expecting a big tip from this couple.

"I'm sorry, Kelly. I didn't mean that. I'm just a little freaked out. This is really complicated."

"I know," she muttered through her sniffles, "I've been trying to think of a way out ever since Friday." Sensing that this was the opportunity to discuss another option, I leaned in and whispered.

"You know, there may be another solution to this," I said softly. I reached for her hand again and this time she let me take it.

She looked up and wiped the tears from her cheek with the back of her hand. I continued carefully.

"Have you considered your other options? Like the possibility of ending the pregnancy?"

She pulled her hand away again.

"I can't do that," she answered firmly.

"Why not?"

"I just can't. Don't try to convince me. That is something I feel very strongly about. I believe that's a sin. I can't. I won't." Her voice was rising.

"It was just an option. You don't have to get angry."

"It's not an option for me," she said, "I wasn't raised that way."

"You were raised to believe that getting an abortion is wrong, but that it's okay to have drunken sex with your boyfriend's fraternity brother?" I demanded, knowing my comment was less than constructive, but unable to contain my frustration. Kelly looked momentarily shocked, but managed to gather her composure enough to respond.

"You are a total asshole. I'm leaving." With that, she stood up, put on her coat, and headed for the door. I rifled through my wallet, found a ten, and tossed it on the table.

"Kelly," I called after her as I grabbed my jacket, cap, and gloves. She was already at her car by the time I caught up to her. She reached into her pocket, fumbling for her keys.

"Kelly, please wait. Listen, I'm sorry. I was a jerk. I realize I'm not handling this as well as I should. But you've got to understand, you've had two days to come to terms with this. I've had less than ten minutes. I'm sorry I mentioned the abortion thing. I didn't know how big a deal that was to you. Please just stop for a second."

She stopped searching for her keys and turned around. The tears on her face were already drying in the cold night air. She seemed so fragile. Despite the streaked mascara, the bloodshot eyes, and the hair that hadn't been washed in two days, at that moment, she looked strangely beautiful. Before I knew what I was doing, I reached out, grabbed her wrist, and pulled her to me. She didn't fight it, instead letting me wrap her up. I hugged her tight. I glanced back at the restaurant. Dot was sneaking a peek through the window. She was smiling. Glad that things had been successfully resolved, she returned to work. After a long time, I let Kelly go.

"Do you mind if I put on my coat?" I asked. "I'm on the verge of freezing solid."

She giggled at that. As I threw it on, zipped up, and put on my gloves and cap, she tried to reassure me.

"We'll figure this out, Jake. We just have to have faith that there is some plan to all this. I was talking to my roommate, Lindsay, earlier tonight and we agreed that everything happens for a reason. I believe that. There must be some larger purpose here that we're not meant to understand yet."

"You didn't tell her about this?" I asked, less concerned with larger purposes than large embarrassments.

"Of course not. Although if there's anyone who would know what to do in this situation, it's her. But I didn't tell her. I didn't tell anyone. All I said was that I was meeting a friend to discuss a problem. But that's not the point of the story. The point is, this is all going to work out for the best. Don't worry. What's meant to be is meant to be."

I was too tired at that point to address the role of fate in our daily lives, so I just nodded. We hugged again.

"We'll find a way through this," I said more confidently than I thought possible. Kelly smiled, apparently easily convinced. I turned and headed for my car. I could hear her fumbling for her keys again. I didn't know how to resolve this thing but I did know that if we could keep this mess between the two of us, there was hope.

There was no way I could have a child right now. Not out of wedlock. Not with this idiot. It would ruin everything. I would wait a while before bringing it up again, but I wasn't giving up on the abortion thing just yet. As long as it was just Kelly and me, I knew I would win out. I'd just wear her down.

The key was to make sure that it stayed just between us. No guilty confessions to Dan. No crying phone calls to Mom. No late night heart-to-hearts with resourceful roommate Lindsay. Just to be safe, I decided to nip that one in the bud. I turned around and headed back to Kelly, who had finally unlocked and opened her car door. Now she was struggling to get the keys out of the lock. It might be overkill, but Kelly had proven that she sometimes needed a little negative reinforcement. I decided one more reminder for her to keep her mouth shut was in order, even if it meant getting in her face.

I walked up behind her and reached out for her wrist. As I did, I slipped on an icy spot. Losing my balance, I grabbed her much harder than I intended, but managed to steady myself. Kelly, startled by the sudden grip on her wrist, yanked her hand away. The sudden motion made *her* slip on the slick parking lot surface. Before I could reach out, her legs flew backward, causing her to fall face-first toward the ground. She let out a little yelp of recognition just before the right side of her head slammed against the asphalt. It sounded like a bowling ball being dropped.

CHAPTER FOUR

Quickly, I knelt down to see if she was all right. Rolling her over to her back, I found that several large chunks of loose parking lot asphalt were now embedded in her skull, just behind the right ear. She must have landed on them when she fell. The sight made my knees wobble and I had to sit down on the ice-hard ground.

I was suddenly very dizzy. I had the sensation one gets after sitting for a long time, then standing up too fast. Everything felt hazy and my vision went black for a few seconds. My hands were clammy and beads of sweat formed on my brow even though it was about seven degrees out. I thought I might vomit or pass out but I managed to take a deep breath of the icy air and the feeling passed.

I looked back down at Kelly. The weird thing, I thought to myself as I sat there, was that there wasn't any blood. Not even around the asphalt pieces, one of which looked to be jammed at least half an inch into her skull. Despite my A+ in

Baby Bio the prior semester, I couldn't tell if she was just un-conscious or dead.

I leaned over and put my ear to her chest. Despite the grisly state of her head, Kelly seemed to still be alive. Her chest rose and fell slowly, then rose again to meet me. I couldn't be cer-tain, but I thought I could hear a heartbeat as well. Once I was confident that she was still alive, I managed to get to my feet. I looked through the Meet & Eat window. The place was vir-tually empty. For a moment, I thought about running inside and telling someone to call 911.

But then I remembered. Barnes Hospital was only a few miles away. By the time an ambulance got here, it might be too late. And what if they didn't have the necessary equipment to help her? Then they would have to drive all the way back to the hospital, wasting precious seconds. It would take double the time than if I just drove her there myself. I made my de-cision.

My glasses were fogging up as a result of my own hot breath. I couldn't see a thing so I took them off for a second to let them clear. Even though my vision was fuzzy, I picked Kelly up as gingerly as I could, gathered her in my arms, and walked quickly to Rick's car. I opened the passenger door, placed her carefully in the seat, and ran around to my side. When I got in, I threw my glasses back on. Luckily the fog had disappeared and I could see again. Praying for the ignition to start, I turned the key. It worked. The engine revved. I threw it into drive and pulled out onto Brentwood.

Now you have to understand that even though I was a senior at Jefferson University and living in St. Louis for the fourth year, I did not consider it my home. I say this because, although the most direct route from the Meet & Eat on Brent-wood to Barnes Hospital might have seemed obvious to a na-tive, it was not so clear to me. So, rather than sit for a second and ponder the best route, I took the path I was most familiar with. That meant that I left Brentwood, turned east on Clayton, and shot down to Skinker. That was at the corner of Forest

Park. I traveled north on Skinker until I reached Lindell, which I knew would take me directly to the hospital. It meant going through the park, but at least I knew it would get me there.

It all worked surprisingly well. Since it was about 11:30 on a Sunday night, there was almost no traffic and few red lights. I ran those anyway, figuring that if a cop pulled me over it might actually help improve my time. By the time I hit Lindell, only about seven minutes had passed since I pulled out of the Meet & Eat parking lot. I punched the accelerator, managing to get Rick's ten-year-old Tempo up to about seventy on a road marked for thirty-five.

I was about halfway through the park when a car pulled out in front of me. I had to hit the breaks violently to avoid a crash. The car began to skid, so I turned into the slide as I let up on the accelerator. The tires magically regripped the road and I was able to get control again. I pushed hard on the breaks and pulled over to the right, managing to ease the vehicle softly into a snowdrift along the edge of the road. I put the car in park and took a moment to catch my breath.

Glancing over at Kelly, I saw that the car's motion had slammed her into the passenger window. Her head stayed there for a moment, then slowly slid down the window, making an odd scraping sound until it came to rest where the window met the door.

It took me a second to realize the scraping sound was from the pieces of rock embedded in her skull sliding unnaturally against the window glass. I could see the tiny scratches in the glass along with the smear of blood that ran down the window. I was no doctor but I guessed that the force of the right side of her head hitting the glass had pushed the chunks in even farther. And with the warmer temperature inside the car, the blood, which was nowhere to be found before, was now starting to trickle down her neck.

For a moment, she stopped breathing and her entire torso was still. For three long seconds it looked like she had died. Then the heave of her chest resumed and I heard a small exhalation. It wasn't until I saw her breathe again that I realized that I had stopped breathing, too. I had to consciously force the air out of my lungs and suck in more. I tried to swallow and began coughing violently. My mouth was so dry that I felt like the insides of my cheeks might actually crack. Unable to move, I stared at Kelly Stone.

She was in bad shape. I pictured myself pulling up to the emergency room doors. I'd carry her into the lobby, someone would put her on a stretcher and run her into surgery. A nurse or doctor would start asking me questions. What happened? How did she get all that junk in her head? Why didn't you call an ambulance? Do you know this woman? What is the nature of your relationship? Does she have any allergies that you're aware of? Does she have *any* medical conditions that you're aware of?

The answers to those questions would be messy. I hadn't really done anything wrong (although I *had* grabbed her kind of hard and was starting to think I should have just called 911) but I knew things would look bad. I'd have to tell them that she was pregnant, which meant that Dan would find out and more troubling, so would Jordan.

All my buddies would think I was a disloyal friend and my girlfriend would never speak to me again. Word would get around. Professors might retract recommendations. Admission to the law schools that I wanted might become iffy. My father would be extremely disappointed. It would not do for the son of the brilliant litigator and pillar of the community, Jonah Conason, to be in any kind of compromising position.

Worse than that, I realized that someone might get the wrong idea. When Kelly and I left the Meet & Eat, we were arguing. Someone might mistakenly think that I was so angry about the pregnancy that I pushed Kelly down. How was I supposed to prove that it didn't happen that way? How could I be sure that I would be believed? If I was willing to betray my girlfriend and my fraternity brother, what was to stop me from going that extra step to keep it a secret? What was to stop me?

Nothing. That's when it hit me, cool and clear and simple. If I took Kelly to the hospital, no matter what happened, whether she lived to say it was an accident or died on the operating table, I was screwed. I might even be charged with something. If I drove up to that hospital now, everything I worked so hard for would be gone. The life I wanted would be over.

But. What would happen if I didn't take her to the emergency room? I looked out on Forest Park—vast, silent. It was almost midnight on a freezing Sunday night. What if I just dropped her off in the park and went home? Could I do that? What would happen? I tried to think it through. I'd been seen with Kelly at the restaurant. But I was pretty sure no one saw her fall or me throw her into the car. Dot had seen us hug in the parking lot, and probably thought everything was cool between us, which it was.

No one had seen me drive off in my car because I was in Rick's car. No one knew I was even using this car because Rick was at his fraternity meeting and likely wouldn't be back tonight. I would have to explain to the police what I was doing with Kelly that night but I could come up with something for that. She had said that no one knew about the pregnancy so I wouldn't be a suspect on that front. If I did this fast and got back to my place soon, I could call someone and create an alibi.

I looked at my watch—11:38. I could drop Kelly off, be back at my apartment and on the phone with Jordan by 11:55. Who would believe that I would attack Kelly in the middle of a restaurant parking lot for no reason, go out of my way to drive her to the park, dump her, and get home less than a half hour later to have a normal conversation with my girlfriend? No one would.

I tried to think of a flaw in the plan. I was sure there had to be one but nothing sprang to mind. The key things were to get this done fast, get home to talk to Jordan, and to have a good story ready when the cops asked me about the meeting. But if any of it was going to work, I had to move now. So I did. I maneuvered the car back onto the road and turned right into the park. I took the main park road, which connected with a smaller one. Pretty soon, I was in a secluded area surrounded by tall, thick trees.

I turned off the headlights and drove about a quarter mile farther, then stopped the car. I got out and looked at the road. It was no longer paved. Instead, I was now on a dirt road covered in chunky gravel, much like the Meet & Eat parking lot. I noticed that the Tempo's tires left tread mark indentations in the dirt next to the tread marks of other cars. I knew I was probably being paranoid but decided that I shouldn't drop Kelly near where the car had been. I looked toward the woods in the distance and saw in the dim moonlight that the road curved all the way around the other side of a wooded area where I could drop her. I decided that I would enter the woods from that side, where there were no Tempo tire marks. To my relief, I found that focusing on the minutiae of the tasks at hand allowed me to keep the larger issues at bay.

I didn't want to get any of Kelly's blood on me, so I popped the trunk to see if Rick had any rags or towels. I was in luck. There was a large, dirty rag resting next to a crowbar. I grabbed it (never taking off my gloves, of course). Then, after thinking for a moment, I grabbed the crowbar, too. I shut the trunk, slid the crowbar inside my coat and moved over to the passenger side.

When I opened the door, Kelly's limp body almost fell out. I had to catch her. The blood coming from the side of her head was flowing more freely now. It was starting to mat her hair and had dripped onto the shoulder of her coat. But from what I could tell in the limited light, none of it had dripped onto any part of the car except the window and door. I wrapped her head in the rag, making sure that none of the blood would drip through onto my clothes when I picked her up. I lifted her into my arms and carried her along the right side of the road, the opposite side from where I wanted to drop her. I walked along the edge of the road, where the dirt and gravel mixed in with the muddy, slushy snow. The ugly combination made identifying boot marks almost impossible but I dragged my feet anyway so as to wipe away any potential tracks.

I followed the curving road until I was on the other side of the woods. When I reached the spot where I wanted to enter, I put Kelly down and took off my boots, leaving only a pair of thick athletic socks. I picked Kelly up again and tiptoed across the gravel road, leaving only slight indentations in the gravelly surface. When I got to the wooded side of the road, I stepped into the snow and walked toward the trees. With each step I took into the foot-deep snow, I squished my feet around, making as big a mess as possible. I didn't want the police to have even an approximate shoe size to work with.

By the time I got to a small clearing in the middle of the trees, my feet were starting to feel a little numb. I glanced at my watch:11:44. I had to hurry. I softly placed Kelly in the snow and turned her on her side so that the right side of her head, with the chunks of asphalt imbedded in it, was facing the ground. I took off the dirty (now bloody) rag and tossed it a few feet away.

I looked down at Kelly. I could see the small stream of blood from her head wound starting to stain the snow underneath. When I was carrying her just before, I could see and hear her soft breathing so I knew that she was still alive. I also knew that if she somehow survived the night and managed to recover, she would be able to say that the last thing she remembered was slipping in the parking lot as I grabbed her wrist. She would talk about how I'd pressured her into having an abortion. She'd say I was the father of that baby even if she wasn't sure it was true. There was no way out of this situation. She had made it impossible.

Who would have thought that such a pretty, innocent-looking thing could so easily destroy my life? I wondered if she was really as broken up as she seemed to be in the restaurant.

She needed me to see her as an emotional wreck, not as some manipulative black widow. Maybe she wasn't as dumb as I thought. She had cajoled that Biology professor into giving her a C and I was pretty sure that it wasn't based on her classroom performance. I wondered if this is what she wanted all along.

Lying in the snow, she didn't look all that innocent anymore. She had played me, just like she always played Dan. Just like Jordan tried to play me the night of the fraternity party. Just like my father played me every time he forced me to do something *he* felt was best for me.

They all fucking played me all the time. It was one thing if it was my own flesh and blood or even my girlfriend, but this little bitch? It was insulting. My life was about to end before it started because of her. She knew what she was doing. She cheated on her boyfriend and she wanted to make it work for her. She wanted me to pay for her mistake. I'd been outsmarted by a bimbo.

I felt my heart beating faster as I ran it over and over in my mind. I could not believe it. The shame and disgust washed over me. I could feel the blood run to my face. My fingertips were tingling from the adrenaline shooting through my body. My teeth were grinding involuntarily. I was sweating right through my clothes on a subfreezing night—that's what this cunt had reduced me to.

I'm not exactly sure when I pulled the crowbar out of my jacket. I know when I pulled it out of the trunk, I'd intended to use it to rip Kelly's clothes off and make it look like an attempted rape. But somehow, without even being fully aware of it at first, I found that I was hitting her with it. I hit her on the arms and the shoulders and all over the chest and back. I must have wailed on her back twenty times.

I just hit and hit until my arms ached. I was in some sort of frenzy and I couldn't stop. I had to purge it from my system so I pummeled her some more. I knew I was crying. I might have been screaming—I'm not sure. I was full of rage and power and hate. But there was something even stronger and closer feeding me. I recognized it well—fear. It wouldn't leave my side.

After a while, I stopped. I stood silently in the park, my whole body heaving, my breathing slowly returning to normal. I felt numb. I couldn't hear anything and the cold was far off in the distance somewhere.

Then the cloud lifted. Suddenly I felt calm, almost meditative. Everything seemed so much clearer now. It was like I was in the most vivid dream I had ever experienced. And because it was a dream, I could do anything. I was free.

Kelly had been dressed warmly for the night and it was a good question as to just how much damage my blows had caused. I could tell she was still breathing. It was possible that she might still live. That couldn't happen. I noticed that my hands had gathered themselves around the crowbar again and that they had a good grip. In the dream, it was obvious to me what I had to do and my body seemed to be leading my mind down the required road.

I took a deep breath, hoping that the cold air would clear the fuzziness that occasionally drifted into my head It did. I could see the spot I needed to aim for, on the left temple at the far corner of her eyebrow. I gathered myself, made sure I had a good footing in the snow, then began.

I lifted the bar above my head and brought it down with all the force I could muster. The blow was a little higher than I would have liked, landing on the forehead about an inch above the desired spot. I had been expecting a crunching sound but it was more of a *smush* than anything else, like when you're working a body bag at the gym.

I also didn't think to compensate for the blood. There hadn't been any when I was hitting her body. Luckily, on that first swing, there wasn't much of it and what there was splattered away from me. Still, I didn't want to take any chances, so before doing anything more, I dropped the crowbar, took off my jacket, sweater, jeans, and cap and placed them about ten feet behind me. I was now wearing only my socks, my gloves, my underwear, and a T-shirt. I figured that if I got any blood on those, I could just burn them and no one would know. But if I had to dump my down jacket or my sweater or jeans, someone might wonder where they had gone. Better safe than sorry.

With that taken care of, I returned to Kelly. I didn't know if she was alive or dead but I wasn't going to get down close to check her breathing. Instead, I picked up the bar and swung again. I don't know if it was the lack of bulky clothing or the reduced nervousness that came from already having given the first whack, but this time I got it dead solid perfect. The blood still mostly splattered away from me. There were a few red flecks on my shirt and something gray had landed on my underwear but all in all, it wasn't too messy. I swung once more and this time there was a lot more give. I must have really gotten through most of the bone on the prior swing because there was almost no resistance. In fact, I was so surprised at how spongy and elastic the target was that I almost lost my balance.

That was three solid hits. I leaned a little to my left to get a better view. Blood was pouring down the left side of Kelly's face. If I stumbled across her while taking a walk, I wouldn't recognize her. I thought about swinging a few more times just to be sure, but ultimately decided it would be overkill.

I stood there for a long moment, letting everything sink in. The blood was pumping through my veins and I could feel the sweat all over my body, only this time there were no heavy clothes to sully the experience. Even at this temperature, it wouldn't evaporate. I looked up at the sky. There were very few lights in the park, so I had only the moonlight as my guide. It was a cloudless night, actually quite beautiful, just as it should be in a dream. Some stars were even visible. I don't know how long I stared up at them. I heard a twig snap and turned in the direction of the sound. A bird flew away but that was all. I held my breath, waiting for what seemed like forever. Silence. I turned back to Kelly.

I saw what remained of her pulpy, misshapen head and suddenly the dream ended. I awoke to find myself in the same place I'd been before, the same place I'd been all along. There was a body on the snow in front of me. It was the body of an innocent girl who'd gotten into a difficult situation. She didn't deserve this. But I had given it to her. I barely remembered doing it. I didn't even recognize that person as me. But it was. The evidence was right there in front of me.

The next thing I knew, I felt a wave of nausea start to overcome me. I wanted to sit down for a minute. I fought both urges. I had to get a grip. I could feel bad for Kelly later. If I wanted to do anything other than feel bad about spending the rest of my life in a cell, I had to focus.

If the police discovered vomit, they might be able to use it to get DNA or who knows what. I couldn't leave any trace. And there was still a little more work to do. I now wished I had done this part before I began the crowbar thing but it was too late for wishing.

I leaned down and unzipped Kelly's jeans. Then I took the unbloodied end of the crowbar and hooked it under her panties and gave a tug so they ripped. After I unzipped her jacket, I pulled her sweater up to her neck and yanked at her undershirt and bra with the crowbar, so that they, too, looked like someone had tried to rip them off.

After all that was done, I took off my underwear and T-shirt and wrapped them in the rag. For a brief moment I was completely naked except for my gloves and socks. As I left the woods, I was careful to step in the same footprints I made on the way in. I tiptoed back across the road and put on my boots again. I looked at my watch: 11:58. It had taken less than fifteen minutes to properly beat a girl to death.

CHAPTER FIVE

I tried to fight the powerful urge to run back to the car and peal out of there. Instead I took a few deep breaths and slowly walked back along the edge of the road to the car. I popped the trunk and grabbed a plastic Saks bag that Rick had left there from a trip to the mall. I stuffed the crowbar and the rag with my clothes inside and wrapped it up tight.

Then I started the car and slowly backed it out from the gravel-dirt road to the small one that was paved. I kept the headlights off until I got back on the main park road. Instead of leaving the park from the same road on which I entered it, I drove farther down to an exit near the hospital, on Kingshighway, where there was more traffic. I figured that people would be less likely to remember a car pulling out of the park at that end than they would on the less-populated Lindell.

I wanted to take the long way around the park, go south, back to Clayton and then take Skinker back north to my place off Delmar, but I decided that time was the most important factor now. It was already 12:05. If I wanted to call Jordan and establish my whereabouts I needed to get to it fast. So I took what I thought was the most direct route home, going north to Forest Park Parkway, then taking that west to Skinker and finally getting to my home Delmar turf. My fears turned out to be unjustified as I made it along that stretch and the rest of the way home without seeing any police cars.

When I parked in the alley behind my place, I looked at the passenger window and door. They were starting to crust over with frozen blood and I wanted to clean them, but I knew I had to call Jordan first. I grabbed the plastic bag with the crowbar and the bloody clothes and bounded quickly up the back steps to the apartment. I tossed Rick's keys back on the table and hurried to my room.

By the time Jordan actually picked up the phone, it was 12:12. Her voice was drowsy on the other end. I hadn't considered that she might be asleep. I should have. It was very late to be calling on a Sunday. I was about to speak when I realized that I hadn't given myself time to calm down from all the craziness. It would sound really weird to call her up this late with tons of energy in my voice, blabbering on about how I had just spent the last hour hanging out with Kelly Stone. I had to be casual.

As Jordan said hello for a second time, I used the moment to exhale and gather myself. But she didn't know that. All she heard was someone breathing heavily into the phone.

"Listen, you sick fuck, whoever you are," she growled before I could say anything, "if you call me again, I am going to have you arrested, do you hear me?"

"I just wanted to hear your sexy voice. Is that a crime?" I asked, hoping I sounded playful.

"Jake, is that you?"

"Yes."

"You know I was sleeping? Maybe you think the late-night dirty phone call thing is clever, but I'd appreciate it a lot more at ten-thirty than at midnight."

"Sorry, I didn't look at my watch. Do you want me to call back tomorrow?"

"No, it's okay. I'm awake now. What's up?"

"It's no big deal. I just had a weird conversation, that's all," I said with as much ambivalence as I could muster.

"What do you mean?" she asked, perking up. My reticence always piqued her interest.

"Well, you know Dan Curson's girlfriend, Kelly Stone?"

"A little bit. I mean she's in my sorority, so we've spoken."

"That's really about as well as I know her, too. But we both took Baby Bio last semester and I helped her out a little from time to time. Every now and then we'd chat about other things, like postgraduation plans, stuff like that."

"Yeah?" Jordan was getting impatient.

"So, last night, at the party, she comes up to me and asks if we can meet, that she has something to talk to me about. She was all secretive about it and asked me not to tell anyone. So I agreed and tonight we got together at the Meet & Eat, which is where I just got back from about half an hour ago."

"Jake, please get to the point," Jordan pleaded. I knew I had her full attention now.

"Okay. So I get there and you know what she wants to discuss? I swear I'm not making this up to sound more impressive to you. She starts talking about how graduation is getting close and how, no matter what she does, she cannot get Dan to take things seriously. She tells me how he has no goals and how he hasn't prepared himself for their future together. She actually said, and you can ask her if you don't believe me, that she wished he was more committed to his future, *like I am.* Isn't that random?"

"Yes. If I were the suspicious type, I'd think you paid her to say that."

"But you're not the suspicious type," I reminded her.

"So what happened?"

"Well, she said some other stuff, gave a few examples of his lack of maturity, things I think she'd rather I not repeat. Then she ended up asking me if I'd sit down with Dan and try to set him straight."

"Are you serious? What did you say to her?"

"What could I say? I told her that I'd talk to him but that I couldn't make any promises."

"And?"

"It got messy. I think she wanted me to assure her that it would be okay. Of course I couldn't. She got pretty upset and even stormed out at one point. I ended up consoling her in the parking lot. I think that in the end they'll work things out. I just don't like being in the middle of it, you know?"

"I don't like you being in the middle of it, either."

"I had a feeling. The truth is, if I had known what this was all about ahead of time I probably wouldn't have gone."

"Yes you would have. If you hadn't you would have beaten yourself up over it. You're like the human guilt machine," she joked.

"I'm trying to get past that."

"Well, tonight was probably not a step in that direction."

I didn't respond to that.

"You know, I should let you get to bed. I don't even know why I called. I guess I just wanted to bounce this stuff off someone and you were the person I immediately thought of. But it is seriously late and I'm going to start feeling guilty if I don't let you get some sleep."

"Like I said, the human guilt machine. I'll see you tomorrow, okay?"

"Okay," I promised.

"I love you," she said.

"I love you, too."

I hung up. It was not the most convincing performance ever. I didn't think I had made Kelly's problems compelling enough to justify a late-night call. And my explanation for why she ran out of the restaurant was weak at best. But Jordan seemed to buy it all. That may have been because she was still sleepy or possibly because she had no reason to think I'd lie.

. . .

As soon as I was off the phone, I went to the bathroom, wet down a couple of washcloths, then grabbed some cleanser and a couple of paper towels. I put them on the kitchen counter, grabbed the bag with the crowbar and clothes and walked to the front room with the fireplace. I got the fire started and carefully dropped the bloody rag and my underclothes in the flames. Then I took the crowbar into my bathroom. I turned the shower to hot and placed the thing in. The blood and some other matter had caked on the end of the bar but it was nothing a few minutes of soaking in hot water couldn't fix.

I grabbed the cleaning stuff and went down to Rick's car. I tried to be as quiet as possible. It was now close to 12:30 and a guy doing a little window washing at that hour would definitely look suspicious. I sprayed the cleanser on the window and door and wiped them down with one of the washcloths. It took a while to get them clean. The blood had not only dried, but frozen as well. Little maroon crystals clung desperately to the glass.

Eventually, that was done. I was generous in using the cleanser, paper towels, and other washcloth to wipe away any trace of blood. The tiny gravel scratches were barely noticeable. I figured that crime scene experts might still pick something up with luminol but decided that if they were checking Rick's car for blood, I was probably out of luck anyway.

I ran upstairs, turned off the shower and used the cleaner of the two washcloths to wipe off any remnants of gunk that might still be on the bar. As I scrubbed, the bar accidentally fell out of my hand and landed in the tub, making a loud clunk. A shiver ran down my spine as I had a thought. I hadn't made sure Rick was actually spending the night at the frat house.

If he had come home for some reason, the noise would definitely have woken him. I doubted I could explain away a bloody crowbar and burned underwear if he came out of his room now. I had to check, so I left the bathroom and crept to his bedroom door, opened it and peeked in. The bathroom light leaked in enough that I could make out a lump on his bed. It took a long, unpleasant second before I realized it was just his comforter. He wasn't home.

Relieved, I returned to the bathroom, took both washcloths and the paper towels and threw them in the fire. I was pleased to see that the clothes and rag were now almost completely gone. After I doused the bottom of the shower with some of the cleanser, I returned to the front room and waited until everything was completely burned. When I was sure, I put out the fire, took the crowbar and Rick's plastic shopping bag and went down to his car again. I threw the stuff in the trunk and headed out.

St. Louis roads in the postmidnight hours on a Sunday night/ Monday morning are always quiet. But as I drove the stretch of Delmar to the Clayton business district, the town seemed almost dead. I made sure to keep within the posted speed limits without looking overly cautious. Even an innocuous traffic stop would completely destroy my minimal semblance of an alibi. I stopped in the parking lot of a bookstore I knew.

The last time I was there I had noticed that their Dumpster always seemed to be full to overflowing. I took the crowbar and dropped it in the corner of the container. It didn't sink all the way to the bottom, but its weight helped it down about a third of the way, where it was out of sight. It was a gamble to throw away Rick's crowbar without replacing it, but buying a new one for him was far more dangerous. Besides, when he finally noticed it was missing, he would probably just assume he'd misplaced it.

I then drove the car to the mall. This was the riskiest part of the evening (not counting beating Kelly to death). The mall was right across the street from the Meet & Eat. But my theory was that the safest place to dump a plastic Saks bag was in a Dumpster next to Saks. I hoped it would go unnoticed. As I shoved the bag into the trash I was pleased to see two other similar bags already there. I pulled out of the mall parking lot just as the security guy drove his car around to where I had been. He stopped and pointed his flashlight in the general direction of the Dumpster.

I pulled over to the shoulder and hit the brakes on the Tempo, concerned that he had seen me and was checking to see what I had dropped in the trash. After a few seconds he turned off the light and started driving again, resuming his normal rounds. When I could no longer see his taillights in the distance, I took my foot off the brake.

By the time I finally got home, It was 1:30 in the morning. I took off the gloves that I had been wearing all this time. It was strange to think that only two hours previous a girl had been alive. And now, for reasons she couldn't understand and I couldn't properly explain, she was lying in the snow of Forest Park, bloody, battered, dead. It hadn't taken very long for our lives to veer off on wildly different courses. Not long ago I'd been advising my little brother on how to avoid the pitfalls of that last semester of school. Suddenly I felt woefully under-qualified.

For the briefest of moments, a strange thought flashed through my head. By doing what I did to Kelly, had I killed my own child? It was an odd question. I didn't know the proper name for the creature at that level of development. Was it an embryo? A fetus? We hadn't covered that in Baby Bio. Or at least I wasn't paying attention that day.

Kelly had said she *felt* that the baby was not Dan's. She *knew* it was mine. I couldn't help but wonder again if that had anything to do with where Dan and I stood in the grand scheme of societal success. I was on my way to a top-notch law school and would be raking in high six figures in five years. Dan wasn't assured of graduating. It felt dirty to ask the question, even to myself, but I couldn't help it. Would Kelly still have *felt* the baby wasn't Dan's and *known* it was mine if I was the slacker and Dan was Ivy League bound? Or would that certainty be thrown into doubt just a bit? More than feeling or knowing, I suspected that Kelly *wanted* the baby to be mine. She *hoped* it would be. She *needed* it to be.

CHAPTER SIX

I managed to get about three hours' sleep, which is three more than I expected. I thought I might have nightmares, but I didn't. I was up at seven, but my first class of the day, Legal Ethics, wasn't until 10:30. I didn't have a reputation as an early riser and had actually tried to set up my schedule so that I didn't have a class before noon. But the only time the Sheridan class was offered was Monday, Wednesday, and Friday-10:30–12, so I had to throw my dream of no A.M. classes out the window.

Still, it would look odd to anyone who cared to see me wandering the campus even minutes before a morning class. Rick, if he returned from the frat house, would definitely be suspicious if he found me making breakfast at seven. So I lay in bed and reread a chapter in my Ethics textbook. Professor Sheridan was a proponent of the Socratic method and I had been embarrassed in her class often enough that I had learned to take every opportunity to better prepare myself for her questions.

I finally rolled out of bed around 9:45. I followed my typical morning regimen. I showered, dressed, grabbed a bagel and headed out. It was cold outside, probably in the mid-teens but the sun was shining brightly and there was no wind. Even if I wasn't having car trouble, I might have chosen to walk on a day as beautiful as this.

It had snowed a little in the early morning hours, just enough to give everything an extra layer of white to cover the dirt and slush and grime. The snow acted as soundproofing, muffling the sounds of the midmorning workday, giving the city a stillness and silence it usually lacked. I didn't even hear birds singing. As I hurried to campus, I couldn't help but admire just how pristine the world could be when it wanted.

I arrived in the classroom a little bit late but Sheridan wasn't there yet. The class only had eleven students since it was an upper-level seminar so Sheridan had picked a room with a big, square conference table rather than the traditional desks. When I got there, only two seats were unoccupied. One was up front near the chalkboard, where Sheridan usually sat. The other empty seat faced directly opposite her. I knew it had been left vacant in a sad attempt by my fellow students to decrease the chances of the professor having them directly in her eyeline and calling on them.

I sat down and pulled out my books and notes. Only then did I realize there might be another reason why the seat was empty. It was next to Evan Grunier, my frat brother and, in case I wasn't clear before, perhaps the smarmiest, most butt-licky, two-faced, snake of a human being I had met in my four years at this university.

"Hey Jake, how's it going?" he asked.

"Good, man. How're you?"

"Not bad. Had a wild weekend. I barely made it today. You?"

"I had a good weekend, too," I said, trying not to engage in anything more than surface chat.

"How's Jordan? You two seem to be doing pretty well, especially after the whole breakup thing."

"I still can't believe how things spread so fast around here. You tell one person something and you'll hear it from someone else an hour later. To answer your question, we're great."

"I'm glad to hear it," Evan said so unconvincingly, I thought it might be intentional, "and I know what you mean about word spreading. I don't think there's any worse place for gossip to grab hold than a small university. It's like a petri dish and gossip is the bacteria."

"That is really quite profound, Evan. Are you sure you picked the right major? Because I could see you wiping the floor with the literature department." I tried to put a joking tone in my voice to temper the sarcasm but for some reason it didn't quite come out that way and all Evan heard was the bite.

He gave me a mean little smile. He looked like nothing so much as Santa's evil elf, all set to give the kids the gift that would make them cry. He was about to say something when Professor Sheridan walked in. I could see him struggle with the choice of whether to speak once class had technically started. Obviously the need was too powerful because he leaned over, even as Sheridan was talking, and whispered in my ear.

"Just like a petri dish, Jake. Makes you hope no one's planning any experiments."

I gathered that his comment was meant to be foreboding, but Evan was such a toad and his little biology lab metaphor was so lame that I couldn't even dignify it with a furrowed brow.

"Whatever," I muttered and turned my attention to Professor Sheridan.

I met Jordan for lunch at the campus deli in Summersby Center. I tried to act normal even though I was a little apprehensive. It was just after noon and I thought that Kelly's body might have been discovered by now. I tried to remember if she had carried a purse last night. I hadn't seen one so I gathered she had kept a little change purse with a driver's license in her pocket. If that was the case, the authorities should have been able to identify her pretty quickly.

If she hadn't been found yet, it couldn't be much longer. The park had seemed awfully lonely last night but I'd been there in the day and I knew that at this hour it was overrun with joggers, bikers, tourists, and people who just wanted to have their lunch in the park. Someone would have to come across the fragile broken body in the wooded clearing. Someone would have to be curious about the crumpled, darkened figure that stood out so dramatically against the whiteness of the snow. I hoped so. The thought of that pretty girl, alone, half-frozen, with people all around, oblivious to her plight, was almost too much for me to bear.

Jordan called out my name from the other side of Summersby. I had to shake myself back into the moment. She ran over and hugged me, clearly not noticing anything out of the ordinary. She gave me a surprisingly long and involved kiss and even slipped in a little tongue for good measure. I was taken by surprise. She looked up at me with naughtiness dancing in her usually innocent brown eyes.

"Maybe you could call me again tonight, Mr. Heavy Breather. I might have a little surprise in store for you."

"Oh?" I asked.

"Just make sure to call before midnight. Before twelve, I can be a nasty, dirty girl. After twelve, I get really sleepy."

"I am making a mental note right now," I assured her.

We wandered into the deli, ordered some sandwiches, and found a table. Jordan went to the restroom and I sat down. The place was crowded and people had to speak loudly to be heard. As I meticulously laid out napkins and plastic utensils, I strained to listen to the conversations around me.

Professor Donnelly was a crabby old bastard. The library was so dusty, someone thought they were going to have an asthma attack right there. The concert on Saturday at Mississippi Nights was "rad." Someone's roommate was such a slob, he actually left used, empty pizza boxes, filled with cheesy residue lying around his bedroom for days.

No one mentioned a classmate or friend who had been found brutally beaten in Forest Park. No one wondered why that pretty girl from class wasn't there today. No one made a comment even slightly out of the ordinary. Everything was normal. Jordan came back and we ate our sandwiches and talked about the party over the weekend.

I even made sure to ask her how the art project she was working on was going. She went on about it in a little more detail than I would have preferred but I could tell she was really excited. This was her big project for the semester. It would essentially determine her grade and bring everything she'd learned in the program to bear. She didn't seem worried about it, just eager to dive in. Her enthusiasm was infectious.

As I listened to her talk, with her arms waving wildly and her eyes blazing, I felt an enormous sense of comfort. I was at ease with this woman. She exuded such confidence and enthusiasm that it was impossible for it not to rub off. She never seemed to doubt herself. And since one of the things she was sure of was me, I couldn't help but feel sure of myself, too. If she loved me, there had to be a good reason. After all, Jordan Lansing was rarely wrong.

She wasn't through describing the project, but I couldn't help it. I leaned over, put my arm behind her head, and pulled her to me. She was so into her description that she kept talking right up until the point when I kissed her. After we pulled apart, she had a perplexed smile on her face.

"What was that for?" she asked.

"I love you. I love you and I just had to kiss you. Sorry."

"That's okay," she said, blushing, "I love you, too."

We didn't say anything for a moment. All around us were the shouting voices of fellow students but we just sat and stared at each other. I think she would have let the moment go on forever, but I broke it.

"So you were talking about how you planned to set up the

base for your project," I reminded her. She smiled, pleased that I hadn't tried to change the subject. She started talking again and it wasn't long before the arms were once more flying about in fits of creative expression.

After my last class of the day, Intro to American Literature, Jeff and I walked back to the frat house. It was 4:15. This was the first class I'd had with my friend of four years and I was pleased to discover that he was a conscientious note-taker. It allowed me the occasional late afternoon daydream. As we walked into the house, it was immediately apparent that something was going on.

There were fifteen guys crowded around the television, none of them speaking. That was very rare. Jeff opened his mouth to make some sort of crack, but managed to catch himself at the last second, sensing that whatever was happening was bad. We exchanged glances and I'm sure he interpreted my expression as a mirror of his own, which was basically, "what the hell is going on?" Of course, that's not what I was thinking. We wandered over to the group and watched what looked to be a breaking news report. A woman was standing in front of the emergency room of Barnes Hospital with a concerned look on her face.

"So once again, Chuck, this is what we know. The young woman was discovered early this morning at about one A.M. by a vagrant in Forest Park. Park police were notified and the woman was taken here, to Barnes Hospital, which is less than a three-minute drive from where she was found. Doctors have informed us that she was severely beaten about the head and body and is in a coma.

"Police spokesman Leonard Ruber has indicated that, contrary to initial suspicions, this does not seem to have been a sexual assault or a robbery. Authorities are unclear at this time as to what instigated the brutal attack. They do say that the woman's car was found a few miles away at a local eatery. They believe that she was abducted there, then taken to the park, where she was assaulted. The vagrant who found the woman is in police custody right now, but authorities are not saying whether he is a suspect at this time.

"Doctors are currently listing the woman in critical condition and refuse to speculate on when, or if, she will regain consciousness. As we told you earlier, the woman has been identified as a student at nearby Jefferson University, but her name is not being released until her family has been notified. Once that has been done, we are expecting authorities to hold a news conference, at which more details should be made available. That's it for now. Live from Barnes Hospital, this is Megan Moses, Channel Eight Eyewitness News. Back to you, Chuck."

"Thanks, Megan. Once again, this breaking news. A Jefferson University student was found early this morning in Forest Park, brutally beaten and clinging to life. She is currently in critical condition at Barnes Hospital. We will, of course, have much more on this story during the five o'clock news. We now return you to *Judge Judy*, already in progress."

The "breaking news" graphic filled the screen for a moment before being replaced by Judge Judy, wagging her finger at a teenager. No one in the living room spoke. Finally, someone asked if anybody knew who it was. Everyone just shrugged. A few of the guys went upstairs to call around. Others wandered down to the kitchen, apparently having recovered from the news, intent on finding snacks. A few more stayed in front of the TV. I wasn't sure if they were waiting for more reports or just into the judge's rant. Jeff gave me a pat on the shoulder and headed upstairs to his third-floor room.

I tossed my backpack on the floor next to one of the couches and sat down to think. She wasn't dead. That was the biggest thing. I had wailed away on her skull and left her in the snow in subfreezing temperatures and she had not died. Yet. And from the sound of things, they didn't know she was pregnant. I wondered briefly if maybe the stress to her body had

caused her to miscarry. Maybe no one would find out about it
at all.

I knew that they would let the bum go pretty soon. They
would have to determine very quickly that there was no way
he could have gotten Kelly from the Meet & Eat to the park.
Besides, if he was responsible, he had nothing to gain by reporting finding her to the cops. I figured he'd be free by tomorrow morning at the latest. I could only pray that he hadn't
seen me. Despite the growing pit in my stomach, I told myself
to calm down. In an area as exposed as that clearing, it was
unlikely that anyone could have seen me without me seeing
him.

With the bum's release imminent, I had a decision to make.
It wouldn't take long for the police to question the people at
the restaurant. They would find out from them, and from Dot
in particular, about the guy Kelly was with and the meal and
the argument and the hug in the parking lot. They may have
already had that discussion. I would eventually be identified as
the guy. I had to take the initiative and come forward. I had
to look as if I was volunteering information. I couldn't be per-
ceived as trying to hide anything.

But should I go in now? That seemed premature. At this
point, no innocent person knew who the beaten girl was. Her
roommate, Lindsay, might be worried since she hadn't seen her
since last night and maybe the thought would have entered
Dan's mind if he had seen the report and had been trying to
get a hold of her. But there was no reason yet for me, as an
innocent person, to make the connection between my meeting
with Kelly last night and the girl on the news. I would wait
until they released her name.

I decided to go up to Dan's room to see if he'd heard yet.
He lived on the third floor, just a few doors down from Jeff.
Brothers who lived in the house got gradually better rooms each
semester. As a freshman, one might have to live with three or
four guys. A double was possible as a sophomore or junior. As
a second semester senior, Dan had one of the best. It was a

roomy single on the top floor, away from all the noise down below and near the end of the hall so people weren't always running by.

It was also conveniently in sight of the fire exit, which was basically a worn-down metal staircase that ran along the side of the house. It made for a great escape route. Many a guy, upon hearing his angry girlfriend was coming up the main stairs, would avail himself of the fire escape to sneak out unnoticed. Dan had used it often.

I stopped in front of his door. I was about to knock when I realized I didn't have any reason to be checking in on him. We weren't very good friends and I had only been in his room a few times the last semester, mostly in groups. Then I had an idea. I went back down to the main floor and checked his mail slot. There were two letters. I grabbed one of them, went back up to his room and knocked. He opened the door.

"Hey, Jake," he said, obviously surprised to see me, "what's up?"

"I found this on the floor in the hall," I told him, handing over the letter. "I don't know if someone accidentally grabbed it or dropped it or what, but I wanted to make sure it got to you."

"Thanks, man," he said, taking the envelope, "do you want to come in?"

"Sure," I said, stepping into the room, "I don't think I've ever been in here sober."

"Yeah, I guess I usually keep things private up here unless it's a party or something."

"That's cool. Why do you think I live off campus? I'd never get anything done if I lived here. You probably love being able to come to your little cave here and get away from everything. Like, I bet last night, after the meeting, you came straight up here and locked the door. Am I right?"

"Naw, man. I'm not some recluse. I hung out downstairs for a little while. But you know how it is—put off studying all weekend so then you have to do it all late Sunday night. So eventually, I had to come back to the lair, you know."

"I know what you mean. Thank god it's our last semester. I'm so burned out on studying, it's not even funny."

"Is that why you're going to school for three more years, Jake? Law school isn't exactly a break from studying."

"I know," I agreed, deciding it was time to cut to the chase, "am I crazy or what? I guess the main thing I'll have to remember wherever I go is not to visit the local park for any late-night studying." It was a clunky transition, but I had to get there somehow.

"What are you talking about?" he asked.

"Didn't you hear? Some girl got attacked in Forest Park last night. Apparently she was beaten up really badly. She's in a coma or something. It was just on the news. They're saying it's a Jeff. U. student but they won't release the name until they contact the family. Freaky, huh?"

"Yeah. That's awful."

"I know. I guess I shouldn't make jokes like that studying thing. After all, it could be someone I know. Anyway, I just wanted to make sure you got your letter. I didn't mean to bum you out."

"No, that's cool. I appreciate this," he said, holding up the envelope I had stolen, "I'll catch you later."

"Later, Dan," I said as casually as possible as I stepped into the hall and shut the door. I stood there for a moment, listening closely. I heard him pick up the phone and dial the four digits to indicate it was an on-campus call.

"Hey, Lindsay," I heard him say, "Is Kelly there?"

I quietly moved away from the door and headed down the hall.

Since I had walked to school that morning, I had to hurry to make it back to my place in time for the five P.M. news. I actually had to run the last little bit. When I got to the apartment, I vaulted up the stairs, three at a time. I got inside, yanked off my backpack, and clicked on the television just in time. It was 4:59. I sat down and waited.

I put on the same station that had run the report. They led with Kelly. The anchor came on, said the same stuff he had before, then threw it to Megan Moses, who was still in front of the emergency room. She began by going over the information she had reported earlier. Just as I began to wonder whether she had anything new to offer, she revealed that a press conference had just been held.

"Chuck, this was Police Spokesman Leonard Ruber addressing the media a few moments ago," her voice announced as a man in a police uniform with an extremely bushy mustache stepped up to a microphone. He cleared his throat and began.

"At approximately 1:14 this morning, a woman was admitted to Barnes Hospital with multiple blunt force trauma to the skull and the body. She was unconscious upon arrival and has remained so. The medical personnel were able to stabilize her. She's currently listed in critical but stable condition. We've identified the woman as Kelly Elizabeth Stone, a student at Jefferson University. We believe that she was abducted from a restaurant in the Clayton district and transported to Forest Park where she was assaulted. There is no evidence of sexual assault or robbery.

"She was last seen at the Meet & Eat restaurant on Brentwood in the Clayton district at 11:30 yesterday evening. She was accompanied by a male, identified as being about six-foot-one and one hundred and ninety pounds with brown hair and blue eyes. (At that point, the spokesman held up a drawing that looked a little like me, but was far from a perfect match. The guy in the picture wore glasses.) If anyone has seen this man or has any information they believe could be helpful please call Crime Information at the number on your screen."

At that point, Megan returned to the screen. She finished up where the spokesman left off.

"Officer Ruber went on to say that the vagrant who found Ms. Stone was released earlier this afternoon and is not believed

to be a suspect. Once again, anyone who has information per-
taining to this case is advised to call the number at the bottom
of your screen."

"Megan," Chuck asked, "do the police have any suspects
in mind now that they've released the vagrant who found her?"

"Not at this time, Chuck," Megan admitted. "My sources
tell me that the vagrant didn't discover the victim until after
the attack and could not help identify the assailant. However,
I was told by one officer that they believe the perpetrator may
be a fellow student, perhaps the man who was seen with Ms.
Stone earlier in the evening. This is Megan Moses, reporting
live from Barnes Hospital for Channel Eight Eyewitness News
at five. Back to you in the studio, Chuck."

Just then, then phone rang. I was surprised it took that long.
As I put the TV on mute and picked up, a thought flashed
through my head—my clumsy attempt to fake a rape had failed.

"Hello."

"Are you watching this?" Jordan's breathless voice asked
me.

"Yeah, can you believe it? I think that picture was supposed
to be me."

"No shit. You better call in quick and tell them what you
know. Jesus, Jake, what happened? Did you see anyone?" she
asked. I listened to her closely, trying to gauge any mistrust in
her voice. I couldn't hear any.

"No. But it was cold. We said good night and I just got in
my car and drove off. She was still fumbling with her keys when
I left the parking lot," I said, then paused as if something dramatic had just hit me. "Oh my god, Jordan, you don't think
she was attacked right after I left, do you? I didn't wait for her
to get in her car. I just left because I wanted to get home to
talk to you. I should have made sure she was safe in her car
before I left."

"Jake," she said firmly, reassuringly, with the confidence I
loved, "there is no way you could have guessed this would
happen. But you can't think about that right now. You need

to hang up and call that number. You have to tell the police what you know. Hell, for all they know right now, you could have done this."

"You're right," I agreed, as if the idea had just occurred to me, "I'll do it now."

"Good. Let me know what happens."

"I will. I can't believe this. Jordan, you know I love you, right?" It was pretty much the first honest thing I'd said in our entire conversation.

"I know you do. Now make that call," she said, then hung up to reinforce the demand.

I hung up the phone and headed downstairs to my car. I decided that if Jordan asked later, I would tell her that I had tried to call but the line was busy. For this to work, I had to deal with everything in person. I got into my car. Here was the crucial part. I didn't want to have to drive Rick's car to the hospital and I didn't want to take a cab. I said a silent prayer in the hopes that my tired, old, dirty white Prelude would start. I turned the key in the ignition and was pleasantly surprised to hear the engine turn over. My battery had returned from the dead. Things were starting to go my way.

CHAPTER SEVEN

I got to the hospital just before 5:30 and parked in the emergency zone, deciding that it wouldn't look proper later if I
spent five minutes trying to find a legal parking space. I ran
into the lobby and asked for Kelly Stone's room. When the
receptionist told me that was confidential, I yelled at her, saying
that I had crucial information for the police. I must have been
convincing because she immediately told me the floor.

I ran to the elevator, jumped in, and hit the button. There
was no one else with me so I took the alone time to get
psyched. After this, I would probably not have a moment to
myself for quite a while, so I would have to be on. Whether
or not I would be charged with attempted murder would de-
pend in large part on how persuasive I could be over the next
couple of hours. I took a deep breath. There was a nervous pit
in my stomach. It reminded me of how I felt just before a big
basketball game in high school. Usually the feeling went away
once I started running up and down the court and got a sweat

going. But sweating was probably not a good idea in this situation.

The elevator stopped and the door opened. I stepped out and looked down the hall. I could see a bunch of people milling about, some in police uniforms. I pretended not to notice, went straight for the nurses' station and asked for Kelly Stone's room. I got the same response as downstairs. Just like before, I upped the volume as if I didn't give a shit about confidentiality.

While the woman awkwardly said she would page the head nurse, I looked around. There was a familiar-looking girl sitting on a chair halfway down the hall. She glanced up momentarily when I raised my voice, then returned to her previous position. Her elbows were propped up on her thighs, with her face resting in her hands. I searched my memory for a few seconds, then it clicked. The girl was Lindsay Donner, Kelly's roommate.

She was the only other person who knew Kelly was meeting someone that night. I'd seen her around campus, even hanging out at some of our parties, usually with Kelly. We'd never formally met. For her to have gotten here ahead of me and already be settled in, she must have left her suite right after Dan called asking for Kelly. Lindsay must have suspected the worst. I wondered why Dan wasn't here, too.

Lindsay was cute. Even under these trying circumstances, there was an unfussy, casual attractiveness to her. She had long, dirty blond hair that cascaded over her shoulders in little ringlets. It wasn't obvious now, with her slouched over, but I remembered that she had quite a body. She was really curvy with nice, wide hips and an impressive chest. She reminded me a lot of Elisabeth Shue in her *Cocktail* years.

I knew that my little encounter with the nurse would have someone in authority heading my way soon, so I used the brief pause in the action to see what this girl was about. I walked over and stood right in front of Lindsay, waiting patiently until she noticed me. Finally, she looked up. There was something about her that threw me. She seemed dangerously self-possessed. Until she spoke.

"What?" she asked, apparently too tired and upset to worry about diplomacy.

"Are you Lindsay?"

"Why?"

"It's just that I know you. I know I've seen you around campus, at parties and stuff. Your Kelly's roommate, right?"

"Yes. We've been going to school together for four years and that's the best you can do? You vaguely remember that I'm Kelly's roommate?"

"I'm sorry."

"What the fuck are you doing here anyway? You and Kelly aren't friends. You and I aren't friends. Why are you here?"

"Kelly and I weren't great friends but we had a class together last semester and we got to know each other a little. And her boyfriend's in my fraternity."

"So what?" she demanded impatiently. I was not doing a great job here. I was trying to be subtle and slowly introduce points one by one, but this girl wasn't having any of it. If she was frustrated with me, I could only imagine how the police would react. I had to get down to business.

"Look, I'm the guy from the news reports. Kelly and I met to talk at the Meet & Eat last night. She wanted my advice on some stuff. Now I find out that I may have been one of the last people to talk to her before all this happened. I wanted to help."

"You were the person she went to see last night?" she asked incredulously.

"Yeah. She told you about that? I thought she wanted to keep it quiet."

"She told me she was meeting someone. She didn't say who or why."

"She just needed to talk to somebody and we had had a few conversations recently. It was a very specific situation," I said, deciding that to reveal any more at that point would be counterproductive.

"I don't see what was so specific that she couldn't discuss it with me," Lindsay said, more hurt than curious. I was rescued from having to go into more detail by a man walking toward us. He was tall, about six-foot-three with closely cropped black hair and frighteningly blue eyes. He was dressed in slacks and a jacket and tie, all of which looked well worn. I knew even before he spoke that the man was a detective.

"Excuse me," he said politely once he reached us, "but the nurse said you were looking for Kelly Stone, that you needed to see her." He looked straight at me. Obviously he had already spoken to Lindsay. I was on.

"Yes," I said, nodding, "I was watching the news and I saw the story and came right over. I can't believe it."

"What can't you believe?" he asked blankly.

"I was just with her last night. I mean we were at that restaurant, talking and stuff, and then this happens."

"Are you saying that you were the man who was with her yesterday evening?"

"Yeah, of course. I mean, we met for a snack and because she needed to talk about some stuff. It was the most normal thing in the world. I don't see how this could happen."

"What's your name?" he asked, pulling out a little spiral notepad.

"Jake Conason."

"Jake, I'm Detective John Cardinal. I'm investigating this case. Do you mind if we step over here for a minute to talk?" he asked, pointing to an unoccupied part of the hall.

"Sure, of course," I said. We walked over to the empty area and he began again.

"So I want to make sure I've got this straight. You're the man who was with Kelly Stone last night?"

"I'm the guy she was with in the restaurant. I mean, I saw that sketch and I guess it's supposed to be me. I freaked out. The news made it sound like I was a suspect or something. So

I thought I better get down here and clear everything up and see how Kelly is. Is she okay?"

"What are you to Kelly, Jake?" he asked, ignoring my question. "Are you her boyfriend?"

"God no. We're not even really good friends. In fact, her boyfriend is one of my fraternity brothers, Dan Curson. I'm sure he's around here somewhere," I said, pretending to look around. "Kelly and I had a class together and sometimes we'd talk after. She asked me for some advice and I tried to help."

"What did she want advice on?"

"Just some stuff with Dan. I guess she figured I could help because I knew him."

"What was the stuff?"

I paused, as if we had hit the first topic that made me uncomfortable. I looked at Detective Cardinal, putting on my best conflicted face.

"I'd rather not go into the details of it. Let's just say it was relationship problem stuff," I said, as if that was the end of it.

"Jake, this woman was viciously assaulted. Don't be coy with me. It's important that you tell me everything that she told you." His voice was patient, but very firm.

"It's just . . ." again I struggled, "it's just that I think she came to me because she felt she could trust my discretion. I don't think she'd want me revealing the personal things she talked about."

Detective Cardinal didn't even speak. He just stared at me.

"Okay," I relented, "I guess her privacy isn't as important as helping you guys. Like I said, it was mostly relationship stuff. She was upset because Dan is kind of easygoing and she wanted him to put out more effort in school. Dan's a smart guy, but he's not exactly the hardest worker. She wanted me to talk to him, to try to get him to take things a little more seriously. I think she hoped they would get married after graduation and she wanted him to have more certainty about his future, you know. She wanted him to take more responsibility."

"And why were you the guy to tell him this stuff?" Cardinal

asked, not even looking up, madly taking down notes in his little pad.

"Well, I kind of have a reputation as this achiever-type. I'm trying to get into law school and I have pretty good grades. And Kelly and I had talked a little because I helped her out some in a biology class we had together last semester. So I guess she thought I was a good person to do it, you know. Because I'd kind of helped her out before and her boyfriend and I are friendly because of the fraternity."

"So you had this talk with Kelly and then you left the restaurant?"

"Yeah, well, I mean, Dan was supposed to meet us, but when that didn't happen, Kelly got kind of upset and stormed out. So I had to run after her."

"Wait, slow down for a second. You're saying that Dan was supposed to meet the two of you at the restaurant that night?"

"That's what she told me. I was actually a little annoyed with her at first. See, she asked me to meet her there at eleven but I showed up a little late. So she tells me all this personal stuff and then she drops this bomb on me that she told Dan to meet her there at 11:15. She wanted us to have the talk right then. So I remember, I looked at my watch and it was like, 11:17 at that second. I was upset, you know. I thought she had kind of forced me into this position without my having a chance to decide for myself if I wanted to help. I said something to that effect and she just started crying."

"She was crying?"

"Yeah. She tried to hide it when the waitress came over but she was pretty emotional. She was all over the map."

"So then what happened?"

"Well, we waited for a while, until I'd say, 11:30 or so and Dan still hadn't shown up. So Kelly starts getting all upset. I mean, she was really freaking. She said that he was probably off screwing some other girl, which I didn't think was fair. I mean, sure, he's not the most faithful guy of all time. I know he didn't want to be tied down and to be honest, Kelly *is* a little clingy. But still.

"Of course I didn't tell her this. What I did tell her was that Dan loved her a lot. Which is true. I mean, he can get really possessive about her. I remember one time, at one of our parties, he saw some guy hitting on Kelly pretty hard and stormed over there like he was going to break the guy in half. It took three or four of us to hold him back. I reminded Kelly about that. But she wasn't convinced. She was still crying. She said he was an asshole or something and ran out."

"So what happened when you got outside?" Cardinal asked.

"Well, I managed to catch up to her and calm her down. I asked her if she had told him what the meeting was supposed to be about. She said she hadn't, so I tried to convince her that maybe he didn't know how important it was, maybe he just fell asleep or something. She laughed at that because that's not unlike Dan, if you know what I mean. I kind of calmed her down, we hugged good-bye and I left."

"Did you see anything unusual when you were leaving?"

"No, but I wasn't really looking for anything, you know. It was cold and I just wanted to get home. Besides, I was getting a headache from my glasses."

"Yeah, you had glasses in the sketch but you're not wearing them now."

"I know. I had already taken out my contacts for that evening so I just wore my glasses to meet her. But the prescription's old, so if I wear them for any length of time, I start to get a headache."

"I see. Now you don't remember seeing anyone else in the parking lot?" he asked.

"I did see some burly guy in a watchcap and heavy coat getting out of a car, but that's it, I think. He didn't look suspicious to me."

"The waitress mentioned a man fitting that description as well. Can you remember anything else about the guy?"

"Not really. I wasn't paying attention. Where was he when the waitress saw him?" I asked.

"Don't worry about that. What kind of car do you drive, Jake?"

"A white Honda Prelude."

"Four door?"

"Two. Why?"

"No reason. So last night, where was Kelly when you left?"

"She was unlocking her door. I remember we waved good-bye as I pulled out of the lot," I said, letting my voice choke and the tears rise to my eyes. It wasn't hard. All I had to do was think about the girl clinging to life only feet away from me. "I didn't realize it might be good-bye forever. I was so oblivious. I just wanted to get home to talk to my girlfriend. I didn't wait to make sure she got in the car safely. Why didn't I wait, Detective? It would have been an extra thirty seconds."

Detective Cardinal looked up from his pad to see the tears streaming down my face. I wiped them away quickly, as if embarrassed by myself.

"You can't think that way, Jake. You couldn't know." He sounded sincere, but I wasn't sure if he was testing me, hoping for some slip up. To be safe, I just nodded and bit my lip. He asked me a few other questions, mostly about the details of the night—exactly when I arrived, when I left, when I got home. He said he wanted to pin down all the relevant times to get a clearer picture of what happened.

He looked to be about done when he asked me, almost as an afterthought, if I had seen Dan today. I'd been worried that he would never get to that. I didn't want to bring it up myself for fear of seeming too eager. But now I had been asked and I had to answer.

"It's funny that you ask that, but yeah, I did. I saw him a few hours ago at the house. I had just seen the first news report about the attack, but they didn't give out the name of the victim and I hadn't made the connection. I went up to his room. I didn't get into the whole issue of why he hadn't shown up last night. I figured that was something between him and Kelly. But I kind of tried to do what Kelly asked."

"What do you mean?"

"Well, I sort of brought up studying in this roundabout way. I thought I could ease into a talk about being more responsible. It was actually really awkward. I gave up after a few minutes. In fact, God, I didn't think about this until just now. I remember I changed the subject because I felt so uncomfortable. I asked him if he'd seen the news report about the attack."

"Had he?"

"He said no. We talked about it for a minute. Actually I talked about it for a minute, how awful it would be if it was someone we knew. He was kind of quiet. How weird that it turned out that we were probably more closely connected to her than anyone, except maybe her roommate, Lindsay. God, Dan must be so upset right now. Is he around here somewhere? Can I talk to him?"

"I haven't seen him," Detective Cardinal said, "but I'm sure he'll be by soon. I want to thank you for all your information, Jake, but I need you to do me one more favor."

"Sure," I said as casually as I could, even though the nervousness that had slowly abated now lurched front and center again. I was certain he needed me to put my hands up against the wall. I saw that Lindsay was watching me closely from down the hall and wondered if she was thinking the same thing.

"I need you to go to Officer Kenner over there and tell him everything you just told me, giving him every detail of last night from the minute you left your place until you got back, including a description of the man you saw in the parking lot. Be as specific as possible. I'm going to give you my card. If you remember anything else, please give me a call. I'll be getting in touch with you again to go over this some more. I may even want you to go to the Meet & Eat with me, to nail down the details of exactly where you were at various moments. Does that sound okay to you?"

"Of course," I told him, "anything I can do to help. Maybe

I can make up a little for leaving early last night. I didn't stop
this from happening. The least I can do is help catch the person
who did it." I walked over to the officer before Detective Cardinal could say anything. I desperately wanted to look back to
see his expression, but managed to fight the urge.

I was also tempted to ask if the news report saying that the
bum hadn't seen the attacker was accurate, but I held back.
There was no way to raise the issue without raising suspicion,
too. Besides, if that bum had seen anything, I had a feeling
Cardinal wouldn't be letting me leave.

The cop led me down to the coffee room. As I passed by
Lindsay, who was still sitting on the chair, I gave a half-hearted
wave. She couldn't bring herself to lift her arm, but did manage
a little nod. As we turned the corner, I glanced back down the
hall and just happened to catch sight of Dan bursting out of
the elevator.

He was still dressed as he had been when I saw him earlier
that afternoon. His hair was disheveled and his wild eyes were
red. Since he was such a burly guy, the sight of him in that
kind of frenzy was kind of intimidating. He saw one of the
uniformed officers and ran toward him. I looked down at my
watch. It was almost six. The news report had come on at five.
For a grieving, innocent boyfriend, he was arriving awfully late
to the party.

CHAPTER EIGHT

That night, I went over to Jordan's. We sat in the living room of her suite and I filled her in on the whole night. Her suitemate, Joanie, was there, too, so I had a full audience. I started with a little lie about having called the number on TV. I told her it was busy so I had just gone straight to the hospital, figuring there were sure to be police there.

From that point on, my version of the events at the hospital was pretty accurate. I may have played up my devastation a bit and made Dan's late arrival seem a little more suspicious than it was, but otherwise, I kept pretty much to the story. I recounted my conversation with Detective Cardinal in as much detail as possible. I figured repeating the words would help reinforce them in my mind.

After I was done, Jordan and I said good night to Joanie and retired to her room. Luckily for us, she had a single. We didn't talk much. Instead we just lay in bed. She cozied up behind me, wrapped her arms around my waist, and hugged tight. Just before we drifted off to sleep, I whispered to her.

"I don't know what I'd do if anyone ever tried to hurt you." The thought of Jordan in pain or danger made me wince.

"Don't think that way," she whispered back, "nothing's going to happen to me . . . or us. Just get some sleep." She kissed me on the cheek and seconds later I was dreaming.

The next day was very odd. By the time I got to my first class at noon, word had spread around campus that I was the guy from the sketch, that I had gone to the hospital to see Kelly and was now helping the police in their investigation. Somehow, the possibility that I was a suspect didn't seem to come up much. Apparently my willingness to come forward and my obvious emotion at the hospital had spread, too, and I had been given, for the most part, a pass.

Most people, if they thought about it all, didn't see any reason why I'd want to hurt Kelly. Already, Dan's late arrival at the hospital, his supposed bad temper and general campus awareness about his and Kelly's brief winter breakup were casting him in a questionable light. I was amazed at the number of people who came up to me, offering their apologies or well wishes. I didn't know if they were sorry for having thought ill of me initially or if they thought Kelly and I were closer friends than we were and that I must be upset. I was approached so often during the course of the day that I started to feel like a minor celebrity. A few people even looked like they wanted to ask me for autographs. No one did.

I learned from one girl that much of the goodwill I was getting was a result of Lindsay. Apparently, her version of last night's events had made me out to be very sympathetic—genuinely concerned about Kelly's condition and incredibly cooperative with the police. I hadn't realized I had made such an impression on her. I decided that I should stop by her place at some point today, to commiserate and continue to sustain a good image in her eyes.

After classes that afternoon, I stopped by the house and used

Jeff's phone to call my apartment and check messages. There was one from Detective Cardinal asking me to join him at the Meet & Eat at five that afternoon to go over the specifics of Sunday night. My watch read 3:20—plenty of time. I called the number he gave and left a message saying I would meet him there.

A bunch of guys wanted to hear about Sunday night's events at the restaurant as well as last night at the hospital. I didn't mind because it gave me one more chance to nail down the details. I tried to cast things in the most effective light without going overboard. Also, I figured that the more people who knew my version of how events transpired, the more likely that version was to be repeated as gospel.

I checked my watch again. It was now almost four and I still hadn't done what I came here for. I told the guys I wanted to check on Dan, to see how he was doing. When I said it, there was a weird silence. I could sense the shift in mood. Nobody said anything, but I could tell that there was an awkwardness, a lack of trust, that had sprung up between Dan and the rest of the fraternity in just the last twelve hours. I headed upstairs, trying to keep the corners of my mouth from curling into a grin.

When I got to the third floor, I could already hear the music from Dan's room. He was blasting the Pixies' "Wave of Mutilation." It wasn't the Doolittle version, but the slower, more mournful take from the *Pump Up the Volume* sound track. I admired his taste but couldn't help thinking that his musical choice was probably not helping to create a reassuring impression among his fraternity brothers.

I had to bang on his door three times before he finally opened up. It was obvious he'd been drinking. His breath smelled strongly of Southern Comfort and Coke. Beyond him, I saw the half-full bottle of SoCo sitting on the coffee table in the middle of his room. He eyed me with dull, suspicious eyes.

"Can I come in?" I asked. He nodded and opened the door

to make room. I sat down in his love seat while he turned the music down and climbed onto his bed.

"Why didn't you tell me?" he asked.

"Tell you what?"

"Why didn't you tell me that you met with Kelly on Sunday to talk about me?"

"Oh man, this is awkward. Listen Dan, I wanted to. But I also didn't want to butt into your business. I didn't know Kelly had asked me there that night to talk about you. And when you didn't show up, I figured you were pissed or something. I just didn't want to get in the middle of it."

"I'm so confused," he said with a bit of a slur, "the cops said you and Kelly were expecting me to be there on Sunday, but I told them, I never talked to her that night. I didn't know I was supposed to meet anyone."

"I don't get that. Kelly told me you were going to be there."

"Did she say she talked to me or left a message?"

"I don't remember," I told him, frowning as if struggling with the memory, "she just said you were coming."

"I am so confused," he said again, closing his eyes in the hopes that the darkness might bring back some nonexistent memory.

"Don't worry, man," I said, using my reassuring voice, "this will all blow over. When Kelly gets better she'll clear everything up."

"Jake, from what the cops told me, I don't know if she's going to get better. And the questions they kept asking me last night, they made me feel like a suspect. I think *they* think I did this, that I could have beaten up my own girlfriend."

"Listen, Dan, maybe they think that now, but eventually the truth is going to come out. You could not have done this. There is no way. I don't believe it and the people who know you don't believe it. I will tell that detective the same thing a thousand times if I have to. You just have to stay cool. I think it's good that you're staying in here. Don't feel like you have to defend yourself to anyone. I think the best thing for you to do right now is just continue with your life. I know it's hard, but you should do your homework, study, chill a little. You don't have to be out there defending yourself to people. When this is cleared up, they'll be coming to you to apologize."

Dan just nodded.

"And listen, buddy. I'm sorry I wasn't straight with you yesterday. I just didn't want to get into what I thought was your private business, you know?"

He nodded again. I got up and headed for the door, making sure to give him one last supportive smile before I left. As I walked down the hall, I heard him turn up the volume again. He had "Wave of Mutilation" on repeat. Not the smartest move.

I got to the Meet & Eat right at five. It was weird to be back here. Less than forty-eight hours earlier, the biggest concern in my life was whether I would get the internship I wanted. Now I was caught up in an assault investigation, which could easily become a murder investigation at any moment. As I got out of the car, I briefly wondered if I should have clubbed Kelly one more time, to make absolutely sure. If she ever woke up, I was screwed. Even if she had brain damage, I knew she'd find a way to point the finger.

As I walked over to Cardinal, I forced the negative thoughts out of my head. I had made certain to dress much as I had on Sunday night. I wore a thin jacket and my glasses. I wanted Dot to remember me as she had seen me in the restaurant. I didn't want her making any connection between me and the burly guy. I was the guy Kelly had eaten with, the one Dot saw her hug in the parking lot. The guy in the heavy coat carrying her to his car (if anyone had seen that) was someone else entirely, someone much bigger who didn't wear corrective lenses.

"Why are you wearing your glasses?" Detective Cardinal asked as I approached him.

"I've always had problems with my contacts when it gets really cold. Besides, I haven't been sleeping much lately and my eyes are always red and irritated. The glasses are just less of a nuisance."

"What about the headaches?"

"To be honest, Detective, I've been having headaches even with the contacts. I'm sleep-deprived, depressed, and I keep having these horrible nightmares. So these things are just one less hassle."

"What kind of nightmares are you having?" he asked.

"Oh, garden variety stuff. I hear Kelly screaming my name, begging me to help her. I see her getting attacked, but my car door is locked and I can't get out to help. I see her, bloody, asking me why I left early, why I didn't make sure she was safe, why I didn't help her. You know, fun stuff like that."

"You should see a counselor at the school or something. If you want I could put you in touch with one of the department's grief counselors."

"Thanks. Let me think about it. Actually, I think the best way for me to deal with this is to help you as much as I can. Maybe once you catch this guy, it'll get better."

"Well then, let's get started. I want you to go over everything that happened from the moment you left the restaurant until you drove off."

I proceeded to re-enact that night. Out of the corner of my eye, I saw a crowd gathering inside, watching my every move. Dot was right in the middle of the group, pointing and talking. I pretended not to notice. I explained all the physical details to Detective Cardinal, veering from the truth only at the end. This time, I didn't turn around to remind Kelly to keep quiet. I didn't surprise her by grabbing her wrist. She didn't slip and fall and land on the hard, frozen asphalt. I heard no stomach-churning thud.

This time, we hugged, said good-bye, went our separate

ways. I walked to *my* car, not Rick's. It was no longer parked at the back of the lot, near the alley. This time, it was right behind the restaurant, where it wasn't visible to the employees inside. It would not be odd if no one had seen my white Honda Prelude because now it had been parked in the shadows, where it would go unnoticed. This time, I didn't carry her limp body to a black, four-door Ford. Instead, I started my two-door Honda, pulled out and waved good-bye to Kelly, who was unlocking her car. She waved back, a little smile on her face. This time I left the parking lot, unaware of the carnage that may have already begun, only yards away.

We went over the evening a few more times, Detective Cardinal asking questions, me answering as simply as possible, occasionally asking him if a certain detail was important or not. I made sure to include the time and content of my phone conversation with Jordan, which I knew Cardinal had questioned her about earlier today. Around six, he thanked me, told me to go home, that he'd be in touch. I left. On the way over I had been so focused on getting to the restaurant on time, I hadn't thought about the significance of the route. But on the way home, traveling the same roads I had taken on Sunday, going in the same direction, making the same turns, I couldn't help but remember.

It was a Tuesday now, in the middle of rush hour. Unlike Sunday night, there were hundreds of cars on the road. I waited at the endless lights on Clayton, glancing at the people in cars around me, wondering if any of them had been out at 11:30 two nights ago. Did anyone look familiar? Did anyone recognize me? I pushed the thought away. Obsessing over something like that would get me nowhere. This time, instead of speeding down Clayton to Skinker, I turned left onto Big Bend. I was no longer on the Sunday route.

As I drove north, I glanced to my right, at the dorms and suites that comprised most of the university housing. I remembered that Lindsay lived there. Without really thinking, I made a right onto Shipson, the street that ran among the various dorms, and found a parking spot. I had checked around and found out that she lived in the suite building called Burleson. I had lived there myself during sophomore year.

As I knocked on her door, an unexpected nervousness hit me. I felt a sudden urge to turn and run. Before I could, someone opened it—Lindsay. Too late for a quick getaway. She looked tired. I suspected she had gotten as little sleep as I claimed to. She seemed a little surprised to see me but invited me in.

Her roommates were in the kitchen, making dinner. When they saw me there was an awkward little moment. But it was over almost as soon as it began and they resumed their cooking. Lindsay led me back to her room. After I entered, she shut the door and sat down on her bed. I didn't know what to do, so I sat on the other bed, not realizing until I was on it that it was Kelly's. Neither of us spoke for a few seconds. I realized that we were bonded in a strange way. She believed that we were the last two people to see Kelly alive and well. I *knew* that we were the last two (not counting Dot) to see her, period.

Lindsay pulled out a joint, lit it, took a big hit, and offered it to me. I thought about it, but declined. She shrugged and took my turn. She looked better than she had last night. She was wearing sweatpants and a white T-shirt that was a size too small and hugged her tightly. I tried not to stare.

"So have you heard anything new about Kelly?" I asked. "How's she doing?"

"She's still in a coma," Lindsay said matter-of-factly. "The doctors don't know if she'll ever regain consciousness."

"I'm sorry."

"Uh-huh," she agreed and took another long drag.

"I don't know exactly why I'm here," I told her, "but I thought maybe we should talk. I thought we should talk to each other outside of a hospital environment."

"You know, Jake," Lindsay said, easing back on her bed, "Kelly never mentioned you. Not once. If not for this whole nightmare, I would never have known that you two knew each other."

"Well, we weren't exactly best friends. I was just trying to help her out."

"With boyfriend problems," she half-said, half-asked.

"Right."

"Kelly and I used to talk about her relationship with Dan all the time. I just can't figure out why she suddenly decided to take you into her confidence."

"Neither can I," I said. We sat there in silence for what seemed like an hour. It was probably about twenty seconds. Finally I gave in and tried another tack.

"So you and Kelly must have been pretty close," I said.

"What makes you say that?" she asked.

"You're roommates."

"So?"

"Well, me and my roommate are good friends. I just figured the person you'd agree to spend a year living with would be someone you liked."

"I guess."

"Lindsay, you seemed a lot more emotional last night. I'm glad you've managed to get control of your feelings."

For the first time in a few minutes, she actually looked at me. Looked through me is more like it. There was something in her light brown eyes that sent a shiver through me. For the briefest of moments, I sensed that she knew. She knew everything. But there was no way she could. And after a second I realized it was the pot making her seem all knowing, not anything internal.

"I think I'm gonna go," I said. "I just wanted to check in on you, make sure you were cool."

"I'm cool," she assured me as she took another hit. "So how's Jordan doing? You know we're in the same sorority."

"She's good," I said, not sure what that had to do with anything.

"Jordan's nice. Maybe a little too cheerful for my taste, but

I'm not dating her. I wouldn't have pegged you two as a couple."

"What do you mean?" I asked, not sure I liked her tone.

"Well, I don't really know you, but I always thought you had some depth. And she strikes me as kind of a lightweight."

"Where do you get that? Do you even know her?" I demanded, "because if you did, I don't think you'd be so quick to dismiss her."

"No offense. I was actually complimenting you. I didn't mean anything by it."

"Well, I take offense. Maybe I should just leave." I waited for her to say something, to apologize, something. She didn't say a word, so I got up and left. None of the other girls noticed as I stormed out of the suite. On the drive home, I tried to get Lindsay out of my head, but the thought of her sitting there on her bed, full of ambivalence and arrogance and unnatural knowledge couldn't help but creep me out.

That night, I got to hang out with my roommate, Rick, for the first time in what seemed like forever. He had been so busy with classes and I had been so busy with the police that I wasn't even sure he knew what was going on. He did. As we made dinner, I filled him in on all the details that he hadn't gathered through the community grapevine.

We sat in the living room, ate our chicken and pasta and caught up. He had learned another Clapton song and promised to play it for me later. I swore to act as if I could tell the difference between good and bad guitar playing. After dinner, he poured each of us a scotch and we sat in the living room with the TV on mute, watching the snow fall outside our front window.

"So what's gonna happen with this Kelly thing?" Rick finally asked, for the first time addressing an issue larger than specific dates and times.

"I'm not sure," I said, trying not to be too talkative because

Rick was a good friend. I didn't want to lie to him more than I had to and I figured he was more likely than most to be able to tell when I was.

"Is that detective going to be asking you any more questions?"

"I wouldn't be surprised. This is a pretty serious case and I don't think he has that much to go on."

"Does it freak you out at all to think that you could have been the victim?"

"What do you mean?" I asked.

"I mean, if Kelly had gotten in her car right away, maybe this guy would have gone after you instead."

"I guess," I agreed, not really wanting to get into the possible alternative scenarios of that night.

"I didn't mean to bring you down, buddy," he said, seeing that I was in no mood to play "potential assault variations." "I'll tell you what, why don't I break out the guitar and you can put that keen intellect to something productive. I'll play and you can judge me and my level of talent."

"That sounds good."

Rick pulled out his guitar and began to play. It was a pretty impressive rendition of "Tears in Heaven." His voice was just beyond mediocre, but he kept it low and soft, refusing to push it too far. And his mastery of the song itself was impressive. He played it for me three or four times, getting better each time. Finally, as he finished up for what had to be the fifth effort, someone began applauding from the hallway. We looked over to find Jordan standing at the edge of the living room. I don't know how long she had been there but she seemed to have caught most of Rick's performance.

"That's pretty good," she said, as she walked over and sat on my lap, "do you know anything else?"

"To what do we owe the honor of your presence?" Rick asked, flattered and trying to hide it.

"Jake invited me over for a little Tuesday evening get together. Didn't he tell you?" she asked, obviously aware that I had forgotten.

"No, he didn't tell me," Rick said, although he didn't seem too upset.

"Sorry, Ricky," I replied, "I invited Jordan over for a little Tuesday evening get together. Do you mind?"

"Of course not. It's always a pleasure to have a chick like her come over and class up the joint."

"Thank you, Rick. That is very flattering," Jordan said.

I went to the kitchen to get her a scotch and Rick eased into a pleasant rendition of Tom Petty's "Free Falling." He was in fine form. As I poured her a glass and listened to my friend's casual, unhurried voice, I felt my body start to relax. It was nice not to be on guard.

After Petty, Rick moved on to Dylan's "Like a Rolling Stone" and, after some urging from me, Van Morrison's "Brown Eyed Girl" which he dedicated to Jordan on my behalf. After he finished that one, I glanced at my watch. It was after ten and I had Ethics the next day. I decided to call it a night.

Jordan and I got up to leave. She started down the hallway to my room but I left her for a second and ran over to whisper something in Rick's ear. He smiled and nodded. Then I hurried to catch up to Jordan before she got to my room. About half-way down the hall, I heard the familiar sounds of Clapton's "Wonderful Tonight." Jordan heard it, too, and turned around. As she did, I caught up to her and scooped her up in my arms as if she were a bride and we were about to cross the threshold. I tried to kick open the bedroom door but managed only to hurt my ankle. Trying not to giggle, she reached down, turned the knob, and pushed the door open.

"Thank you, my darling," I said, stepping inside and shutting the door behind us. We could still hear the song slightly as I carried her over to the bed and slowly eased her down onto it. I turned on the CD player and Etta James's clear, crisp voice filled the room. There are few CDs better for late-night romance than the *Living Out Loud* sound track and "At Last" is one of the major reasons why.

Jordan looked up at me in the half-light of the moon coming in through my window. We kissed. She pulled me down onto the bed, right next to her. Neither of us spoke. I looked into her soft brown eyes and knew that I was lucky to have her. If I had ever doubted whether I was in love with this woman, those apprehensions now slipped away. Of course, Jordan wasn't perfect, but she was perfect for me.

She seemed to read my thoughts.

"Don't worry, baby," she cooed as she caressed my cheek, "soon all this ugliness will be in the past and we'll be able to focus on the good stuff—you and me, me and you."

I nodded. That's all I wanted—to put the Kelly mess behind me and get on with my life. My future—graduation, internship, law school, Jordan—it was all within reach. I just had to grab it and hold on tight, never let go. I decided to take a small step to firming up one part of my future then and there.

"Jordan," I whispered, trying not to grin as I said it. "I don't know if I want to make love yet. I think I'd rather talk about art history. How was class today?"

She smiled. There's no more effective way to ensure your girlfriend will sleep with you than to pretend you're not interested in sex, that you'd rather just talk. Of course, I wasn't trying very hard and Jordan wasn't fooled *or* in art history mode at that moment.

"That's sweet," she said, "even if it is completely transparent and self-centered. I'll tell you what, after we're through, we'll have a nice long chat about impressionism, okay?"

"After what?" I asked innocently as Etta's voice trailed off and was replaced by the funky strains of Brownstone's "If You Love Me."

She didn't answer. Instead, she pulled my shirt off and began to nibble at my chest. She licked and bit and kissed, all in perfect rhythm to the music. I closed my eyes and let myself go, concentrating only on her lips pressed against my tingling skin. At that moment, all was right with the world.

CHAPTER NINE

Detective Cardinal called at nine the next morning and asked me to come in to answer a few more questions. When I told him I had class and asked to come in that afternoon, he said I would have to miss class. I tried to convince him to at least let me go to Legal Ethics. Professor Sheridan hated it when students skipped. He said I had a good excuse, that he'd even give me a note but that I was to be at the station at ten o'clock.

I had never been to the police station and was surprised to find that, apart from all the cruisers outside, it looked just like any other small office building. I walked in, trying to act as casual as possible under the circumstances, and told the desk officer who I was and that Detective Cardinal wanted to see me. He said to have a seat—the detective would be out momentarily.

I sat down on the wooden bench. Next to me, an exceedingly obese man seemed to be sleeping sitting up. There was a form in his hand that had become crumpled as he involuntarily squeezed his fingers into a fist in his dream. I turned away and tried to focus on my own situation. I wasn't sure why I was here. When Cardinal called, the tone in his voice had made me uneasy. He didn't sound as conversational, as friendly as he had at the Meet & Eat last night. Obviously he had come across some new information that portrayed me in a bad light. I tried to think of what it might be.

The most likely possibility was that when Dot had seen me again yesterday, she realized that I was the guy in the coat and watchcap. I had convinced myself that because I didn't wear the huge coat or the cap or the gloves inside the restaurant that night and because I wasn't wearing the glasses outside after the accident, she hadn't made the connection. Maybe I had been premature in my optimism.

There was also the possibility that despite my best efforts, I had screwed up in some way in the park. There was a period there where I kind of lost it. My memory of that brief stretch of time was still foggy. It might even have been something beyond my control. Maybe the bum that found her *did* see me in that clearing. If that was the case, I was screwed. If they knew it was me, then even as I sat here, they were probably searching my apartment.

Their tests would find leftover bloodstains in my shower. They would find remnants of bloody clothing in the fireplace. They would surely check Rick's car and almost certainly find bloodstains that I thought I had removed. If they wanted to prove it was me, they would be able to.

My breathing grew shallow and my heart started to beat faster than normal. I was officially rattled. Cardinal opened the door from the back area. He didn't see me yet, was walking straight for the desk officer. I had to get a fucking grip. I had come this far. It was almost sixty hours after the attack and they hadn't brought anyone in since the bum. I'd heard somewhere that almost all crimes are solved within the first twenty-four hours. I didn't know if that was true, but I chose to believe it at that moment.

I'd played everybody so far. I'd worked Lindsay and Detective Cardinal at the hospital and did it again with Cardinal at the restaurant. I'd tricked Dan, Rick, and even Jordan, who knew me better than anyone. I had all of them walking around clueless. I had even turned one of them into the main suspect.

I was good. I did not want to be in this situation. I did not choose it or ask for it, but I was in it now and if I had to be here, I was going to make it work for me. I was supposed to be in law school a year from now. I was supposed to be on my way to being a litigator. I was supposed to be engaged to Jordan. And if I was worthy of all those things, I had to prove it now. I had to win now. If I couldn't clean up this mess, then I didn't deserve to get out of it. This was a challenge. And I was up to the fucking challenge.

Cardinal spoke to the desk officer briefly, who pointed in my direction. Cardinal waved and walked over to me. I had the juice rolling around in my belly now but forced myself to remain calm. I didn't officially know why I was here yet. Maybe he just wanted to follow up with a few more innocent questions. It would look bad for me to get defensive before he had made any accusations.

"Thanks for coming in, Jake," he said, shaking my hand. "Let's go to the back. It's more private."

"I may have to get that note from you when we're done. I don't think Professor Sheridan will accept anything less," I told him jokingly as I followed him down the hall from the lobby to the back area.

"We'll see what we can do," he said without turning around. He led me through a cavernous room with a maze of desks, most separated only by elevated corkboards intended to give the illusion of privacy. The place bustled with activity. People walked by like they had somewhere important to be. Others had phones pressed to their ears, madly scribbling notes on pads. There was an intensity to the environment that was shockingly at odds with the casualness of campus life. Even during finals, there was never this level of institutional anxiety.

Detective Cardinal led me past all this into another area. There was a row of doors along the back wall. I pretended not to get it, but I knew, *knew*, those doors led to interrogation rooms. Cardinal spoke to a uniformed officer for a second and I acted as if I was awed to be in a place like this. I craned my head all around, like a kid visiting Disneyland for the first time.

"Let's step in here," Cardinal suggested, opening the door to one of the rooms.

"Wow, you have your own private office?" I asked, making sure not to look inside as I posed the question. When I actually got in the room, it became clear to even the most naïve person that this was not an office. It was small, with the obligatory mirror against one wall. In the center of the room was a small metal table bolted to the ground. Three chairs surrounded it. That was all. It didn't look like anything out of *NYPD Blue*. It was cozier. I doubted more than four people could be in here longer than a few minutes before dramatically affecting the room temperature. The walls looked thick, like they were soundproof, and the lighting was fluorescent, although one of the bulbs was on the fritz, flickering intermittently, like a lazy strobe light. I wondered if that had been done intentionally.

"I'm guessing this isn't your office," I said, looking around. My tone made it clear that I'd figured out we weren't here for a friendly chat. I hoped he believed I'd only just come to that realization.

"Have a seat, Jake," he said, not directly addressing my comment, "we have a bit of a problem."

"What's that?" I asked as I sat, deciding it was finally appropriate to let my real feelings of apprehension and budding fear become visible.

"You haven't been completely honest with me about something," he said, clearly enjoying this moment of power.

"What's that?" I asked.

"We discovered last night that Kelly is between six and eight weeks pregnant. Did you know anything about that?"

He studied me closely. I knew that this moment would

come eventually, I just wasn't sure when. I figured that even if Kelly lost the baby, the fact that she'd been pregnant would be discovered. And obviously, if the baby survived, the pregnancy would come to light. But I hadn't had the chance to do any research on how long that would likely take. I was worried that I might be watched or followed. If I checked out any books on pregnancy from the library or went online, that would leave a surefire trail.

So I had been stuck in the difficult position of not knowing when the information would come to light. Now it had, in less than three days—pretty impressive. I'd never really had a chance to properly prepare my exact reaction at the moment the pregnancy was revealed to me. And now it was here. Cardinal was still watching, waiting.

"Yes," I said softly, with my eyes cast downward, "I knew."

"And you chose not to share that?" he asked, trying to keep the accusatory tone out of his voice for the time being.

"I didn't think it was important."

"You didn't think it was important? A girl is brutally beaten, you know she's pregnant, and you don't think it's important to mention that little detail?"

"It's complicated," I said, knowing it was a risk not to spill everything at once. But I held firm. He had to draw it out of me.

"What do you mean, it's complicated?"

"I was trying to protect Kelly," I muttered, with a little hitch in my voice.

"What the fuck are you talking about, boy?" he shouted, losing his patience.

I didn't answer. An innocent man who felt guilty would not respond to that kind of attack. He would retreat. I put my head down on the table, covering my face. Cardinal realized his screaming had been counterproductive. Out of the corner of my eye, I saw his head swivel to glance in the direction of the mirror. He had lost his edge for a second. He tried again.

"Jake, I need you to tell me the truth. Now don't make

me pull teeth here. Explain what you mean by protecting her. Tell me what happened." His voice was quiet now. An unbiased observer might have thought he was pleading. I looked up at him, as if deciding whether to trust him. He wasn't breathing. Finally, I sat up and began the story.

"Detective Cardinal, everything I told you before was true. Everything happened exactly as I said it did. But what I didn't tell you before was what Kelly and I talked about that night. I mean, I told you a little. Remember how I said that Kelly was upset because Dan wasn't being serious about stuff, about how he had a problem with accepting responsibility?"

"I remember," Cardinal said.

"Well, she wasn't just worried about him being responsible about getting a job and being a husband. She was worried about him as a father. She told me that she was pregnant. I was shocked. Like I told you before, we weren't super close friends and Dan and I weren't that close either. I still think she told me for the reason I explained earlier. I have this reputation as a guy who can solve problems and I knew both of them. I think she felt that I could be neutral about the whole thing."

"But why would she want to involve anyone other than Dan in such a private matter?" Cardinal asked.

"I wondered that, too. I even asked her. She told me that she was worried that Dan would get scared, that he would ask her to have an abortion, which she said she was morally opposed to. I guess she thought that if someone else knew, he couldn't make that kind of demand on her."

"I don't know, Jake," Cardinal said, sounding less than convinced. The good thing was, he didn't seem to doubt what I was saying. Rather, he seemed skeptical about Kelly's reasoning.

"Listen, Detective, it didn't make much sense to me either. She was very emotional. It was around the time where she talked about the abortion thing that she got all upset and ran out, saying that Dan was probably off, screwing some other girl. She wasn't all that coherent. Anyway, like I told you before, I went outside after her and calmed her down. I made the joke about Dan probably being asleep because he didn't know how important the meeting was. I told her I would talk to him the next day about the baby and try to help as much as I could."

"Did you specifically make reference to the pregnancy when you were talking in the parking lot?"

"Yeah," I said, after taking a moment to "recall" the conversation.

"How loud were you talking?"

"I don't remember. It was cold out. We were close so I don't think that loud. But she was upset, so I wanted to sound firm. I wasn't yelling, if that's what you mean."

"No, not that. Do you think someone else in the parking lot might have overheard your conversation, what you were talking about?"

"I guess they could have. But I wasn't really paying attention to that."

"Do you think," Cardinal asked, "that if someone overheard your conversation, that they might have misconstrued what you were saying?"

"What do you mean?"

"I mean, did you say 'I will talk to Dan tomorrow about him taking responsibility for getting you pregnant' or did you say 'I will talk to Dan tomorrow about the baby?' "

"More like the second," I told him.

"And you said the other day that you hugged her before you left?" he asked.

"Uh-huh," I said. "What difference does that make?"

"Just double-checking," he said dismissively. I was pretty sure I had him. This had gone better than I expected.

"Are we done?" I asked. It was a mistake.

"Not quite. I still don't see why you didn't reveal the pregnancy to me that night at the hospital."

"I thought I made that clear already, Detective," I said with a little too much exasperation.

"Clear it up for me again, if you don't mind," he ordered. All my hard work, down the drain.

"Kelly is very religious. I didn't want to make her seem promiscuous. She told me about this whole thing in confidence. Her body had already been injured. I didn't want to have the same thing happen to her reputation."

"Did it ever occur to you that her pregnancy might have had something to do with her being attacked?"

"Not that night. I thought she was attacked by a bum, like the news said."

"But you must have had some other ideas once we let that man go."

"I don't know what I thought, Detective. I was trying to do the right thing by Kelly. If I made a mistake, I'm sorry. I haven't had much sleep lately. Maybe my loyalties got confused."

"Maybe you obstructed justice," Cardinal said, throwing the possibility out there as if it were real.

"What?" I asked.

"What you did could be considered a crime, Jake. And I'm starting to question if I can believe anything you tell me. How do I know your loyalties aren't getting in the way of revealing other information important to this case? How do I know you're not protecting a fraternity brother?"

I knew he was mostly trying to scare me, to make sure I had given him everything I knew. I had even expected it a little. But he raised the option with a little more conviction than I liked. He sounded like a guy who didn't have much of a case and wasn't above rooting around in some kid's life if he thought it might make him look good. No matter how certain I was that he was bluffing, I couldn't have a homicide detective questioning my professors, my friends, school administrators. Even a hint of impropriety could damage my reputation and my law school chances. This would have to stop now.

"Detective Cardinal, what *exactly* are you suggesting here?"

"I'm not suggesting anything. I'm just wondering," he said, clearly pleased with his word choice, "if I have reason to doubt your forthrightness. And I'm wondering if I need to pursue that further."

"Detective," I said, trying to keep my voice from getting too cold, but failing. "I came here voluntarily. I've helped you in every way possible. I even let you interrogate me in this room, which is clearly an *interrogation* room, which I believe is generally used to interrogate *suspects*. I was under the impression that I was a *witness*. I allowed all this to happen because some-one I know, someone who came to me for help, is on the verge of death. I wanted to help the police in any way I could so that the monster who did this could be caught."

"Jake, I'm not suggesting you haven't been helpful, but you have to admit you've been less than completely truthful with me." He could see me getting defensive and was trying to ease up a little, take the pressure off, but it was too late.

"I admit that I held back some information which now looks to be important. I apologize for that. I was trying to protect the privacy of someone who placed her trust in me. Maybe that was a mistake. But I don't like where this is going. If you're suggesting that I'm guilty of something worse than bad judgment, then I am going to have to exercise some *good* judgment for my own protection."

"Oh really, Jake? And what do you propose to do?" he asked, clearly amused by my words.

"Well, I may have to start by getting a lawyer. I'll probably call my father, who I'm sure you're familiar with. You've heard of Conason and Skellner down in Texas, right? I may have him recommend someone in this city whom he respects and ad-mires. I'll retain that lawyer and tell him about the 'wondering' you've been doing. I have a feeling he'd tell me exactly what I'm about to tell you. If you decide to test my forthrightness by questioning the people I know, by investigating me, by ha-rassing me, you had better go all the way. You had better have something legitimate to pin on me."

"Are you challenging me, Jake? It sounds a lot like you're challenging me," he said, not so amused anymore.

"I'm not challenging you, Detective Cardinal. All I'm saying is that I'm a dean's list student with an impeccable reputation. I'm waiting to hear back from several Ivy League schools
about entering their law programs. I'm about to begin my professional life. And all I have in this life is my reputation. By
wandering around campus, asking questions and hinting that
I'm covering for someone, you throw that reputation into question. If I lose that, there's no way to regain it. If you ruin my
name, it's ruined for good."

"Listen to me, Jake," Cardinal said, still trying to keep
things from getting too ugly, "if you're being straight with me,
you shouldn't have anything to fear from my asking around a
little bit. You should tell your buddy Dan that, too."

"Maybe you should tell Dan that yourself, Detective. What
I'm telling *you* is that if you try to ruin my name and you don't
have the goods, then I have to pursue some form of recourse.
Do you understand? (I looked directly at the mirror when I
said this). You know why? Because in my world, your reputation counts, your credibility counts, your personal moral authority counts. Your good name *counts*. And if you rob me of
that, you rob me of everything. If you try to do that and you
can't back it up, there will be consequences. Now I'm sorry
to be so blunt, but I wanted to make sure you understood
where I stand on this."

When I first started my tirade of indignation, Cardinal had
opened his mouth a few times to interrupt me. Now, as I finished, his mouth was still open but there were no words coming
out. He just sat there, looking at me. My reaction was obviously
unexpected. I heard the door open and looked in that direction.
An older man who I assumed to be Cardinal's boss stepped in.

"Jake . . ." he began.

"I think I'd like to be referred to as Mr. Conason from now
on," I interrupted.

"My name is Lieutenant Edward Wendell. I understand
your frustration," he said, choosing not to address me by name
at all, "but you have to understand that we are conducting an

investigation here and we have to pursue all areas of inquiry."
He didn't even consider hiding the fact that he'd been watching
the entire interrogation from behind the glass.

"I understand all of that," I told him, in my most brusque,
professional voice, "but I also understand that I've been nothing
but helpful to you people and now you're threatening me."

"Nobody's threatening you, Jake," he said, then realized he
was being too familiar with me again.

"*He* threatened me," I said, pointing at Cardinal, who now
seemed to have regained control of himself, "and I bet my as
yet unhired lawyer would agree."

"Look," Lieutenant Wendell said, "I can't make you any
promises. And I won't allow members of my department to be
threatened themselves. What I can tell you is that this force is
very professional and from what I know of this case, your concerns about destroyed reputations are overstated. I think you'll
find that everything we do in this investigation is in accordance
with proper department guidelines."

"I hope so," I said, allowing myself to be placated.

"I think it's time for you to go home now. If you hurry,
I'm sure you can still make some of your classes."

"Okay," I agreed, and stood up. Wendell extended his arm
to me. I let it hang out there in the diplomatic void for an
extra second before I took it.

"We appreciate you coming in," he said. I nodded and
headed for the door. Just before I left, Cardinal piped in.

"Jake," he said, his confidence restored, "please make sure
not to leave the jurisdiction without permission."

I felt the heat rise to the back of my neck but managed not
to react. Instead, I gave his boss my best "see what I mean"
face and walked out without saying a word. Wendell shut the
door behind me. Even though I know the room was soundproof, as I walked down the hall, I could have sworn I heard
his voice. I could have sworn I heard him yelling.

CHAPTER TEN

As I drove home, I tried to determine the success of the interrogation. I knew I had taken a big risk by challenging Cardinal. Until now, he had viewed me as a likable, fairly smart kid caught up in an unpleasant situation beyond his control. That persona was gone now, replaced by something less benign. I suppose he could have taken it a step further and surmised that someone who was willing to confront the detective investigating him was also capable of other unexpected acts. But I doubted he'd make that leap. He likely assumed I was just the cocky, spoiled son of a big-time Texas lawyer.

They had nothing on me. And the only way they would be able to get something was if they really started checking into every detail of my story and Dan's story. From the look on Lieutenant Wendell's face, I was betting that after today, the investigation of my story would be pretty limited, which was the whole point. I had to weigh seeming like a connected, uppity brat and getting the questions to end with seeming like a likable student and risking more dangerous questions. The choice was clear.

I have to admit that, regardless of the strategic risk of what I did in that room, it felt damn good. I was so tired of the endless questions, not just from the police but from my brothers, other friends, and people on campus I didn't know. I had even received a few calls from some reporters, all of whom got a "no comment." I had spent the last three days reacting and I liked it when I got to take the initiative. The expression on Cardinal's face when he realized that I might sue was magical. Besides, I think I deserved the right to dish out a little righteous indignation. I had put up with enough questioning looks in the last three days to last a lifetime.

I could tell that people wondered if I had done enough to help Kelly. Maybe I'd seen the attacker and left anyway for fear of being hurt myself. Now that the pregnancy was about to come out, I'd get more looks. Why hadn't I told the authorities about it? Didn't I care if the baby lived? I bet some people might even suspect that I was in cahoots with Dan, which seemed to be where Cardinal was going.

In his own casual way, Cardinal was relentless, like a shark chasing you in bloody water. I've heard that sometimes the best way to survive a shark attack is to turn around and give it a whack on the nose. So I gave Cardinal his whack. It was a little rash. It was a lot risky. But it felt great, really cathartic to go at the bastard.

I also felt pretty good about where I stood at this point. Unless Cardinal wanted to risk a lawsuit or possibly even disciplinary action, the investigation of me was probably over. The most they seemed to suspect me of was cowardice or some warped code of fraternity loyalty. The focus would continue to tighten on Dan. That was good, but it was also a problem. The truth was, no matter how hard I tried to make it so, Dan had not attacked Kelly. And if there was any way he could prove that, then the investigation would have to turn elsewhere.

I imagined that a paternity test was on the menu in the near future. I wasn't worried about the test itself. No matter what the result, I was confident that I was still in good shape. If it showed that Dan was the father, he was screwed. Nothing he could say would overcome that fact. If it turned out, as Kelly "felt," that he was not the dad, he still had problems. Cardinal was obviously considering the possibility that Dan had been lurking in the parking lot, overheard our conversation and misunderstood. If Dan thought Kelly had cheated on him and I was the father of her child, he might have gone into a rage and attacked her.

Of course the second scenario had flaws. If Dan wasn't the father, the cops would probably want to find out who was. And high on their list of people to check out would be yours truly. That would be bad. I felt reasonably sure that even if a test showed me to be the father, I could still avoid suspicion on the assault. I could say Kelly never told me it was mine. I could say Dan told me afterward that he had attacked her and threatened to hurt Jordan if I came forward. There were options.

But those were options to avoid being charged with attempted murder. They did nothing to help me with Jordan. If she learned that I had slept with Kelly, it would be over. Of that, I was certain. I would be a pariah on campus—the guy who cheated on his girlfriend and his fraternity brother. No explanation would salvage my reputation. Even if I was free and clear legally, the credibility I had harped on to Cardinal would be shot.

So it was clear. There was no way that I could be discovered as the father of that being growing in Kelly's belly. It was unlikely that such a discovery would be made, but it wasn't impossible, especially if Dan decided to get off his ass for the first time in his life and try to save himself. More than anything else right now, Dan was my biggest problem.

By the time I got back to school, it was a little after noon. I had one more class today, but not for a few hours, so I went

to the deli to grab a sandwich. It was the first week of February
and even though snow still covered the ground, the sun was
peeking out from behind the clouds. I decided to eat outside.

I found an unoccupied bench and sat down. Even with the
sun, it was still only in the forties and pretty soon my cheeks
were starting to feel numb from exposure. I chewed my sandwich harder, hoping that the champing motion would get the
blood flowing through my cheeks and restore a little feeling. It
was probably amusing to an observer to see some guy chewing
extra vigorously as his cheeks got redder and redder. I was so
immersed in the activity that I didn't notice that I did have an
audience.

"Trying to eat your tongue?" an unpleasantly familiar voice
asked. I looked up to find Evan Grunier looking down at me
with amused disdain. I considered explaining to him what I was
doing but then decided not to waste my time.

"How's it going, Evan?" I asked, after I swallowed my latest
big bite.

"Good. We missed you in Ethics today. Sheridan was asking
where you were. I said you were probably off at the crime lab."

"I was actually answering some more questions for the police, but I appreciate your confidence in me."

"You really seem to be the point man on this thing," he
said.

"What do you mean?"

"Well, you were the person with Kelly that night. You went
to the hospital. You've been consoling Lindsay. You took the
police to the crime scene to give them background."

"So?"

"So, I'm just saying you are really on the ball. Hey, if they
catch this guy, I wouldn't be surprised if that detective gave
you a recommendation to law school. I'll bet there aren't many
other candidates who will have that in their application."

Evan had been worrying me a bit, right up until that last
comment. I realized that he wasn't making accusations about
my possible guilt. He was merely charging me with using this

tragedy for my own personal gain. The thought had never occurred to me. The idea was actually offensive.

Evan was a very smart guy, but, in this instance, he reminded me of one of his biggest flaws. He had other flaws, like arrogance and cruelty and more envy in his heart than in the populations of many small countries. But in terms of his current and future success, his greatest flaw was that he didn't see the big picture. He only saw Kelly's attack in terms of how it affected my chances of getting into a good law school, which affected his chances of getting into that school. He only saw my questioning down at the station as an opportunity to make points with Professor Sheridan. He had made me break out in a sweat on a cold day with his "point man" comment. But I wasn't worried now. That forest for the trees saying had been invented to describe people like Evan.

"Evan, I'm not even going to dignify that. This is a girl that we both know, that I, at least, like. For you to suggest something like that . . . well, I think I'm going to pretend I never heard you say it."

"You did seem fond of her," he said, not in the least deterred by my scolding.

"What?"

"I'm just saying that I agree with you. I mean, of course I liked the girl, although I have to admit that I didn't know her very well. But you seemed to be very close to her, from everything I've seen."

He was smiling as he said that. For one of the few times since this mess began, I found myself completely at a loss. I could not read him at all. He could have been suggesting any one of a thousand different things. But in my mind, he was suggesting one thing in particular.

To give myself a second to think, I took another bite of my sandwich. I chewed it slowly. Evan stood directly in front of me. He was still smiling. I continued to chew. I made it last as long as I could. The longer I took, the more his smile faded. By the time I swallowed, the corners of his mouth were even again. I stood up. I had needed every second of that time to think of something safe to say.

"Evan," I said, hoping I didn't sound flustered, "I don't know if you've noticed, but every time you talk about Kelly, you refer to her in the past tense. She's not dead. And some of us are still praying for her. Maybe you should think about that."

I lifted the hood of my jacket over my head to protect my now frozen cheeks. Before Evan could say anything, I turned and walked off in the direction of the house. As I left, I tossed the last of my sandwich in the trash as if I was too disgusted to take another bite. But as I walked across the huge field in the center of campus, it wasn't disgust I was feeling. It was fear.

When I got home that evening, I found an amazing message on my machine. The firm of McHenry, Solis & Steiner in New York wanted me to interview for their summer internship. And they wanted me to interview on Friday. They were offering to fly me into the city Friday morning, do the interview that afternoon, put me in a hotel and have one of the current interns show me the city on Friday night. I would fly back on Saturday.

Even though it was past eight in New York, I called and left a message saying that I was definitely in. Then I called my parents to give them the news. My dad was even more pumped than I was. He sounded really proud. I couldn't remember him ever being that pleased with me. Next, I called Jordan, who was genuinely happy for me. I also told her about the interrogation. She was pissed at first because I had kept the pregnancy thing from her. But she seemed to understand when I explained how I was trying to protect Kelly's privacy and, especially, her reputation.

She offered to come over but I said she better not. I was already behind in Legal Ethics and having the sexiest girl in the world over for the night would not be conducive to my catching up. Professor Sheridan would expect me to know the material, whether I was being questioned by the police or not. I had already suffered scholastically on more than one occasion as a result of Jordan's influence.

Last year, on my twenty-first birthday, a bunch of my friends threw a "guys only" party at my apartment. It was a Thursday night and I had a big test the next morning but Jeff and Rick made me feel guilty, saying they'd already planned the whole thing, ordered kegs and even hired a stripper.

So I gave in and we all got trashed. When the stripper arrived, they sat me in a chair in the middle of the main room. She came in wearing a police uniform. She had long brunette hair, huge sunglasses, and a police dress cap. Then, with forty of my closest friends whooping it up, she put on Prince's "Kiss" and started to dance. She took off her slacks but left the shirt and panties on so she looked like a girl from one of those old Van Heusen commercials. At some point, she managed to cuff my hands behind me. Then she unbuttoned my shirt and started kissing my chest, much as Prince suggested.

She stepped back as the song wound down. Dozens of rowdy guys chanted "take off your top." She undid her top button, then paused, playing with the next one. The song ended. She held up her hand. She had something to say. The chanting slowly petered out.

"What is it?" Rick asked.

"I don't think my boyfriend would want me to take off my top in front of all you guys," she teased.

"Don't worry. We won't tell him," someone shouted.

"Maybe I should ask him, just in case," she said.

There was a collective groan from the crowd. The stripper took off her sunglasses and cap. Then she pulled off the brunette wig to reveal (no surprise here) . . . the reddish blond hair of Jordan Lansing. Apart from the sound of my handcuffs clanking against my chair, there was total silence in the room.

"Happy Birthday, sweetie," Jordan said. Still, no one spoke. Then, some freshman in the back of the room finally broke the spell.

"Oh my god. You have the greatest girlfriend of all time!"

There was universal agreement on the point. After the handcuffs were removed, Jordan and I went back to my room to celebrate privately (we took the cuffs with us) while Jeff and Rick, who were in on the joke, let the real stripper in.

I didn't sleep at all that night and ended up getting a C– on the test the next day. But it was absolutely, unquestionably worth it. Even my father would have understood that grade, if he'd ever found out. Tonight though, I couldn't afford to partake of my favorite distraction. With everything going on, I had to keep Jordan at arm's length. Even without the cop outfit, she was dangerous.

So I studied for a few hours, then chatted with Rick, who had spent most of his evening studying "Sunshine of Your Love." It wasn't until I was in bed, drifting off to sleep, that I remembered Evan and our little chat. I slept fitfully that night.

CHAPTER ELEVEN

The circumstances that resulted in my scurrying silently up the fire escape entrance to the Kappa Omega house two nights later, dressed mostly in black and wearing a blond wig, are a little complicated, so please bear with me. It started when I got a call back from the travel coordinator for McHenry, Solis & Steiner on Thursday morning telling me to pick up my ticket from the travel agency.

Unlike most people these days, the firm did not use e-tickets. They liked to have paper copies of the ticket for accounting purposes. Furthermore, they had some sort of deal with one of the airlines where they got a discount if they pre-purchased a bunch of tickets each year. So the ticket I picked up from the agent didn't have my name on it. Instead, it simply said "M, S & S passenger."

It had me leaving at 9:30 in the morning, St. Louis time. I was supposed to get into LaGuardia around one and take a cab to the firm's Manhattan offices. The travel person told me to get receipts for everything and I would be reimbursed. I was to spend Friday night at the Roosevelt Hotel in midtown (which would bill the firm directly—I didn't even have to formally check out) and leave New York on Saturday at noon. I would be back in St. Louis (after the time change) around two in the afternoon, with time left to enjoy the rest of the weekend.

There were a few problems. I had to call the police to get permission to leave town, which really burned me and I'm sure greatly pleased the recently stymied Detective Cardinal. Luckily, I spoke to one of his colleagues who clearly wasn't aware of the animosity between me and his buddy. After that was resolved, I had to talk to my professors to warn them. Sheridan was annoyed since that would be two consecutive missed classes, but in the end, even she understood.

The only downside to leaving was that I was missing Jordan's party. She and her suitemates had been planning this big blowout since the start of the semester. At the beginning of the week, after the Kelly news broke, they had considered canceling it. But ultimately, they all agreed that it would do everyone some good to have a little fun. They made sure to specifically invite Lindsay and all the girls from Kelly's suite. Even though the party was on South Campus (which is mostly dorms and suites), many of the Greeks were expected to attend. It was going to be huge, but I wouldn't be there.

The rest of the week would probably have gone exactly as expected if I hadn't stopped by Dan's on Thursday afternoon to check on him. Part of the reason I went over was because I was sincerely interested in seeing how he was doing. The general consensus around campus was that he had tried to kill his girlfriend. Now word was spreading fast that she was pregnant and he may have done it because he didn't want to get stuck with a kid.

The other reason I went to see him was that I wanted to keep the buddy vibe going. I needed Dan to see me as an ally. I was the guy who had revealed pretty much everything that was damning him right now. But I needed him to consider me someone he could trust, someone he could confide in. If he started to view me as an enemy, there could be trouble.

He was not in good shape. I had to bang on the door a few times before he heard me over The Smiths' "How Soon Is Now?" He let me in and I could see that he was drunk again. It was four in the afternoon. He opened his fridge to offer me something. Inside, there were four jugs of orange juice and two bottles of vodka. That was in addition to the half empty bottle on top of the TV. I asked how he was doing.

"They say Kelly's pregnant," he said, trying not to slur. "They say you told them that."

"Yeah, she told me that night. But she made me swear not to tell anyone. I realize now that I should have, but I've been so confused this week."

"I know what you mean, man. My life is confusion. I wish you would have told me though." I was surprised at how easily he let it go.

"So you're going to be a dad?" I asked.

"I guess. They want me to come in for a paternity test next week just to make sure. They say that she's between one and a half and two months pregnant. There's some test they can do to tell for sure if I'm the father but they have to wait another two weeks before they can safely do it on her."

"So you're going in when?"

"On Monday. Then, when they test the baby later in the month, we'll know for sure."

"I don't know what to say, Dan." My brain was racing too fast for me to concentrate.

"I don't know either."

"Listen, man. I gotta go. I'm going to New York tomorrow. Do you think maybe you should get out for a few hours? You know, Jordan's having that party tomorrow night. Maybe you should go."

"Are you kidding?" he asked. "Everyone there will be thinking I tried to kill my pregnant girlfriend. That party is the last place I plan to go. I'll probably spend tomorrow night right here in this room. It's starting to feel pretty comfortable."

I nodded, gave him a friendly guy-hug and left. As I walked downstairs and headed to my car, I tried to stay calm. I don't know if it was the adrenaline high from my confrontation with Cardinal that clouded my judgment, but it was now obvious to me that I had been far too cocky afterward. The conclusions I had drawn immediately following the interrogation now seemed Pollyanna-ish.

If Dan submitted to a paternity test and it turned out that he was not the father, things would get very complicated. I didn't know if the authorities had to have a person's permission to conduct such a test but his volunteering certainly wouldn't hurt his credibility. By the time I got home, I had come to a decision. I was going to have to change the course of events.

Rick dropped me off at the airport on Friday morning. He offered to pick me up tomorrow but I said I'd take a cab. At the gate, I gave the attendant my ticket and she gave me a boarding pass. She didn't even ask me for ID. I guess it was pointless with these prepurchased tickets. My flight left on time and I was in the offices of McHenry and his pals by 1:30 that afternoon.

It was weird. If I didn't have so much else on my mind, I probably would have been nervous about the interview. But other things were competing for my attention. I think the interviewers misinterpreted my lack of focus as confidence and I could tell from their expressions when we were done that it had gone well for me. For the briefest of moments, I wondered if I should get consumed by police investigations before all my important interviews. It seemed to serve me well. The lawyers told me they would have an answer for me sometime in the next few weeks.

For the rest of the afternoon, a second-year law student named Henry something showed me around the city. I took out several hundred dollars from an ATM. I didn't have to use any of it. After I checked in at the hotel, he bought me a nice dinner on the firm. I slipped away briefly to call the airline. Afterward, he asked what I wanted to do on Friday night in New York City. I think I surprised him when I said I wasn't feeling that well and wanted to just go back to the hotel for the rest of the night. He was disappointed. I think he'd been looking forward to a night on the town at the firm's expense.

Nonetheless, we said our good-byes at the hotel. He wished me luck and headed off to find a good time he could afford. I went up to my room, glanced through the yellow pages, showered, dressed, threw back the covers on the bed and made a mess of the sheets. Then I grabbed my bag and left the room.

I took the stairs instead of the elevator. When I got to the lobby, I left through a side door, and walked the few blocks to the costume store I had looked up in the phone book. I bought a blond wig and a beard to match. I still had a lot of cash. I stopped into a McDonald's, bought some fries and went to the bathroom, where I put on the wig and the beard, which didn't look as ridiculous as I thought they would. I took a cab to LaGuardia and arrived around 7:30. I looked at the departures board and saw that the flight I had checked on earlier was still leaving for St. Louis at 8:15.

I got to the gate and sat down to get a good look around. This was going to be the hardest part of the plan. I had to pick the right person. It didn't take long to find my hero. Sitting in the corner of the gate area, wearing a ratty T-shirt and faded jeans, was a guy I gathered to be in his late twenties. He had a huge duffel bag, which made me pretty sure he hadn't checked any bags. I approached him and sat down in the seat to his left.

"Hey man, can I ask a favor of you?"

He gave me a skeptical, but not hostile look.

"I'm not interested in anything you're selling," he said.

"No man. I'm not selling anything. Just hear me out for a second. If you don't want to give me a hand, then you can tell me to fuck off and there'll be no hard feelings, okay."

The guy seemed to think this was a reasonable proposition and nodded.

"Cool. So this is my situation. I'm scheduled on a flight that leaves tomorrow around noon. I managed to get a good deal because it's this pre-bought thing. The problem is, I'm going to St. Louis to see my sister, who's supposed to give birth to her first baby sometime in the next twelve hours. They were originally going to induce labor tomorrow afternoon, but I talked to her best friend on the phone a few hours ago. She says there may be complications and they're going to do it sooner."

The guy seemed intrigued so I kept going.

"Her boyfriend skipped out on her a few months ago and her friend's the only one with her. I want to be there for her. But with this ticket, I'm locked in. Because I got this cheap rate, I'm the last person on every standby list. The chances of my getting out of here tonight are pretty shitty.

"So what I'm hoping is that you'll switch flights with me. I noticed you already have your boarding pass so showing ID's not a problem. My ticket is through this company so they won't ask me for ID tomorrow. I don't know if you have some emergency that you have to get to St. Louis for, but I do. I would eat the cost of this ticket and buy a spot on this flight but it's sold out.

"Now I have two hundred dollars here that I'd be willing to throw in just to make the hassle of the extra half-day worth your while. I know it would be a pain for you to stay here overnight, but it would really help me out a lot. I would thank you, my sister would thank you, and my nephew, should he make it, well he'd thank you, too."

The guy listened to the whole spiel without interrupting and I saw as I told my story that the more I talked, the softer his face got. By the time I finished, he looked like the idea didn't seem that crazy. I had a shot. But I didn't want to risk him backing out so I went in for the kill.

"Now if you think this is too weird or shady, I totally un-

derstand and I'll leave you alone and go back to the information
desk and try again like I have been for the last few hours. But
I just saw you and you looked like a decent person and I
thought I had to at least try, you know, for my sister."

The gate attendant announced that boarding on Flight 263
to St. Louis would now begin with first class, bonus-club members, and anyone with small children who needed a little extra
time getting down the jetway. Her timing could not have been
more perfect.

"How do I know that they'll let me on the flight tomorrow?" he asked.

"They will. I use these things all the time and they never
ask for ID. They don't even like to make eye contact with
people using bargain tickets. Plus, I'm giving you two hundred
bucks. That will get you most of the way to another ticket if
something comes up, but I guarantee you won't need it. There
won't be a problem."

It wasn't long before the attendant was on the speaker again,
this time announcing rows twenty-five through thirty. The
guy's boarding pass said he was in seat 16-B. He looked at me,
at the people lining up to get on the plane, then back again.

"Okay, man. I may regret this, but okay."

I hugged him.

"You will not regret this, I swear. You are helping out a
whole family here. What's your name?"

"Ted."

"Ted, you now know my nephew's middle name. Count
on that." The gesture seemed to touch him. I gave him my
ticket and the two hundred bucks and he handed over his
boarding pass.

"Now don't forget," I said before getting into line, "don't
give them ID. It'll just mess things up."

He nodded. I got in line and smiled at him. When I got to
the ticket agent, I turned around and waved good-bye and
thank you to Ted. He waved back. He knew he would be
spending the next sixteen hours in this airport, but he had done

something good for another human being. And that made it worthwhile.

With the time change, my (actually Ted's) flight arrived in St. Louis at ten that night. I got a cab and had it take me to a ratty motel on Forest Park Parkway, about a mile from campus. I had called the place from a pay phone on Thursday night to make sure they took cash and didn't require ID. It turned out that it was the kind of establishment that preferred things that way.

The beard was starting to itch but I fought the urge to scratch. I changed into the clothes I had brought especially for the occasion. I wore a black sweatshirt with a hood and roomy pockets, black sweatpants, also with deep pockets, and gloves. I was underdressed for the weather but that's the way it had to be. I put the hood over my head and began the walk to campus. With the snow and the traffic, it took twenty-five minutes.

By the time I actually reached fraternity row, it was about 11:30. The place was quiet. One of the frats at the end of the row was throwing a party, but because of the cold, they had shut their doors and the sound of the music was muffled. Just about everybody else had gone to South Campus for Jordan's party and the other smaller parties that inevitably sprouted up around a large one.

By the time I got to the house, I was sufficiently spooked. I had seen so few people that I began to wonder whether this was some sort of trap. But as I hid next to the Dumpster behind the house near the fire escape, I saw a couple wander by in the direction of South Campus. Just seeing two people set my mind at ease a little. I took off the hood and casually ambled over to the escape steps. I was worried that the hood would make me look like a thief. The risk of not wearing it was that even with the wig and beard, I might be recognized and identified later.

I tried not to think about that as I hurried up the steps as quickly as I could while still looking like I belonged. When I got to the top floor, I took a second to catch my breath. It was at about that moment that the oddness of the circumstances I referred to earlier hit me. But here I was. I started to reach for the door when I realized that I had not brought my house key with me. If the door was locked, as it was supposed to be, then this whole elaborate scheme would be for naught. Over three hundred dollars and hours of ulcer-inducing worry would be wasted. I wanted to kick myself for my stupidity.

I grabbed the handle and turned.

CHAPTER TWELVE

It gave and the door opened. Apparently the constant re-minders at meetings to lock it had fallen on deaf ears. I peeked inside. There was no one in sight. I quickly stepped into the hall and tiptoed my way to the small third-floor rest-room. Once inside, I locked the door and turned on the light. Looking in the mirror, I saw that the beard was on the verge of coming off completely. I tried to peel it back slowly but it hurt. I decided I might as well just rip it off like a Band-Aid.

The sting was intense but I managed not to make a sound. I removed the wig and fixed my hair as best I could. Then I stuffed both the wig and the beard in the deep sweatshirt pock-ets and waited until I was sure there was no noise in the hall. I could only hear the sound of loud music somewhere in the distance. As I stepped out of the restroom, I realized the sound was coming from Dan's room. This time it was Metallica. I hurried in that direction and knocked on the door loudly, glancing around and praying that no one would walk by. I heard Dan call out, asking who was there. I didn't dare say anything and instead banged again, only harder this time.

After a few more seconds, he opened the door. Before he could say a word, I stepped inside and shut the door behind me. When I turned around to face him, I could tell that despite the fact that he was stone drunk, Dan was surprised to see me.

"I thought you were out of town," he muttered.

"I was," I told him, "but I came back early. I figured I should check on you and see how you were doing."

He made a sweeping gesture as if to say "take a look."

"What do you think?" he asked.

I surveyed the room. It was a sty. There were dirty clothes lying all over the place and there was a vague, soiled smell in the air. Two empty vodka bottles and a carton of orange juice sat on the top of his mini-fridge. I walked over and opened the door. Inside were another nearly full vodka bottle and one more jug of juice.

"It looks like you've been busy," I remarked. "Do you mind if I join you?"

"Be my guest," he said with a dismissive wave as he slumped down on his bed. It looked like he might pass out. That wouldn't be good.

"Hey, Dan, get up. I'm not drinking unless you drink with me."

He sat up.

"I don't think I can drink anymore tonight," he admitted. "That one vodka bottle was almost full this afternoon."

"Listen man, there are guys in this house who could down a bottle of vodka in a tenth of that time and be ready for more."

"Fuck those guys!" he shouted.

"I thought *you* were one of those guys. It sounds like you've gotten soft in your old age."

"I haven't gotten soft," he assured me. "It just takes a lot more for me to forget these days." He was only making partial sense. I decided to go wherever he took me.

"Well, why don't the two of us see if we can't get a blackout going, huh? We both have a lot we'd rather not remember right about now, don't we?"

"What do you want to forget?" he asked.

"I want to forget that Sunday as much as you do, Dan. Don't you think I wish I could turn back time? Sometimes I wonder what would have happened if I'd never met Kelly at the restaurant that night. She wouldn't be dying right now, I'm sure of that."

"You think I tried to kill her, don't you?" he asked, resigned to the label the world had placed on him.

"No, Dan, I don't think you tried to kill her. Whatever you did or didn't do that night, I know you never wanted to hurt her. Maybe it was just a mistake."

"What mistake?" he demanded. "Her head was bashed in. That doesn't sound like a mistake to me."

I looked over at him. Despite the fog of drunkenness, he seemed genuinely upset and angry. I don't know why that surprised me. I guess I'd briefly forgotten that he didn't have any idea what was going on. But I was also a little annoyed with him. I was doing my best to make this less painful for him, to make things right. And he was throwing cold water on my sincere efforts. It was very frustrating. I allowed that feeling to gestate.

"Hey, let's not go there. I'm going to pour you a drink and we're going to talk about happier times."

"Fine. But I gotta take a piss first." He got up, stumbled to the door and after a little struggle with the knob, wandered out and down the hall. I got up quickly to shut the door again. Then I pulled the baggy with the crushed Lomotil out of my sweatpants pocket and carefully poured it into Dan's empty thirty-two ounce plastic cup. After that, I filled the cup a third of the way with orange juice and the remaining two thirds with vodka. I mixed it up with a plastic spoon, then threw in a few ice cubes. I took a little whiff but couldn't smell anything.

Lomotil is a drug that helps fight diarrhea. One of our fraternity brothers, Dale Sykes, got a huge stash of it from his doctor father for our spring break trip to Cancun last year. Nine of us went, including Jeff, Dan, and me. Dale had given each of us about a half dozen of the pills but warned us that they were dangerous when mixed with alcohol. As it turned out, none of us used any of the pills because getting drunk was a higher priority than not getting the runs. Besides, the resort we stayed at was pretty nice and the water turned out to be fine.

So we all had these little collections of this potent drug when we returned. I didn't think about it again until winter break, when I got a little sick because of a bad oyster in San Antonio. I got terrible runs and wished I had some of that Lomotil right about then. When I got back, I checked and found that I still had all of the pills. There were actually eight total and they were all still in the little baggy I'd wrapped them in for the trip.

I didn't know how many of them it would take to cause a bad interaction so before I left for New York I had ground them all up, except one. I was a little concerned about carrying a dangerous drug in powder form on a flight but my fears ended up being baseless. There was a noise at the door. I saw someone fighting with the knob and hastily shoved the baggy back in my pocket. Dan stepped inside and shut the door behind him. He didn't look any more aware than he had before.

"That feels better," he said, although he didn't look better.

"I made you a drink," I told him and handed over the cup.

"Jesus, this is huge," he said. "I'll never finish the thing."

"Sure you will. In fact let's make a bet. I bet I can pour myself a little concoction *and* finish it in the time it takes you to finish your drink."

He looked at me with slow eyes, as if the wager was too complicated to comprehend, then glanced over at his bookshelf, which held several bowls, cups, and plates.

"Which cup are you gonna use?" he asked. No fight. No argument. No refusal.

"Well, to be fair, I think I should use a cup about half the size. I'll take this one," I said, grabbing a medium-sized red plastic one. "Do we have a bet?"

"What do I get if I win?"

"What do you want?"

"A boy."

"Excuse me?" I said.

"I want the baby to be a boy. I want a boy."

"I don't know if I have that kind of power, Dan. How about this? If you win and it's a boy, I'll buy him a little football."

"And if it's a girl?"

"If it's a girl and you win, I'll buy her a little necklace, a cute little one with a heart. How does that sound?"

"Okay, what if you win?" he wanted to know.

"If I win, you have to buy a baby gift for my firstborn. Fair?"

"That's fair," he said.

"Then let's get started. You ready?" I asked.

He nodded.

"Ready, set, go!" I half-shouted (but not too loud). He began to chug his screwdriver. I opened the refrigerator and grabbed the orange juice container. I pretended like I was having trouble getting the top off. After it was open, I poured the cup halfway full. Dan was really getting into it and glugged even more aggressively when he saw me go for the vodka. I turned away so he couldn't see that I hadn't actually taken the top off the bottle. I tilted it so it looked like I was pouring. Then I feigned putting the top back on. As I threw the bottle back in the fridge, Dan stopped to take a deep breath. He looked over at me. His eyes were blazing with adrenalized intensity. For the first time all night, he seemed to be truly alive.

"Here goes," I said as I put my glass to my lips. "I'm gonna catch ya."

That was all it took for him to dive back into action. I probably could have beaten him if I had tried. My glass was only about twelve ounces and, despite his Herculean effort, Dan was starting to slow. I had to act as if I was swallowing while I actually kept my mouth shut and I stopped a couple of times to take fake gulps of breath. On the second recovery breath I gasped that I was almost done. I saw Dan's eyes widen at that and he put even more effort into the contest. I made sure to wait until he pulled the cup from his mouth before I took my last sip.

"Damn, I almost had you," I said, mustering enough conviction to fool someone who was sauced but no one else. I could tell he wanted to say something but it was taking a while for him to catch his breath. For a second, I thought he might throw up. Instead, he let out an enormous burp and started to laugh.

"You owe me a mini-football," he said.

"That," I agreed, "or a necklace. Let's hope you get your wish." Neither of us spoke for a minute. I assume he was thinking about the baby he would never see and I took the down-time to give the room a once-over. His computer was in sleep mode but it was on. I fought the urge to move in that direction and looked back at Dan. He was staring at my hands.

"Why are you wearing gloves inside?" he asked.

"Oh, I have a circulation problem. It takes forever for my fingers to warm up after I've been outside so I leave the gloves on for a while once I get indoors."

"Aren't they warm yet?"

"No, not quite. I think I'll give it a few minutes more."

He nodded, satisfied.

"Maybe we should go to that party after all," he said, completely out of the blue. "I'm feeling a lot better than I did before."

"I don't know if that's such a good idea. You're pretty drunk, Dan. It might not look too good."

"What do I care how anything looks anymore? My life is fucked. I might as well have a good time while I still can, right?"

"Don't talk like that," I scolded, "your life is not fucked. You never know what the cops might find. You could be vindicated tomorrow. If you stop fighting, who's going to do it for you?"

"You will."

"No, Dan. I won't. The only person you should count on is yourself. If you give up, then how can you expect anyone else to stick with you? It's important that you keep going."

"Why? It doesn't seem worth it."

"Of course it's worth it. If you do fight, you might win. You might lose. But if you quit, you'll lose for sure. The minute you think you're out of options, then you are. I don't care if they're getting set to give you the needle, you have to keep fighting anyway. Do you hear me?" It wasn't until I finished the lecture that I realized how much I'd raised my voice.

I shut up and waited, listening for the sounds of a door opening or footsteps coming our way. Nothing. All I could hear was the chorus to "The Unforgiven." I got up, walked to the door and opened it a crack. There was no one in sight. I shut the door and locked it.

When I turned around, I saw that Dan had crawled up onto his bed and was lying in the fetal position, facing me. His eyelids opened and closed slowly the way they do when a person is just drifting off into sleep and making a cursory attempt to battle it. Then they closed for good. When it came to Dan, even that fight was half-assed.

I sat down at his computer and began to type. Every now and then, I heard a groan or unintelligible muttering from the bed to my right, but I didn't look up. I had memorized what I wanted to write a while ago and it didn't take long to finish. After I was done, I studied the screen. This is what it said:

I have decided to end things. Its just to hard to continue with everything thats happened. I can't face all the stares and the stuff that
people say. I loved Kelly alot and I wanted to be with her but I guess

that can't happen now. I wish that I could take back all the things that have happened latly. I'm sorry for everything and I pray for my baby. Goodbye.

I wondered whether the typos were too much. Dan wasn't a great student but he wasn't an idiot either. I chose to leave them. After all, it was actually pretty cogent for a guy who had just downed a ton of vodka and some pills. I hit print. While the page printed out, I took the last Lomotil, broke it into several pieces and scattered them around the room. I put a small chunk next to Dan on the bed, dropped another one on the floor next to him and placed the last piece on the top of the fridge next to the vodka bottles. Then I took one of his bath towels and wiped out the inside of the glass I had used, making sure to pay special attention to the rim. After I put it back on the shelf and returned the towel to the rack, I checked the note to make sure it had come out properly. I decided it would be best to leave the page in the printer. They'd find it.

I did one last room check, like when you're on vacation and checking out of a hotel room. Everything seemed to be in order. I moved over to Dan and leaned in close. He was still breathing. I considered rolling him on his back so that if he started to puke, he might choke to death on the vomit. Ultimately, I decided it wasn't worth the chance that moving him might wake him up, especially now that the note was done and the room properly prepared. I didn't want to overdo it. Just let the chemicals do their job.

I stepped back and took it all in. I felt like maybe I should say or do something as a kind of good-bye. I had been so pressed for time with Kelly that I never got the opportunity to make peace with her. That night was like a fever dream that I still wasn't quite able to wrap my mind around. Even now, I couldn't believe I had done those things to her. But I had, just as I was doing these things to Dan now. Only it didn't feel so alien to me this time. It felt . . . familiar.

I thought about saying a little prayer but that seemed in-appropriate. In the end all I could muster was a half-hearted "sorry, buddy." I know that probably seems weak but I had spent so much time thinking about all the other aspects of the plan that coming up with some kind of last rites hadn't ever entered my mind. Finally, I decided I had to go. Maybe I could say something at the funeral.

This was the most important part. I cracked open the door again and waited. No one was visible and there was no sound but James Hetfield and his musical accompaniment. I made sure the doorknob lock was set so that no one could just come in and turn off his music. It would be an ordeal to get into this room. Then I slid the hood back over my head, stepped out, shut the door tight, and walked casually to the fire escape. When I was at the door, I pulled the wig out and put it back on underneath the hood.

This was it. I opened the door and made my way down the stairs, ambling as if I didn't have a care in the world. As soon as I got behind the house, I headed down the hill in the direction of Delmar. I crossed Forest Park Parkway and made my way back to the motel. I didn't take off the hood and wig until I was safely back in my room. I looked at the clock by the bedside. It was almost two in the morning. I stripped down to my underwear, turned off the lights, and got under the covers. Exhausted, it wasn't long before my eyelids were fight-ing that little flittering battle against sleep. Just like Dan, I gave in, at least for tonight.

CHAPTER THIRTEEN

On Saturday, I took a cab from the motel to the airport, then another back to my place, where I quickly unpacked. After that, I went over to Jordan's suite. I parked on the street behind South Campus. I wandered casually through the dining center, trying to listen in on conversations and catch word as to whether Dan had been discovered yet. There was no mention of him. I wasn't surprised. Not many people had been stopping by to see him in recent days. It might not be until he missed his appointment for the paternity test on Monday that anyone would check up on him.

Jordan's place was surprisingly clean when I arrived. There wasn't the usual mess associated with a post-party environment. In fact, other than three huge hefty bags sitting by the door, there was no evidence that there'd been a party. That didn't include the girls, who all looked disheveled and worn out. I smiled politely at them on my way to Jordan's room. I was impressed to find her at her desk, typing. She had already showered and dressed and looked to have no ill effects from the prior evening.

"Wow, you recover quickly," I said, startling her as I abruptly broke her study silence.

"I was the hostess. I had to maintain some level of coherence."

"It looks like you were the only one with that idea in mind," I said, nodding to the living room full of hungover lasses.

"I suffer that they may not have to. Of course, they're the ones suffering this morning."

"Where's Joanie?" I asked, "I didn't see her out there."

"She's been in the bathroom for a while. I check on her every ten minutes or so. It's not pretty."

"I'll bet. That girl doesn't seem familiar with the concept of moderation. So I'm guessing that the party went well?"

"Very well. We had some wine and cheese. Then everyone gathered in a circle to discuss the early work of Kandinsky."

"I'm sorry I had to miss that," I said, less than convincingly.

"Oh, don't worry. I had Joanie tape the whole evening. We'll be watching it together later."

"I think I'm busy then."

"When are you busy?"

"When did you want to watch it?" I asked, happy for this brief moment of levity.

"Tonight."

"Yeah, I'm busy then."

"Okay, how about . . . ?"

"I'm busy then too," I assured her.

"Fine, you're off the hook for now. Seriously though, I think it was really good for everyone to have a chance to let off a little steam. Things have been so tense around here recently, it was nice to just have one evening where everyone could kick it and not have to think heavy thoughts, you know?"

"Yeah, I do."

"So how was New York? How did the interview go? You think you got it? Did you see any sights?"

"New York was good. The interview went pretty well. I don't know if I got it but I don't think I embarrassed myself. And I had a stomachache last night so I didn't really get to take in any sights. I pretty much went back to my hotel room and crashed. I slept most of the flight back this morning, too."

"Poor baby," she said with mock motherliness that didn't mask her real affection, "how are you now?"

"Much better, now that I'm back with you." I meant it.

"Well, unfortunately for you, our time together will be brief today. I have to finish this paper for Monday and with the party and all, I am seriously behind."

"I understand," I said, giving her a little good-bye kiss on the forehead, "I just wanted to check in with my honey to see if she was still sweet."

"Oh my god, that is terrible. Get out now before *I* end up heaving in that toilet." She tried to sound disgusted but the smile on her face was broad and dare I say it . . . sweet.

"I'll call you later," I promised and headed out the door, grabbing one of the trash bags on my way.

I started back to my car when, for reasons I can't explain, I changed my mind and turned in the direction of Lindsay's suite. I knocked on the door and she answered.

"Where are all your suitemates?" I asked.

"At a vigil for Kelly down at the hospital chapel."

"How come you're not there?"

"For me, every waking moment is a vigil so I don't feel an obligation to go to any formal ones."

"Fair enough," I said, not wanting to say anything else to alienate her. "Did you get a chance to stop by Jordan's party last night?"

"I made a brief appearance. I thought it might take my mind off things."

"Did it?"

"Not really. I noticed that you weren't there."

"I had an internship interview in New York. I didn't get back until today."

"How did it go?"

"What?" I asked.

"The interview."

"Not bad. I won't know for sure for a few weeks."

"That's great, Jake. Are we done here?"

"What do you mean?" I asked.

"I mean, we're not really friends. We hardly ever spoke before this Kelly thing and now you keep stopping by my place, like you're checking on me, making sure that I'm not cracking up. Well, you can stop worrying. I'm not losing it. And I don't need some *fake* pretending to give a shit about me."

"What do you mean, 'fake'?"

"I mean, I still don't believe that you and Kelly were ever friends. She told me everything. And if you guys were hanging out in a casual, 'hey pal' kind of way, I'd have known about it. So that means that you're here for another reason. I don't know exactly what it is, but I do know that your motives are not as pure as you'd like me to think."

"Jeez, you are really a piece of work, you know that? It may be hard for you to accept that Kelly didn't share every detail of her life with you, but guess what, she didn't. Did she tell you everything about what was going on with Dan? No, she told me. And do you know why? Maybe it has something to do with the fucking judgmental way you react to everything people say. Maybe she thought she could get a less biased, less bitchy opinion from me than she could from you. Maybe I could help her work out this thing with Dan better than you could. Maybe she just thought what I think."

"What's that?" she demanded.

"That you're a self-righteous, suspicious snot who can't seem to accept that people make mistakes and that sometimes they need help rather than criticism."

"You know what I think?"

"I'm afraid to ask."

"I think you want to fuck me."

"Excuse me?" I wasn't entirely sure I had heard her.

"You heard me," she said, putting that to rest. "I can smell it. You've got a stink coming off you."

"A stink?"

"That's right. You've got 'I wanna fuck you' oozing out of your pores."

"I'm leaving," I said without moving.

"Go then and take your stink with you. I think it's about time you started being honest with yourself, don't you, Jake?"

"What is wrong with you? Your best friend is lying in a coma. Your suitemates are holding a vigil for her. A decent guy comes by to make sure you're okay and all you can do is accuse him of being a fake and talk about how he has a fuck stink about him?"

"All those words you're saying now, you know they're just for your own benefit, right? Because I know what you're really saying with your eyes and with what you won't say. You know that you're having a one-way conversation right now, don't you?"

"You are so messed up. I'm amazed that you and Kelly were ever friends."

"Please go. You're wasting both our time." She turned and headed toward the kitchen.

I didn't know what else to do so I started to leave. As I pulled the door shut, she called out to me.

"By the way, Jake. You say Kelly and I were friends. We weren't. We were roommates. There's a difference."

Not interested in hearing about the subtle distinctions of Lindsay Donner's female relationships, I shut the door and left.

That afternoon, Rick and I went to see a movie. He wanted to see *Scream 3* and I just wanted to get off campus (even though

I had been in another state less than twenty-four hours earlier). He spent most of the movie trying to figure out who the killer was and kept whispering "I think it's . . ." and changing the name every five minutes. I didn't even try to guess. In my experience, the killer can be anyone with a mask and he's never found out until the last reel anyway, so I just settled in and waited.

After it was over and the killer was revealed (he took off the mask), we headed home. Rick asked if we could stop by the row. He'd left his backpack at his house on Friday and wanted to pick it up. When we pulled into the parking lot, there was an ambulance and several police cars in front of my house. Rick and I looked at each other and got out. As we got closer, I saw the paramedics wheeling someone out on a stretcher. His face was covered and they weren't rushing, sug- gesting that the person was dead.

We walked up to the courtyard and asked what was going on. Jeff, who had a dazed, disbelieving look on his face said that Dan had been found dead in his room. It looked like su- icide. There was a note and everything. I had tried to pretend (even to myself) as we walked up to the scene that I didn't have any clue who was under that sheet. I wanted my reaction to be real.

I sat on a bench in the courtyard without saying a word and just stared at the ground. I tried to imagine how Dan's folks would feel when they learned that their son, who, until re- cently, had such a promising future, was dead by his own hand. But try as I might to picture them at the morgue, identifying the body, I felt nothing. I was numb.

I glanced up at Rick, who wasn't paying any attention to me. He was with Jeff, asking him questions, most of which Jeff couldn't answer. Out of the corner of my eye, I saw Detective Cardinal leave the house. He saw me and motioned for me to come over. I followed him as he retreated inside to the corner of the house, so that we were standing behind the bar. The smell of stale beer was overwhelming.

"Is it true?" I asked before he could hit me with a question of his own.

"Is what true?"

"Is Dan dead? Did he really kill himself?"

"He's dead. And it looks like he did do it himself."

"Jesus," I muttered.

"Had you spoken to him recently?" Cardinal asked, trying to sound conversational but ruining it by taking out his notepad and pen. I pretended that his question was intended purely for informational purposes and that we had no animosity. I put on my best helpful, dismayed face and tried to think back.

"Actually, yeah, I did. I stopped by to see how he was doing Thursday afternoon. I was going to New York for an interview on Friday, I think you knew that, and I just wanted to make sure he was okay."

"And was he?" Cardinal asked, not commenting on the trip thing.

"He was really drunk. He kept saying everyone on campus thought he was a murderer. He was out of it. I tried to talk him into going to a party my girlfriend was throwing the next night, that is last night, Friday night."

"I get it. What did he say?"

"Basically, no. He said no one would want him there. He was probably right."

"Did he say anything specifically about possibly taking his life or about his involvement in Kelly's attack?"

"God, no. If he had even hinted at killing himself, I would have taken him to the hospital. And if he'd admitted anything, I would have called you. Well, not you specifically, but the police."

"Okay," Cardinal said in the most pleasant tone of voice he could muster, "that's all for now."

I didn't even try to match him. Instead I just nodded and wandered back outside. It was pretty clear that Lieutenant Wendell had laid down some very specific rules for Cardinal's interactions with me. I guess they *had* heard of my father this far north. Rick had retrieved his backpack and was waiting for me.

"You want to go home?" he asked. I nodded again and we headed off to his car.

CHAPTER FOURTEEN

Sunday's fraternity meeting was canceled for obvious reasons so I ended up not leaving the apartment all day. Rick sensed that I wasn't in a talkative mood and left me be. Monday was unpleasant but I got through all my classes without being called on. Sheridan actually looked sorry for me, which was good because I hadn't done the reading for Ethics or anything else for that matter.

I got home at four and immediately checked mail and messages. There was nothing from the internship people and of course, nothing from Harvard, Stanford, or Yale. I did a little reading but my mind kept wandering. At five, I gave up and moved to the living room to catch the local news. The Dan story had led the newscast on Saturday night and gotten a mention on Sunday. It looked like it wouldn't be discussed at all today, but with two minutes left, the anchor said they had late-breaking news.

Sources said that Dan Curson's death was officially being ruled a suicide. Preliminary results of the toxicology report indicated he'd taken an opiate in combination with large quantities of alcohol. Curson had apparently consented to a paternity test just days before he died. The test would still be done. Police sources said if the test showed he was the father of Kelly Stone's unborn baby, they would likely close her attempted-murder case with a non-binding finding that Curson was responsible for the attack on her.

The report was primarily good news. I was disappointed that the authorities hadn't completely dropped the idea of doing a paternity test. I'd hoped that with him gone, they would think there was no need. But it wasn't the end of the world. They'd still have to wait a few weeks before testing the baby and in that time anything could happen. They could close the case. Dan's parents might oppose the test. I didn't know if they could stop it but it could certainly mess things up for the police if they tried.

The key thing was that Dan was dead and the cops had ruled it a suicide. It would now be difficult for them to find anyone else responsible for Kelly's attack with all the circumstantial evidence against him, especially the note. Plus, Dan was no longer around to protest his innocence. And there was no one who was going to do it for him. His silence while alive did him great harm and in death it would indict him even further. For that reason alone, despite the risks and the potential drawbacks, it was worth it.

I was in the mood to celebrate so I called up Jordan and told her I was picking up dinner and would be at her place at seven. She sounded surprised but said to come on over. I knew I'd have to tone down my enthusiasm by the time I got there, at least for a while. But after a few drinks, I felt sure that I could safely relax and we could have some fun, even if she didn't know the real reason I was so energetic.

I picked up Chinese and headed over, parking on the same street I had on the afternoon after her party. I cut through The Bird's Nest (the South Campus snack bar) to grab some napkins. As I was leaving, I bumped into Lindsay and two of her suitemates. They muttered muted hellos and got in line. Lindsay let them go and held the door open for me as I stepped outside. She didn't go inside.

"How's it going, Lindsay?" I asked, as if our last conversation had been completely normal.

"It's going," she answered cryptically.

"Funny running into you here," I said, mostly to avoid silence.

"You really can't stand awkward moments, can you?" she asked, half smiling. I was about to make some sort of defensive comment when I realized that she hadn't intended it as an attack.

"No," I replied, "I can't." She looked a little surprised by my honesty.

"Well then, I won't make this one last any longer than necessary," she said, stepping through the door to join her friends. "Take care," she added, almost as an afterthought. She sounded almost sincere.

"You, too," I said, watching her turn and join her friends, who were waiting to order cheese sticks.

The Chinese food was good and while the wine was not, it had the desired effect. By nine, Jordan and I were huddled in her bed. We didn't speak, but Jordan could tell I was troubled.

"You know you couldn't have done anything, right?" she asked.

"About what?" I played along. She was trying to help but she was on the wrong track.

"About Dan killing himself. Hell, you were the only person talking to him at the end."

"I know, but I couldn't help him or Kelly. I feel like everyone I try to help ends up worse off."

"What about that girl at Formal last year? She's better off because of you," Jordan reminded me.

She was talking about the fraternity's big blowout last

spring, held at a lodge in the Ozarks. Everyone was bussed out there. We had a great time but on the way back, a tire blew out on our bus and it was taking forever to replace it. While we waited, some guy's freshman date, who had too much to drink, passed out. We tried to wake her but she was really gone. It turned out to be alcohol poisoning.

Nobody had brought a cell phone so I ended up sprinting the three miles back to the lodge to call for help. What Jordan conveniently forgot was that *she* really saved the girl. She kept everyone calm and when the girl started to vomit, she turned the idiot on her side and dug the puke out of her mouth with her fingers. The girl rewarded her by spitting up all over her and involuntarily biting her. Even after that, Jordan took care of her. She even rode with her in the ambulance.

"Jordan, I'm not the one who went to the hospital with that ditz even though she threw up all over me. That was you, if I remember correctly. If not for your willingness to endure vomit, that girl would probably be dead now, no matter how fast I ran."

"I think you're way too hard on yourself," she said, ignoring the unsavory details of that evening. I didn't want to spend the night discussing guilt and blame so I stopped talking and dove under the covers. I was just starting to get fresh when Jordan threw me a curveball.

"Are you planning to go to the memorial service for Dan tomorrow?" she asked.

"Yeah, I think I am."

"Why?"

"Why?" I repeated.

"Yes, why would you go to that?"

"Do you really want to get into this? I thought were going to play naughty games."

"Not until you tell me why you're going to this thing tomorrow."

"I'm gathering from your attitude that you won't be joining me."

"I'd say that's a safe assumption."

"Why?" I asked, trying to turn the tables.

"Oh, I don't know. How about for starters, he tried to kill his pregnant girlfriend."

"We don't know that," I said with more indignation than I thought possible.

"Maybe not to a legal certainty, but we know it, Jake. Why else would he kill himself? That note was pretty conclusive." The note had been leaked to a reporter and therefore, the world.

"He never admitted to it in the note," I reminded her.

"Not in so many words but it was pretty clear what he was trying to say. I think he just couldn't bring himself to put the truth down on paper."

"Look," I said, refusing to address that theory, "maybe he did this thing and maybe he didn't. Even if I knew for sure that he had, I would still go. You know why? Because he was my friend."

"Jake, he was barely an acquaintance."

"At first that was true. But after Kelly asked me to help them and after she was attacked, I spent a lot of time with him. He was a guy in pain, Jordan. He felt like the whole world was against him. He didn't deserve that. Maybe he did do it and if he did, obviously that's terrible. But I can't believe he set out to do something to her. It must have been a moment of passion thing."

"That makes it okay?"

"No, of course not. But it makes it understandable. All of us do things we regret in moments of passion. Sometimes we lose control and it's not until later that we realize what we've done. We all make mistakes, bad choices. This one was worse than most. But that doesn't mean he was a bad person. A month ago, we all would have said he was a good guy. We couldn't have been completely wrong."

"Maybe we didn't really know him," Jordan said, "maybe

he always had this darkness in him and he just managed to hide it for twenty-two years."

"Do you really think that's possible?" I asked, genuinely interested in the answer.

"I don't know. It's hard to imagine he could keep it hidden for so long. But maybe it took something this drastic to bring it out in him. Regardless, I don't think I could go to some service and really mourn him, knowing what he's done."

"Well, I'm going. I hope you'll reconsider."

"Don't hold your breath," she said. We went to sleep. There were to be no naughty games tonight. Even I didn't feel like it anymore.

CHAPTER FIFTEEN

I was in my Tuesday European Politics class when I heard the news. Kelly Stone and her unborn child had died. I got word from someone who walked into class late and whispered it to the person next to me. Even though I wasn't supposed to have heard him, I asked if he was sure. He said that he had heard it from someone on the quad. Everyone was talking about it, he said.

But this wasn't high school and there was no intercom to announce this sort of news. I thought about leaving class and going to find out for sure. But something about that seemed inappropriate. I couldn't behave as if I had a vested interest in knowing for sure whether she was dead. Besides, I told myself, if she was dead, an hour of European Politics wasn't going to change that. By the time I got out of class, the information would likely have gone from rumor to fact. I could wait.

The first thing Kelly's death meant (if it was true) was that the doctors could now test the dead baby to see if Dan was the father. I didn't know how long it would take but my hopes of the day before were quickly becoming unrealistic. This was now a murder and regardless of Dan's parents' wishes or public opinion, the test would be done. And if it turned out that he wasn't Daddy, the lingering question of who was would remain. It would keep tongues wagging and that could only hurt me.

The second thing her death meant was that there would now be a wave of mourning for Kelly Elizabeth Stone. It would be like Princess Diana in the heartland. Dan was lucky he was dead. If he were still up in his room drinking screwdrivers, he might be in danger of a lynching. The frustration everyone would feel about the man who did this going unpunished would be intense. Heaven forbid, they discover that someone else was responsible. That person would be in for a very ugly time.

The third thing her death meant was that, technically, I was now a murderer. If the truth were to ever get out, I would no longer be charged with assault or attempted murder, but actual murder. I might even be charged with two counts if they tried to include the fetus as a victim, which was not out of the realm of possibility. That was when another thought resurfaced briefly. If Dan's paternity test came back negative and I was the father, that meant that, in the strictest sense, I had killed my own child. I pushed that thought out of my head and tried to focus on things I could control.

I would still need to go to the service for Dan. Kelly's death didn't change that. But after it was over, it was probably best not to defend Dan anymore, not to Jordan or anyone else. I would need to act sad but in general keep a low profile. If the paternity test did not go well, I wanted to be way under the radar when the authorities started thinking about whom else to chat with. When class finally ended, I had determined that my policy for the next few weeks would be to make myself as scarce as possible.

When I got out of class, I decided that the best place to go to get the correct information was the house. They would surely have the news on. They did. The gist of the story was that Kelly had died around seven in the morning and that the fetus, far too premature to survive on its own, was gone minutes later. They also reported that the unborn baby had been a girl. No football this time out.

A paternity test, considered a formality at this point, would be done immediately. They also announced that there would be a memorial service for Kelly on Friday morning in the campus chapel. They tagged the story by mentioning that a service was being held this afternoon for the alleged killer, at an undisclosed location.

The location was actually not a secret to anyone interested in going but the station must have thought that revealing the site might lead to protests. In fact, the service was being held at a small church in the Central West End in less than an hour. I had to hurry home to change into a suit. I arrived at the church just before one, the scheduled start time.

In the front pew on the left were Jeff and Kevie Poo, along with a couple of Dan's buddies from back home who also went to Jefferson. On the right was an older couple I didn't recognize but suspected were Dan's parents. Next to them was a young girl, about sixteen. I assumed she was Dan's sister although we'd never discussed our families. Much to my surprise, in the pew behind the family sat Jordan. And even more shocking, beside her was Lindsay. I slid into the seat next to Jordan.

"Changed your mind?" I whispered.

"I decided that if this is important to you, it's important to me," she whispered back. I grabbed her hand and squeezed it tightly. I could feel eyes on me and glanced over to see Lindsay staring at me. I gave her a little smile and a nod. She reciprocated. I still had no idea why she was here.

Dan's body was waiting at the airport, ready to be shipped back home for burial. As I would later learn, his parents had not opposed the paternity test. They just wanted to get it over with and get him in the ground. The pastor began to speak. I heard Dan's mom start crying and figured that was the perfect time to tune out. The whole thing lasted less than twenty minutes. After it was over everyone filed out slowly. No one knew quite what to say to the Cursons about their son, so everyone just nodded sympathetically. I knew that it violated my low profile edict, but I couldn't help but walk over to the family. They looked up at me, astonished that anyone was willing to speak to them.

"I didn't know Dan that well," I said to them, "but what I did know of him was that, despite everything, he was a decent person. There was good in your son, Mr. and Mrs. Curson. You have to believe that." Mr. Curson shook my hand and Mrs. Curson gave me hug. Both of them fought back tears. His sister didn't even try. I turned away quickly and hurried out. Jordan started to follow me but Lindsay held her back. Once outside, I looked around and saw a hedge near the back of the church. I ran back to a spot where I knew I was out of sight and then, when I was sure I was alone, I threw up.

Midweek was quiet. Everyone was waiting for Kelly's memorial service on Friday. All the local stations and a few national outlets were going to be there. The chancellor was going to speak and a writer in residence from the English department had written a poem in her honor. In a weird way, there was a kind of excitement in the air. I was apprehensive about more than just some service. In the wake of all the media attention surrounding the case, the police were sure to be pushing hard to determine the paternity issue. Even if the results were not what I was hoping for, I just wanted it resolved.

Plus, I still hadn't heard back from the internship people. It had gone well and I hoped to hear something soon. Add to that the nervousness surrounding law school itself. I had heard nothing from Stanford, Yale, or Harvard. I knew that they had until late spring to let me know but a few people had already gotten responses. My father knew this, too, and I began dreading his weekly phone calls even more than usual. Every day with an empty mailbox was a killer.

I was having trouble focusing on classes. They didn't really seem all that consequential in light of recent events. Jordan noticed that I was withdrawn but assumed I was just bummed about Kelly like everyone else. She didn't bug me about it. I was glad because I didn't have the energy to deal with her if she started asking questions.

Strangely, I'd recently found that the best place to get away from it all was Dan's room. On the Thursday afternoon before the funeral, I ended up going to the house and heading straight there. Police tape covered the door but I ignored it. Obviously, no one else in the house wanted to take his room and there was talk that it might be completely redone over the summer. But for now, everything was the same as last Friday night. I sat down on the bed and thought about nothing for about half an hour.

When I got home, I found three envelopes on the kitchen table. One had a New Haven return address—Yale. It was thin. I went through the formality of opening it even though I already knew what it said. "Unfortunately, we are unable to offer you a place in our program . . ." I set the thing down and looked at the other two. The second one was from Stanford and said essentially the same thing as the first letter. The last one was a phone bill. I owed $56.21. I went to my room to lie down.

I woke up three hours later to a ringing sound. I hadn't meant to drift off but I hadn't been sleeping well and I guess my body just decided to take charge. I rubbed my eyes and reached for the phone. The sun had gone down and my room was pitch-black. I fumbled around, knocking the receiver to the floor. It took me a few seconds to retrieve it.

"Hello," I mumbled.

"Jake? Hey, it's Lindsay." Even in my groggy state, I could tell that she lacked her usual confidence.

"Hey, Lindsay, what's up?" I asked even though I didn't really care.

"Are you busy right now?"

"Not really. I accidentally fell asleep and I'm a little out of it."

"Could you come over here? I don't want to sound like a dork but with everything that's going on right now, I'm kind of freaking and you're the only person I think knows what I'm going through."

I couldn't very well say no outright after I had just told her that I wasn't busy. Sleepiness was a surprisingly effective truth serum.

"What time is it?" I asked, trying to buy some time.

"It's 8:30. Please, Jake, I know it's an imposition, but with the service tomorrow and everything, I just really need someone to talk to." I expected her to say more but she didn't and the abruptness with which she stopped talking caught me off guard. There was an unpleasant silence.

"Of course I'll come over. Give me a few minutes to wake up. I'll be there by nine."

"Thanks, I'll see you then," she said, hanging up before I could respond. I sat there for a minute, awake but dazed. When my brain began to function again, I decided to call Jordan to get her take on how best to deal with what was likely to be a pretty emotional encounter. I got her machine, so I hung up. The clock said 8:34. I got up to wash my face.

I arrived at Lindsay's right at nine. The first thing I noticed was that the place was empty. Lindsay looked like she was in much better shape than when we spoke on the phone.

"Where are all your suitemates?" I asked.

"I thought you knew. They're all at the sorority planning meeting. They're deciding exactly what they want to do at the service tomorrow. We'll probably end up singing. Jordan's there, too."

"Why aren't you there?"

"I work in the admissions office and they had me there late tonight. This is their busy time."

"I didn't know you worked there," I said.

"Yep. This year that's my only job. My first three years here, I also worked in the alumni office."

"That must have been exhausting," I said.

"I'm afraid it's my cross to bear. Someday I'll marry into money and look back fondly on these hardscrabble days."

"Really?" I asked.

"No, not really. Hopefully I won't look back on them at all. But for now, this is my life. Not all of us have rich lawyer fathers."

"I wasn't saying you . . ."

"I know. I'm sorry. That wasn't fair of me. The truth is, I only used work as an excuse to miss the sorority thing tonight. Like I told you before, it's all just too much for me," she said, sitting down on the sofa and motioning for me to join her. "I didn't think this was going to get to me so much but I guess I was wrong."

"Listen, Lindsay, I know it's rough right now but you're going to get through this. This service will be a good way for you to say good-bye."

"Like Dan's service was for you?" she asked. There was a strangeness to her tone I didn't like.

"Exactly. Going to that helped give me some closure for what was a painful experience. I'm sure it helped you a little, too."

"Not really," she admitted, "I only went to the thing because I was worried that no one else would show up and his parents would be there all alone. That would have been too sad."

We sat there for a few seconds, neither of us saying a word. I got the bizarre sensation that Lindsay was fucking with me. Everything she said seemed sincere enough but I didn't get the feeling that there was anything real behind her words. It was like she was putting on an act for me but not trying too hard. I didn't want to offend her if I was wrong, but I had to find out, so I asked a question.

"Lindsay, forgive me for asking this, but not too long ago, in this very apartment, you said that Kelly was your roommate but not your friend. Now you seem to have had a change of heart. What happened?"

"I may have overstated things before. If you'll remember, I was a little pissed. Kelly and I had some really good times together. We also had some really bad times together, and I mean that in the best sense. I remember she took me home with her one weekend and we had the best, nastiest time together. Kelly could get really dirty sometimes. Especially when she was drunk. There was one night . . . ."

"Maybe this isn't the right time to be sharing tales of debauchery." I heard myself say.

"Jake, that's what Kelly and I had. Endless tales of debauchery. Spring Break '97, the '98 summer in Spain, winter break in Aspen that same year. If I can't recount tales of debauchery, there's not much left to remember."

"I didn't realize Kelly had such . . . history," I said carefully.

"No more than the average college girl. Well, maybe a little more. I guess that's what I meant before. We weren't just roommates. We were party pals but I'm not sure if that made us friends. Like you said, you're the one she came to when she had real problems with Dan, right? I didn't have a clue."

I didn't say anything in response to that. Without warning, Lindsay slowly leaned over. I automatically pulled back. She gave me an amused smile as she grabbed the pillow behind me to prop behind her back. I could smell her perfume. I thought it odd that she was wearing perfume on a Thursday evening when she had no plans to go out.

In a less than subtle gesture, she arched her back as if it were stiff and she was trying to get out the kinks. I couldn't help but notice that she was wearing a V-neck sweater without anything underneath. I could see the freckles on her chest. Either she had been sunning herself in the thirty degree St. Louis winter days or she'd been going to a tanning salon. I hated tanning salons. But I liked the freckles.

She stretched for quite a few seconds so I also couldn't help but notice what I initially remembered that night in the hospital. She was very well proportioned. Hell, she was fairly bursting out of her two-sizes-too-small sweater. I caught a whiff of her shampoo, which created a nice combination with the perfume. Her tight, curly blond locks actually glistened in the unusually soft light. I imagined her hair would be very soft to the touch but fought the impulse to reach out and make sure. I got the distinct impression that Lindsay Donner was no longer in need of consolation in the conventional sense.

"Why is it, Jake, that Kelly would share her innermost concerns with a relative stranger? Just because you're good-looking and well liked? I don't think so. And you don't really strike me as one of those good listener types."

"I don't know," I said, "maybe she just felt comfortable with me."

"That could be it. Is that why Jordan's with you, because you make her feel comfortable? Or is it because you're so smart? Everybody always says how smart you are. I also hear you can be very funny, although I haven't seen it. Is she with you because you make her laugh, Jake?"

"I couldn't tell you, Lindsay. I think I just got lucky."

"That's possible. She *could* have just about any guy on campus if she wanted. But somehow, I don't think it was luck that brought you two together. I think she sees you as quite a catch, Mr. Conason."

"I think she might disagree with you. Besides, Jordan doesn't think that way," I assured her.

"No? I bet she does. Everyone does. She sees that you're headed for big things. I think that's what draws her to you. And I think she's right. You ooze potential."

"Thanks, I think."

"There you go again, doing that avoid the awkward moment thing with the offhand remark. But there's no need for it now. I'm just complimenting you. Why should you feel awkward? Can't you take a compliment, Jake?"

"Thank you for the compliment, Lindsay. It's very nice of you to say that I ooze potential."

"You're going to go far, Jake Conason, but not without help."

"What do you mean?" I asked.

"I mean that you need a little guidance to get where you want to be. I don't know if you have the killer instinct."

"You have no idea," I said, almost laughing, shocked at my own lack of discretion.

"There's a difference between self-preservation and a killer instinct," she said without missing a beat. A cold shiver shot down my spine. I did not like where this conversation was going. It was like this girl could see right through me. I had no idea whether she was legit or just a great actress but I didn't want to stick around to find out.

"I think I should go," I said, starting to get up.

"What are you afraid of?" she asked, grabbing my wrist and pulling me back down on the couch. "Did I get a little too close to the secret place?"

"I'm just not comfortable with this conversation," I said, pained by my own prudishness. I tried to recover. "What is this anyway? You invite me over to talk and all of a sudden you start throwing all these spears at my psyche. It's not normal. Who do you think you are?"

She laughed at that. I noticed that she still hadn't let go of my wrist.

"Throwing spears at your psyche? You really are dramatic, aren't you? My name is Lindsay, I'm twenty-one years old, just like you. I just know what makes you tick."

"You're like a witch or something." I was only half-joking. This girl had a gift for making me sound ridiculous and, knowing that, I couldn't understand why I hadn't left yet.

"I'm the witch who's casting a spell on you," she said, enjoying the imagery. "Is it working?"

Before I could answer, she leaned in and kissed me. It was one of those really intense kisses where tongues are flailing all over the place and lips are being bitten. I wouldn't exactly call it romantic. More like brutal, animalistic. As we kissed, she took my arm, the one she had never let go of, and pulled it up to her chest. She grabbed my hand and placed it on her breast and squeezed . . . hard. She took her hand away and I discovered that mine stayed there, still squeezing, even harder than she had.

I heard a little moan of delight and before I knew it she had climbed on top of me. She rolled my sweater up to my neck and began licking my chest with a ferocity that almost hurt. She took my hand and slid it down her jeans, which she had unbuttoned somewhere along the line. As she pulled my hand down, she glanced up at me. Something in her eyes frightened me. She looked like she might actually devour me if she could.

This was not the same person who had called me forty-five minutes ago. That other person had been an act, as surely as my entire existence over the last week and a half had been an act. And she was a better actor than I ever was. She was playing me. I had no idea what she was after but this Lindsay witch-woman was totally manipulating me, just as I had with Kelly that chilly night at the frat party back in December. I don't know how that memory popped into my head but now I couldn't get rid of it. I snapped out of my haze of lust and sat up, pulling my hand out of Lindsay's pants as I disentangled her tongue from mine. At first she thought I was just teasing and tried to force her mouth back onto mine. Finally, I had to push her off.

"What?" she demanded, as I stood up. Her nose was bright red, as if she'd been outside in the cold and protected every part of her face but that one.

"I can't do this." I said.

"Of course you can. You just proved that. Now it's just a

matter of finishing the job." She was still flushed.

"I can't. I won't. I love my girlfriend. I can't believe I even came over here. I don't know what I was thinking."

"Don't give me that shit," she said, her voice rising, "you knew exactly what you were in for when you came over here. It's what you wanted, even if you didn't know it."

"This was a huge mistake," I told her as I quickly threw on my jacket, "I can't be here."

"Don't be a pussy, Jake." She was pleading and mocking me at the same time. I headed for the door.

"This is not who I am," I said more to myself than to her.

"Are you sure? Isn't this exactly who you are? I think we both know it is."

I turned and looked at her closely. I couldn't tell whether she was talking about this evening or making reference to another night with another girl two months ago. I wasn't sure if she was just throwing out comments for effect or if she really had some special key to unlock the terrible thoughts that were bouncing around in my brain. I was completely lost. As weird as it sounds, in that instant, as I slammed the door and ran down the stairs, I actually believed in witchcraft.

CHAPTER SIXTEEN

Kelly's memorial service started at ten on Friday morning. The crowd was huge. The only reason I even got a seat was that the powers that be had created a reserved section for special guests and I had somehow made the list. I didn't really know anyone sitting near me so I kept to myself. Jordan and Lindsay, along with all of Kelly's sorority sisters were up on the pulpit, waiting to sing their song of tribute. The odd sense of excitement that pervaded campus all week long had reached a fever pitch now. It felt like a rock star was about to step onto the stage.

A hush fell over the crowd. The chaplain had stepped up to the podium. He made some very heartfelt comments about Kelly, even though I doubt he'd ever met her. He was followed by the chancellor, who talked about the contributions Kelly had made to the school in her four years, how many people she had touched and how she would never be forgotten. After that, the professor from the English department got up and read a very flowery poem that I'm told she stayed up all night polishing. I didn't really get it and from the expressions of those sitting next to me, I don't think I was alone.

Then the chaplain got up again and introduced the ladies of Delta Theta. They stood, and accompanied by the hundred-year-old organ the chapel housed, began a rendition of the lovely but overused "I Will Remember You" by Sarah Mc-Lachlan. I have to admit that despite all the clichés at work, the service was well done. It went off without a hitch.

After it was over (the whole thing took about forty minutes), I waited by the exit for Jordan so we could leave together. Much to my dismay, I saw that walking with her down the aisle was none other than the witch woman of Jefferson University, Lindsay Donner.

"Are you ready to go?" I asked Jordan when they got within earshot. She nodded and I took her hand, hoping desperately that Lindsay had kept her mouth shut. We stepped outside the chapel door only to be immediately accosted by a familiar-looking platinum blond. I tried to move but she stood right in front of me with a microphone jammed in my face and a camera directly behind her.

"Megan Moses, Channel Eight Eyewitness News. What does this event mean to the university? Is it inspiring to see so many people turn out to honor Kelly Stone?" she asked with an aggressiveness usually associated with paparazzi at a premiere.

"It's good that people care," I muttered halfheartedly as I tried to sneak past her. Instead of letting me go, Megan stepped directly in my path and tried again.

"Did you know Ms. Stone? This must be incredibly painful for those of you who spent the last four years laughing and learning with Kelly."

I looked at Megan Moses. She just wasn't going to let me go without a comment. I stifled the urge to say something flip. That would not serve me well considering that I could still be tried for killing the girl at issue. I took a moment to gather myself and leaned toward the mic, making sure that I was staring straight into the camera.

"The death of Kelly Stone is a tragedy. For those of us who knew her, this is a particularly painful time. Partly because we can't help but remember how she was brutalized by a vicious attacker, but also because we are forced to see her brutalized once again by media jackals like yourself. Please, have the compassion to let her rest in peace, finally. Turn off your cameras and let us mourn privately. Haven't you done enough?"

Megan was sufficiently taken aback that she let Jordan and I pass without any more hassle. Lindsay followed close behind. As we walked away, I saw Detective Cardinal leaning against the wall of a nearby building. He'd obviously heard my diatribe. When he saw that I noticed him, he walked over.

"Did you mean all that?" he asked, nodding in the reporter's direction.

"Detective, I know you don't believe me but I'm not some fraternity purist who puts brotherhood before justice. If Dan killed Kelly, he deserved to be punished. I would never have covered for him."

"You made some poor decisions, son. You made some questionable choices."

"I know that now, but at the time I thought I was doing the right thing. I was trying to help Kelly, Dan, and the police and I ended up not helping anyone."

"That's not true," Jordan whispered. I kissed her forehead gratefully and turned back to Cardinal.

"Detective, do you remember those nightmares I told you about, the ones where Kelly is screaming for my help, but I'm locked in my car?"

He nodded.

"Well, I still have them. All the time. This case may be basically closed for you, but it's not closed for me. I don't think it will be for a long time." I tried to read his expression, to determine if he was buying my bullshit. He didn't seem outright skeptical but I didn't get the sense that he wanted to give me a big hug either.

"I've got to get back," he said.

"Thanks for coming, Detective," Jordan said before he walked off. When he was out of earshot, Lindsay, who'd kept silent the whole time, turned to me.

"That was pretty impressive," she said, "it sounded like it came straight from the heart."

"Are you being sarcastic?" I asked, incredulous.

"No," she answered, taken aback, "I was talking about how you handled that reporter."

"Oh, sorry."

"She's right, Jake," Jordan added, "I think you really nailed her. I don't know if it did any good but at least you got your point across."

"Thanks. I just wanted to give her a taste of her own medicine."

"Hey, Jake," Lindsay said as if the idea had just occurred to her, "the sorority is having a reception in Kelly's honor. I'm sure Jordan already told you about it. We'd love to have you."

"I appreciate the offer," I told her as if she weren't a girl I'd almost had sex with the night before, "but I think I'm just gonna go back to my place and take it easy. I don't really feel like being around people. You understand, right?"

"Are you uncomfortable being around other people who cared about Kelly?" she asked, refusing to let it go. Jordan jumped in.

"Lindsay, I think Jake's just had enough for a while. I mean, you know better than anyone the tough times he's had. Let's not ask him to do anything he's not comfortable with."

"Are you uncomfortable coming?" Lindsay asked me directly.

"I'd just rather not," I said. Nobody said anything for a few seconds, so I added, "I think I just need a little alone time."

"There it is again, the uncomfortable silence avoidance thing," Lindsay said, "I thought you'd gotten over that one, Jake."

"What's this?" Jordan asked.

"Oh, nothing," I said, "Lindsay has this theory that I have a problem with uncomfortable silences."

"He does," Lindsay reiterated.

"I'll have to work on that another time. Right now I'm going home. Jordan, you want a ride?"

"That would be nice," she said as I grabbed her hand and led her away without looking back.

Classes were cancelled on Friday so I had the whole afternoon to myself. I lay in bed, whiling away the hours, going over the events that had gotten me to this place. I thought about Kelly, about Dan, about last night with Lindsay. I was amazed that after everything that had happened to me and everything I'd done in recent weeks, I wasn't sitting in a jail cell right now. I tried to remember how I had managed to avoid it to this point but it all began to run together. It was difficult to separate the sensation of a crowbar smashing into soft brains from the feeling of lips pressed against lips.

I gave up on figuring out how I got here and tried instead to concentrate on why. That was clearer. I had to graduate and get a good job. My father would demand nothing less. If I was to eventually join his firm, I had to prove that I was really worthy of that honor, so there could be no complications.

But most of all, there was Jordan. All this, everything I had done, was to make sure that the woman I loved didn't leave me. I couldn't lose her. If I lost everything else, it wouldn't matter as long as I still had her. Unfortunately, losing everything else almost certainly meant losing her, too.

And then I realized, there was a way to solve that problem. There was a way to make sure that Jordan and I would be together forever. It was an option I had not seriously considered until now but it was one that made perfect sense. I made reservations for the following night at Tarino's, just off campus. It was far from the fanciest restaurant in St. Louis but it was the site of our first official date and I thought it would be appro-

priate for what I had in mind. Then I called her. She wasn't
in, so I left a message telling her not to make any plans for
tomorrow night, that we were going out to dinner.

Then I went out to do a little shopping. I didn't get back
until late. There were several messages on my machine. One
was from Jordan, confirming tomorrow night. The next was
from one of my fraternity brothers, saying that despite the
events of the last week, there would be a house meeting on
Sunday. The third message started out with a long silence. I
was about to delete it when a familiar voice asked, "How's that
for a long, uncomfortable silence?" Then she hung up.

I think Jordan suspected what was going on from the second I
picked her up. I tried to act normal but I was jumpy and I
couldn't keep the goofy grin off my face. If there had been any
doubt, it was removed when we pulled into the Tarino's parking lot. She remembered its significance as well as I did. I tried
to act casual but I even reserved the same table as our first date,
so by the time we got our menus, there was no suspense left.
I managed to wait until after we had ordered before I went for
it.

"Jordan, you and I have been together for twenty-one
months. And while I admit not every second of that time together has been perfect, I can honestly say that I never feel as
happy when I'm without you as I do when you're with me. I
know that I can be self-involved and neurotic. Hell, you've
told me that I can be self-involved and neurotic. But I hope
that recently I've proven to you that I can be more than that."
At that point, I got out of my chair and knelt down next to
her. She didn't speak. In fact, it didn't look like she was even
breathing. I continued.

"It took some very weird stuff for me to realize this, but
there isn't another person in my life as important to me as you.
If every other person on the face of the earth died today, I
could deal with it if I knew that you were still here and that

you wanted to be with me. What I'm getting at is that I love you and I would be honored if you would be my wife. Jordan, will you marry me?"

I pulled out the ring I had bought yesterday and waited. Since she knew what I had in mind a while ago, she had some time to formulate an answer. One tear trickled down her cheek, then another. She was crying. Not audibly, but the tears were there and I could hear her make a cute hiccupy sound every few seconds. Finally, she gathered herself and spoke.

"First of all, get off your knees. Now, I had a sneaking suspicion that you might be heading in this direction so I've been thinking about what I wanted to say if you did." She somehow managed to be both warm and businesslike. "Let me start by saying that I'm not saying no. But I'm not saying yes just yet either. What you said is true, we have had our problems and things haven't been perfect. But you've made a serious effort to change the stuff that drives me crazy and for that you deserve major credit.

"But, as you know, I'm waiting to hear about the master's programs at NYU and Miami, as well as the position at the museum here in town. My life is very much up in the air and I'm hesitant to make any firm decisions about anything until I know exactly where I stand professionally.

"Having said that, you are the sweetest, most loyal, most loving person I have ever met and I want to spend the rest of my life with you. So here's what I'm suggesting. Let's give it two months to see where we're both at in terms of profession and location. If everything's still looking good then, I would love to be Mrs. Jordan Lansing–Conason." Having finally gotten the whole thing out, she waited and more important, breathed. I could tell she was apprehensive about my response.

"That is the least romantic semiacceptance of a marriage proposal that I've ever heard in my life," I said, smiling to let her know I wasn't upset. "You should be ashamed of yourself. If I weren't such a sweet, loyal, loving person, I would really have a few words for you. But I am so I don't. Nothing has ever been easy with you missy, so why should I have expected anything different in this situation?"

"You shouldn't. Now what do you say we make this meal to go and head back to your place?"

"I like the way you think," I said, motioning for the waiter.

When we got back to my apartment, Jordan was greeted by about twenty scented candles burning in my room. I had even changed my sheets in anticipation of the evening. Although she knew that she was going to give me only a conditional marriage acceptance, Jordan hadn't skimped on the appropriate postproposal attire. As I watched from the bed, she slowly undressed, revealing a negligee that I had never seen before and suspected she had purchased specifically for this evening's activities.

"Where's the Enigma?" she asked, referring to our favorite nighttime music.

"Getting it," I said, nearly falling over myself as I hurried to throw the CD (the Roman numeral one with the song about the principles of lust) into the stereo. After the music kicked in, Jordan resumed her dance of insatiable desire, as I liked to call it. I tried to behave like a good boy despite a strong urge to jump up and ravish her right then and there. She was in a zone and I didn't want to mess with that. Eventually she made her way over to the bed and pointed in the direction of her shoulder strap, which I took as a sign that she wanted me to remove it. She didn't protest so I slid the other strap off and before I knew it, my semifiancée was standing naked and proud in front of me.

She then proceeded to undress me. Unfortunately I had not thought ahead and was wearing my everyday, non-lingerie boxers. She didn't seem to mind. We got under my (clean) covers. Unlike Thursday night, there was no biting. Everything moved wonderfully, achingly slow. We kissed forever. It took about twenty minutes to get to where Lindsay and I had gotten in twenty seconds.

At one point, Jordan took a candle and let one drop of wax fall onto my chest, followed by another, and another. It burned, but only for a second. When one drop splattered and I gasped slightly, she pulled the candle away and leaned over to blow on the sore spot. She didn't apologize. She didn't ask if I was okay. She just blew softly on my chest. Then we did other things.

The candles burned out before we did. It was almost dawn when we finally drifted off. Jordan was curled up in my arms and fell asleep before me. I could hear her soft, deep breathing and waited with anticipation every time she exhaled and her back brushed against my chest. As I watched the first rays of the morning sun sneak past my blinds, I relished one of the few moments of true peace that I'd had in weeks. The truth was that the police could break in right now, put me in handcuffs and take me away forever and it would have been worth it for tonight alone. All my crimes had been worth it if they allowed me to lie here now. I felt my heavy eyelids close. I tried to fight it. I didn't want the moment to end. But despite my best efforts, I did fall asleep. And no one broke in. No one called. Not even a whisper interrupted our perfect slumber.

CHAPTER SEVENTEEN

It didn't take long for my perfect little universe to start crumbling. It began on the following Monday, barely twenty-four hours after all seemed right with the world. Everything seemed okay at first. I had spent most of Sunday catching up on the work I'd neglected over the previous week. I'd even finished early enough to make the fraternity meeting, which was surprisingly uneventful considering that it was the first one since one of our brothers supposedly committed suicide after trying to kill his girlfriend and unborn child.

I got up early on Monday and managed to catch the morning news before heading off to Ethics. If I hadn't been paying attention, I would have missed it completely. Halfway through the newscast, one of the anchors made a passing reference to Dan Curson's paternity test coming up negative. Apparently, authorities were still confident they had the right killer but would officially leave the case open pending determination of the real father. They had a few leads they wanted to follow up.

This was obviously not good news. I assumed I would be

one of the leads they followed up on. And after having seen my unedited postmemorial service performance on Friday's evening news, I gathered that I looked like a guy who was pretty upset that Kelly had been killed. I had only intended to sound like a typical, frustrated student, but onscreen, I seemed more like an angry protester. It was way too high profile. The only good thing was that the guy most likely to be suspicious, Detective Cardinal, didn't seem to be reading it that way and had apparently been ordered not to pursue it, even if he was suspicious.

When I arrived on campus (for the first time since that Friday morning), I found that my comments had given me some marginal celebrity. Much like the day when my name was mentioned after Kelly's initial attack, people approached me on the quad to offer congratulations on my brave words. Unlike last time, no one felt the need to temper their enthusiasm. I was the guy who had told off a pushy reporter. Cool. Awesome.

With a few exceptions ("Kelly is smiling down on you for what you did"), no one seemed to remember that what I said was in defense of a dead person's dignity. It was almost as sickening as the interview. Even Professor Sheridan let me off easy. I could have been mistaken but it seemed like she actually threw a few warm glances my way. I was genuinely bummed that she didn't call on me. I had really studied the case at hand and knew the answer to every question she posed.

After class, I had a meeting scheduled with my advisor, who wanted to see how I was holding up. His office was at the other end of the main campus near the administration building and I was in such a hurry that I didn't hear Evan jog up next to me. He walked with me for a few steps without saying a word. Finally I got frustrated and gave in.

"What is it, Evan? I have somewhere to be."

There was something about Evan Grunier that gave me the creeps. Apart from being a mean-spirited jerk, he had a way about him that made me uncomfortable. I didn't like how he looked at Jordan when he thought I wasn't watching. It was how I imagined a child molester might look at a potential victim.

I'd seen him look at other girls that way, too, although I never made much of it. Evan was an odd bird. I'd never known him to have a girlfriend, never even seen him on a date. He seemed to prefer to covet from afar. And I wasn't the only one uncomfortable around him. Jordan once told me that she knew girls who wouldn't go to our fraternity parties out of fear that Evan would approach them.

Beyond the general creep factor, something else bothered me about Evan. We'd been in the same pledge class, so we were required to spend lots of time together and get to know each other well. That's how Jeff and I became such good friends, sharing stories while being tortured by upperclassmen. You have to find some way to pass the time while locked in a storage closet for hours with ten other guys.

But Evan never shared any stories. I remember he was even reluctant to tell us his hometown. It was like he thought that the more he told us about himself, the more likely we were to use it against him. He was so guarded. Evan was an intelligent, resourceful guy who'd done many good things for the house, but he and I would never be pals and I was fine with that.

"Catch the news this morning?" he asked in his patented smarmy manner, jarring me out of the past.

"I guess. Why?"

"Did you see the report that said that Dan was ruled out as the father of Kelly's baby?"

"Yes." I thought it was majorly insensitive for him to be talking to me about the subject.

"Well, I thought I might have a few leads to offer the authorities on where else to look."

I felt a little hitch in my walk but managed to correct it before Evan noticed. I kept up my brisk pace and waited for him to say something else. No response I made at that point would've helped me much.

"So," he continued, "I wanted to wait until the results of

that test came back before I said anything because I didn't want to cause any trouble, but now I feel like I have to come forward."

"How can you help?" I asked without slowing down or looking at him.

"Well, since you ask, it just so happens that on the last night before winter break last December I walked outside our fraternity house during a party to get a little air, but there were still too many people around for my taste. So I wandered over to the soccer goal. You know, it's the one with the view of the side of the house. Anyway, I was out there shivering in the cold, having a smoke, when I noticed a girl leaning against the side of the house. She seemed to be crying. I could barely make her out because of the shadows. But when she turned a certain way I realized it was Kelly Stone.

"Not long after that, I saw a guy who looked suspiciously like you come outside. He sat on a bench in the courtyard for a few seconds, then glanced in Kelly's direction. He must have heard her crying. He walked over to her and the two of them chatted for a little while. Then, much to my surprise they began kissing. They kissed for quite a while. I know this because I had to light a new cigarette since I'd been standing on that field for so long. I briefly considered walking quietly around them to get back inside but was concerned that they would see me. Then, all of a sudden the guy was helping Kelly pull down her jeans. She even started pulling down her panties when it must have occurred to the guy that they were getting carried away. He glanced around to see if anyone was nearby but he didn't look over to the soccer field or he probably would have seen me standing there. The girl pulled her pants back up, but instead of going back to the party as I thought they would, having now returned to their senses, the two of them wandered off to the north, in the direction of your apartment."

I kept walking, not saying a word. Evan's memory of the evening was actually crisper than mine. While I walked, I tried to force my brain to come up with some kind of response. I couldn't admit anything, but a flat-out denial would be more for show than anything else. One thought popped into my head. Evan had known about my tryst with Kelly for months now. He could have come forward at any point during the murder investigation with the information. Why hadn't he?

I figured that part of the reason was that he couldn't be sure that Kelly and I had actually had sex. We could have backed out at any point. He didn't know for certain. No one else had seen what happened that night. If he claimed that we had gotten together and demanded that I take a paternity test only to discover that Dan was the father, he would become a joke and a pariah. It was only after the official report on Dan came out that he felt sure enough to proceed.

To someone who suspected me, all my behavior made sense if I was the father. The late night get-together at Meet & Eat where we discussed issues that may have set Dan off if he was listening in. My emotional upset upon learning of her attack. The way I tried to defend Dan when everyone else abandoned him (out of guilt over my indiscretion). And of course, my outburst after the memorial service. They would all lead a reasonable person to assume that we'd had sex and that I'd gotten Kelly pregnant. I could only hope that was as far as his assumptions went. Evan hadn't spoken for some time. I guess he was letting it all sink in for me. But now he resumed his little monologue.

"Anyway, I don't think I need to spell out the logical conclusions that can be made from what I saw and what I know. I don't want to be crass. So here's what I'm thinking. I could go to the authorities with the information I have. Many people would argue that's the only ethical course of action. But if I did that, then your reputation would be left pretty much in tatters. I doubt you'd get into the school of your choice. Your friends would view you as a hypocrite, a liar, and a bad brother. The authorities might even charge you with something. And your girlfriend would never, ever speak to you again. Your life, or at least the life you want, would pretty much be over."

"Listen Evan," I began, "you have no idea . . ."

"Hold on. Just let me finish before you say something you might regret. Letting that happen to you, while it may be just, doesn't strike me as especially merciful. And all semester, Sheridan's been saying that justice should be tempered with mercy. I believe in that. So I've come up with another solution to our little dilemma." He paused for dramatic effect. "I want you to break up with Jordan. You'll tell her that you realize you don't really love her and that you two aren't right for each other. You'll tell her these things, then never speak to her again. If you don't comply with my request, I'll tell her and the police what I just told you. If I ever see or hear of you speaking to her, even a simple hello when passing through the hall, I'll tell her and the police what I know. On the other hand, if you comply with my request, and never speak of our arrangement to anyone, I'll do the same. As long as you stay away from Jordan Lansing, your secret will be safe from her and more important, from the St. Louis police."

"Are you done?" I demanded, desperately pretending to be bored.

"Not quite. I know this is a huge thing to take in all at once, so I'm not going to ask you for an answer right away. Come around to my room around nine this evening and we can discuss our plans. But let me warn you, Jake, I'm not kidding around here. You'll do what I ask or you will suffer the consequences."

He didn't wait for me to respond. Instead, he broke off and started back in the direction of the house. I continued walking, refusing to glance back at him, refusing to look rattled. When I was sure he was out of hearing distance, I opened my mouth to gasp for air. I'd been holding my breath without realizing it.

I kept up my brisk pace so that I wouldn't be too late for my advisor meeting. Obviously, I had a lot to think about in the next few hours but for the next fifteen minutes I refused to let myself be consumed by Evan's ultimatum. The one pleasant thought I allowed myself as I hurried through the main quad was that if Evan had even a vague clue as to what I was capable of, he would never have tried to blackmail me. He would have known better. If he knew what I could do, he would be in Detective Cardinal's office right now.

After my advisory meeting and my other class that day, I went back to the apartment to evaluate my options in peace. Clearly, the most important thing for Evan was having Jordan. Getting me in trouble, being the man who solved the mystery of the dead baby's parentage, all those things were secondary to Jordan being with him. I'd always known he had a thing for her. But, until now I had no idea how deep it ran. To come up with a plan like this, he must have been thinking about it for days, even weeks. For him, Jordan was the Holy Grail. I had to remember that winning her would guide all his actions. As twisted as Evan obviously was, I couldn't help but admire him for how far he was willing to go. Truth be told, she was worth it.

So what to do? The first decision I made was that there was no way I could concede to his demands. I would not allow myself to be blackmailed. I couldn't trust that Evan would keep his end of the bargain. I was at his mercy. He could change his mind at any time and go to the cops or let the truth slip to Jordan. There was no way I could guarantee he wouldn't do that. In fact, the likelihood is that he would at some point.

Besides, even if I thought that Evan would deal straight with me and even if I thought I had no other options, I still couldn't do it. There was just no way I would let that little shit get the upper hand on me like that. I'd resort to drastic measures before I'd let him embarrass me.

For the time being, I didn't allow myself to go down that road either. I had already resolved too many problems with unsavory means and each resolution seemed to bring up new, more challenging problems. Eventually, I might be forced to make a dramatic move, but that time hadn't come yet.

There was another possibility. It would require me to be on top of my game. And it would require me to deceive a person I hated lying to. I could go to Jordan and tell her a very modified version of the truth. It was a risk to tell her anything of course. But I was pretty certain that even if Evan didn't go to the cops, he would at the very least tell her. Now that he had told me what he knew, he couldn't sit on the information very long for fear that I would find a way to weasel out. If I could convince her that my time spent with Kelly had been innocent and that Evan was a freak (that wouldn't be too hard), I might have a shot at defusing his accusations.

But there was still the paternity issue. If Evan went all the way with his claims and I ended up having to be tested, I was screwed—at least my reputation was. The test was his trump card. Of course, if Evan really had that much faith in his charges, he would have already told Jordan, the cops, and every local station he could get to listen. He hadn't quite reached the point of risking his own name over this thing. His conversation with me this morning was his first tentative foot dipping in the water. He could still pull back with little fear of consequence. But he had to know that getting in any deeper could do him as much harm as good. He hadn't played at this level before, which was a big advantage for me.

I didn't want to have to bluff. Evan was concerned about looking foolish but he was also love struck and bitter and jealous and cocky and any of those factors could lead him to make rash, emotional decisions. I would have much preferred to find a surefire way to guarantee that he wouldn't talk.

Because of his tight-lipped nature, I didn't know much about his background before Jefferson or even much of what he had done since coming here. There had never been any rumors of cheating on tests or hidden gay rendezvous or shoplifting convictions, but I doubt anyone had much of a reason to look into his past before now. I would need to investigate, but that had to come later. My primary responsibilities were to reassure Jordan that nothing happened and put the fear of god into Evan.

I had been so involved in my mental masturbation that I didn't notice the letter sitting on the kitchen table until I came out of my room to make dinner. It was from the New York firm and it was thick. I ripped it open. It was a letter of acceptance to their summer internship program. I sat down and waited for the wave of joy or relief or whatever was coming to wash over me, but there was nothing. I felt nothing. That is if you don't include the anxious ball in my stomach that had developed from the second I realized what I had to do tonight. Nonetheless, I called the Harvard Law School admissions office and left a message saying that I had been accepted into a prestigious internship program and would fax them written verification tomorrow.

After that I called Jordan to see if I could come over that evening after dinner. We hadn't actually seen each other since Sunday morning. There was no answer so I left a message telling her I needed to talk to her. I said I would be over there by seven and to call if there was a problem. After that, I called my folks at home. I knew they wouldn't be home yet which was fine because I didn't really feel like talking to my father. I left a message with the good news. I said not to call that night, that I had a ton of work and would call them again later in the week. Then I ate dinner and did the dishes. Rick wasn't around, so I spent the extra time alone going over everything in my head again, and again, and again.

CHAPTER EIGHTEEN

I got to Jordan's a little before seven. She and a few of her suitemates were still eating and watching some TV. When I arrived she got up and gave me a big hug and a kiss. I looked at the other girls. They all had goofy smiles on their faces like they knew something, but no one said a word. We sat back down and everyone watched the end of *Jeopardy!* Afterward Jordan took my hand and we retreated to her room. She sat down on the bed and patted the spot next to her as a sign to join her.

"So what's up?" she asked with surprising perkiness. I'd been a little apprehensive when I first arrived at the suite, worried that Evan might have already spoken to her. Her reaction when I walked through the front door set me at ease, and from her behavior now, I could tell that she definitely hadn't heard anything.

"I heard something disturbing today and I wanted to talk to you about it before anyone else did."

"Ooh, this sounds juicy," she said, clearly not aware of the magnitude of what I was about to say.

"Jordan, you're not going to like this. I didn't like it either. But I have to tell you because you're going to hear it anyway. Before I start, I want to make absolutely clear that what I'm about to say is not true and that I am livid about it."

"I'm a little confused," she said, no longer playful. "Maybe you should just spit it out."

"Okay. This morning Evan Grunier came up to me after class and tried to blackmail me."

"What?"

"Just give me a second to explain," I said. "Remember last December, the night of the end of semester party?"

"The night we had the fight," she said.

"Right. Well after you left I went outside looking for you. I didn't know that you had left. I saw some girl crying by the side of the house and thought it might be you. It was actually Kelly Stone."

"Oh?"

"She was really upset because she said she knew Dan had gone off with some other girl, that he was cheating on her. You know, all the stuff that she told me again that night at Meet & Eat, only on this night she was also really drunk. So I tried to console her. We talked for a while. I told her it would all work out. I even mentioned how you and I had just had an argument to prove it could happen to anyone. I told her that she shouldn't let a few roadblocks get in the way of a relationship she believed in.

"We hugged and I gave her a little kiss. She asked if I'd take her home and I said yes. We started halfway down the hill heading north when I asked where she lived. She said South Campus. I don't know where she was leading me but I think we might have ended up in Illinois if I hadn't asked."

"You talked to her about our relationship?" Jordan demanded.

"Yes, but that's not the point. Please, sweetie, let me go

on." Jordan shifted a little on the bed but said nothing. I continued.

"So I walked her back to her suite. She demanded that we go the long way around, along Big Bend. She said she didn't want people to see her in that kind of shape. I got her all the way to her building. She said she could handle the rest on her own. So we hugged again and I told her anytime she needed to talk again to just let me know. She thanked me and asked me to keep our conversation to myself. I said all right and left. I actually thought about going to your place but it was late and I was tired and I figured you were still pissed and I *knew* I was still pissed. So instead, I walked all the way back to my apartment, falling a few times along the way, mind you."

"Okay, that's a really nice story. I don't see what has you so livid."

"Here's what. When Evan approached me today, he said that he saw Kelly and I that night. And he says that we were more than just friendly. He said that he saw us kissing and that Kelly even started undressing. Then he says we headed off in the direction of my apartment." I watched her closely as I said all this, trying to discern her impression. She looked shocked, which I had expected, but beyond that I couldn't tell much. I continued.

"So I'm processing what Evan's just said to me, trying to reconcile what he was saying with the actual events of that night. I was about to tell him that he must have been seriously mistaken and make a suggestion for an eye doctor when he went on. He said that in light of the police announcement that Dan was not the father of Kelly's child, he felt obligated to tell you and the police what he had seen. He said there was reason to believe that I was the father.

"So now I'm just dumbfounded. What had seemed like an error a few seconds before had suddenly turned into some horrible nightmare. I knew that Evan and I were never best buddies, but for him to make an allegation like that seemed beyond the pale, even for him. I didn't even know how to respond.

But as it turned out, I didn't have to. He still wasn't finished."

"Wait a second, Jake," she interrupted, "if this is some sort of lame joke to get me back for not saying I'd marry you right away, you can quit it now. It's not funny."

"I wish I was kidding, but I'm not. Just please let me get through this. So Evan tells me, in a voice that would generously be described as sarcastic, that he feels a duty to report all this but that he wouldn't under certain conditions. He says that the main condition for him keeping quiet is that I break up with you. He says I should tell you that I don't love you and that we're not right for each other.

"Of course, when he made this demand, I'm guessing he was unaware that just two days ago, I asked you to spend the rest of your life with me. Then he said that after I break it off, I am never to speak to you again, not even if I see you walking in the hall. He says that if I ever even try to talk to you he'll tell you and the police about his charge. Finally, he says that as long as I don't violate his conditions, he won't tell anyone about what he 'saw.' "

"I cannot believe this," Jordan muttered. I didn't know what to make of that so I just pressed on.

"So at that point I realized several things. First of all, his version of what happened with Kelly that night had not just been a simple misinterpretation, as I initially thought, but a willful lie. He had taken something completely innocent, made it seem dirty and added lies to it to make it sound even worse. Then, of course, there's the fact that he is obviously obsessed with you. To come up with this elaborate story just to get me out of your life on the off chance that he might somehow sneak into your affections is a scary sign. It tells me that he's at the very least, a little off."

Jordan was still listening but she stood up and wandered over to her dresser. She stared absently at her reflection in the mirror. I decided now wasn't a bad time to give her some good news.

"Jordan, this scheme shows that he's not thinking clearly. If

I had really done what he claimed, then he would have no reason not to go straight to the police. Doing that would have the same effect as what he's doing now. You wouldn't come near me and I would probably be charged with something.

"His problem is that he would only come to me if his allegations *weren't* true. He wants to be a lawyer. He knows that if he makes these kinds of claims to the authorities and he can't back them up that he's open to the possibility of being expelled, prosecution, not to mention, potential mental observation.

"So he goes this route, hoping I won't want to risk even the hint of impropriety. He knows you and I had an argument that evening and that you might believe I'd do something stupid. He knows only three people were outside the house that night and one of them's dead so it's just his word against mine. And he knows that even if his charge turns out to be false, which it would, just an insinuation that I was the father of that baby or that I'd slept with her would do untold damage to my reputation and my future."

Jordan finally tore her eyes away from the mirror and looked at me. I motioned for her to sit down. She hesitated, looking at the bed as if it might bite her. Reluctantly, she shuffled over. I continued.

"But I think he's losing it because he's forgetting a few things. He's forgetting first and foremost that his charge isn't true, so that ultimately, no matter how ugly it gets, I'll be vindicated. And he's forgetting that there's no way in hell that I'd ever just give you up. Not because of some lame threat, not for any reason. He's banking on my concern that even if nothing else sticks, you might still believe I slept with Kelly. After all, there's no way for me to prove I didn't. But he's ignoring something."

"What?" she asked.

"He's ignoring that of course I'm going to risk you thinking I cheated if the alternative is not being with you at all. What do I have to gain by doing what he says? If I do, I lose you anyway, so I might as well be straight. Evan seems to think that just making an accusation of infidelity is enough to ruin your trust in me. I don't believe that."

I paused for a second to see if she would say I was right. But she obviously wasn't ready to say that just yet. I moved on as if that didn't bother me.

"Anyway, after he told me all this, he said he wanted an answer from me by nine this evening. Then he walked off, leaving me to wonder exactly how my world had collapsed in less than a minute. So I went home, took a nap, woke up, made some dinner, and called you. I figured the best way to deal with this was head on. I briefly considered going to the cops myself but then I realized that he could deny that we ever had the conversation. I would look like the crazy one and he could accuse me of defamation or something. So what do you think?"

The whole time I'd been talking, I watched her closely to see if she was having trouble buying anything that I said. The real moments of distress were the ones I expected—when I described what Evan said Kelly and I had done and when I admitted that there was no way I could prove I didn't sleep with her. Other than that, she seemed to be handling the whole thing surprisingly well.

"This is quite a lot to take in," she said.

"I know. It was for me, too."

"Can I ask you a few questions?"

"Of course. Anything."

"Why didn't you tell me about that night until now?"

"For the same reasons I didn't tell the police. One, because Kelly asked me not to. That didn't seem like such a big deal because she didn't tell me anything that night that she didn't say later. I also didn't mention it at first because I didn't know that Dan was going to be a suspect and I didn't want him to find out that his girlfriend, in a coma at the time, thought he was cheating scum. But the main reason I didn't tell *you* was that I didn't want you to be mad that I had mentioned our fight as a way to help her. I thought you might consider it a violation of our privacy."

"I do."

"I know. I felt the same way as soon as I said it. I guess I might have been trying to reassure myself that everything was going to be okay between us even as I was doing the same thing for her."

She sat quietly for a moment. I took the time to do a brief internal status report. I seemed to be doing okay. She wasn't visibly angry and she didn't appear to think that everything I had just said was bullshit. I watched her turn the whole mess over in her mind and prayed that I hadn't missed something.

"Would you be willing to take a paternity test to prove that you weren't involved with her?" she asked, wincing as the words escaped her lips. She obviously knew that this was a touchy question, but she had to ask it. I would have been disappointed in her if she hadn't.

"Of course, if that would make you happy. I will take any test at any time if it helps you maintain your faith in me. But just to let you know, that could get messy."

"How?"

"Well, I can tell you from being down at that police station that nothing stays private. Dan's suicide note got out. The results of his toxicology report got out. Even if I went in there voluntarily, it would look bad. It would get out that Jake Conason was tested for paternity of Kelly Stone's baby. They might include the fact that I volunteered, they might not. Even if they do, the question will still be out there—why did he feel the need to volunteer to be tested? Was he involved with the victim? And from there it gets ugly.

"My prospective law schools will ask the same thing. So will my family and your family and friends. No matter how pure our motives, there will be a taint. Ruining my reputation may only be Evan's secondary goal, but if I take this test, it's the one he's most likely to accomplish."

"Do you really think all that would really happen?"

"I don't know for sure. But remember what happened to Dan. Imagine if he had actually been eventually proven innocent. By the time that fact got out, he would have been screwed. The truth is, he was screwed no matter what, just by the belief that he *might* have killed her. I'm not saying that things would get that drastic for us, just letting you know that it's a possibility.

"Regardless, I'll do it. I don't care what the consequences are. As long as we're together, law school doesn't matter, what people think doesn't matter. I only care about what you think. And if my taking this test will make you believe in me, then let's do it."

"I hate this," she said. "If I make you do this, you're going to think it's because I doubt you and you'll resent me. And if it gets out, that will hang over us no matter what." I liked the way her mind worked.

"That's not true," I protested, "I could never resent you. And I would totally understand if you wanted me to do this. The truth is, I have no way of proving to you that I never slept with Kelly. That's what makes Evan's plan so insidious. Even when I pass this test, it doesn't prove I didn't sleep with Kelly. It only proves I didn't get her pregnant. In the end, it's still up to you to decide what to believe."

"Then let me ask you this, Jake. Did you sleep with her?" I saw her gulp and actually hold her breath. This is where I had been leading the whole conversation. I knew before I came over to Jordan's that I would have to present the possibility that I had cheated on her, even if I did it in the softest terms.

And I knew that to get out of this situation unscathed, I would have to get her to ask me if it was true. *She* had to pose the question. I couldn't ask her if she thought I cheated. It would seem too defensive. But the issue had to be addressed, preferably with my answer settling everything for good. I settled it.

"Jordan, I swear to you, as your future husband, that I did

not sleep with that girl. I would never jeopardize what we have, not for a second. It's not true."

I left it there. She didn't say anything but her eyes welled up. She grabbed my hand and pulled me to her, hugging me tight. I wasn't sure if she was reacting this way because she believed me or because she wanted to believe me. It was too early to know if anything I'd told her would stick. I hugged back, maybe harder than she did. After an eternity, I stood up. She wiped the tears from her cheek. As I moved to the door, she asked where I was going.

"Evan's."

CHAPTER NINETEEN

It was only 8:15 when I knocked on his door, but I figured showing up early might throw him off a bit. When he opened it, I could tell he was surprised. I looked around his room. It was immaculate. One of the textbooks from Sheridan's class was lying on his bed. I was impressed. We didn't have that class again until Wednesday and I, for one, rarely did the reading until the night before a class. But Evan and I were, as I was quickly discovering, very different people.

"I didn't expect you this early," he said, stating the obvious.

"I was in the neighborhood and I thought I should just stop by so we could resolve this."

"That sounds good. Just let me run to the bathroom for a minute, okay? I'll be right back," he said.

I watched him hurry out. I couldn't tell whether he really had to go or whether this was a stall tactic to let him get his thoughts together. A little of both, I bet. I sat down in his easy chair and glanced around. I had been in his room one or two times before but had never really studied it. The place was pretty sterile. He didn't have posters or paintings up on his walls. There was a nondescript area rug that covered the area between his bed and door, but otherwise the room was free of decoration.

I was settling into the chair when it occurred to me that a college senior not having any of the standard room accouterments wasn't just unusual, it was suspicious. I remembered my earlier commitment to learn a little more about my fraternity brother's background. There was no time like the present. Quickly, I jumped up and shut his door. Then I moved to his dresser and gave it a once over.

There wasn't much there—a little loose change, a lighter, some cigarettes, and a tube of Clearasil. I opened the medicine cabinet above the dresser to see if he had anything more damaging there. There was the standard Advil bottle, a pack of condoms, some nasal spray, nail clippers, dental floss, and assorted contact lens solutions.

I heard footsteps in the hall and quickly closed the cabinet. The steps continued past Evan's room and down the hall. I thought hard. Where else would Evan keep something incriminating? The room wasn't big but there were a thousand hiding places. I remembered all the odd nooks and crannies I'd used when I was in high school and needed to keep things safe from my parents. It would have taken them hours of searching to discover all my contraband.

I looked under his bed—nothing. I opened his closet—nothing. This was getting me nowhere. I stopped for a second and closed my eyes. Where would I hide something embarrassing in here? I glanced over at the bookshelf to see if there were any gay porno mags mixed in with his subscription to the *National Review*—nothing. He would be back soon. Where did I hide things? Where? Where? I looked back at the dresser. All the drawers were completely closed. It was so tidy, not a single piece of clothing sticking out accidentally. He was meticulous.

I opened his top clothes drawer. Socks. I felt around in the back of the drawer. That had been my secret condom spot back in the day. I couldn't reach all the way back so I pulled it out a little farther to get a full view. Nothing. I was about to slide the drawer shut when I noticed something odd. One of the pairs of tube socks in the very back corner was incredibly ratty. It had so many holes around the toes that they were no longer worth wearing. Evan wasn't a "hole in the socks" kind of guy. I squeezed them. There was something hard in the rolled-over top section.

I unrolled it and found another smaller Advil bottle. The expiration date was May of 1995, almost five years ago. I opened the bottle and found six whitish pills, each with a small indented line across its center. I have little interest in chemistry in general or pharmaceuticals in particular, but for some reason I couldn't quite explain, those pills seemed oddly familiar. I had seen them before but couldn't remember exactly where. It was on the tip of my brain.

Whatever they were, Evan obviously wanted to keep them a secret, which meant they were almost certainly illegal. I stole one, then refolded the socks over the bottle to approximate the way they looked before. I put the socks back in their corner of the drawer and closed it. More footsteps. They stopped at the door. I stuck the pill in my jeans pocket and jumped back into the easy chair just as Evan opened the door.

"Why did you shut the door?" he asked suspiciously.

"I didn't think you wanted everyone to see me in here and wonder why."

"I think you should be more concerned with that than me," he said in his best condescending tone. "So I gather you've given my proposal some thought."

I didn't answer at first, partly to keep him guessing and partly because I had just come up with an idea. Of course, I still intended to go through with my initial plan, but with the discovery of the mystery pills, I began to consider another tack as well. I needed a little time to find out what they were and whether they could help me. I still needed to bluff Evan and to put a little fear into him, but I also needed to stall for time.

The last thing I wanted was for him to call my bluff before I had a chance to see exactly what chemical concoction he'd been hiding in his sock drawer.

"I have."

"And what did you decide?"

"I decided not to call the cops myself," I said, letting the comment hang in the air before going on. "Listen Evan, I've spent most of the afternoon trying to figure out why you would lie about something like this. Could it just be that you want Jordan? Is it as simple as that? She wondered the same thing."

He was clearly taken aback by the last statement. His eyes widened and he opened his mouth to speak, but nothing came out. I continued.

"That's right. I told Jordan all about your little threat. I told her what you accused me of and what really happened. That is, I told her how I consoled a distraught girl and took her home. I told her how the girl was so drunk that she initially led me in the wrong direction, away from her suite. I told her how I gave the girl a small, sympathetic kiss. I told her how you somehow tried to make that seem tawdry."

"You and I both know that's not what went down. I saw you. I know the truth." His voice was less convincing than his words.

"You claim to have seen something. But let me ask you something, Evan—did you actually see Kelly I having sex? Because *I* know whether or not we did and *I* know whether there's any chance that I'm the father of that dead baby."

"It doesn't matter," Evan said, trying to get his bearings even as he spoke. "It doesn't matter whether you're really the father or not. When you take the test, it's going to look bad for you. People are going to talk."

"No one's going to talk because I'm not taking any test. I offered to Jordan but she said no. She said she believed me. Plus she pointed out what you just said. If I did take that test, word would get out and I'd look bad. That would hurt my reputation, which could hurt my future—my law school chances, my future earnings success. Hell, Evan, she's just an art student and she knew that anyone who'd put my future at that kind of risk would be in serious danger of facing a civil suit if those allegations proved false. Now, of course, I would never sue Jordan. If she wanted, I would take that test in a nanosecond. But if someone else were to make those kinds of reckless claims and my reputation was injured as a result, I might have a cause of action."

I paused for a moment to let it all sink in for the guy. He was doing a pretty good job of pretending like I wasn't getting to him but his eyes gave him away. They were darting all over the place, like he was looking for a way out. I waited until he came to the point I knew he would eventually, inevitably reach. I could tell when he did because those darting eyes suddenly froze. I spoke slowly now.

"So here's what you have to decide, Evan. How confident are you in what you saw and in what you think happened later? Because if you're wrong, you'll be taking a big risk. All the bad stuff that could happen to me if I did fuck her will happen to *you* if I didn't. *You'll* be the guy with the awful reputation who tried to stain the honor of a fellow student, a fellow brother. *You're* the one whose academic standing and future will be in jeopardy. *You're* the one who will be facing an expensive lawsuit.

"You've already lost any chance of ever being with Jordan. Do you think she'd really be with a guy who would blackmail someone to get her? Or for that matter, a guy who would resort to blackmail at all rather than take relevant information straight to the police? Even if she believed it was true and ended it with me, there's no way she'd take up with you. You're compromised."

I watched him try to find a way out of the maze. His brain was in overdrive. I decided to add a little gas to the tank.

"You could tell her you never threatened me but I doubt she'd believe you. Why would I make that up? Why would I risk my relationship for a lie that only hurts me? I wouldn't.

She knows what you did now. You've lost her before you even got off the ground. So let's put Jordan behind us. She's over for you.

"What you need to focus on is this: You have two choices. You can go to the cops with your suspicions. They may believe you. They may not. They might ask me to submit to a test. They might not. They also know that lawsuits are a reality these days. My father's firm loves lawsuits. But maybe they'll go to the mat for you and maybe you'll be vindicated. Of course, even if I did test positive, that doesn't help you much. You'll still look like a jerk to every person on this campus. You'll seem like a guy who dredged up unpleasantness for no good reason."

"But . . ." he started.

"No buts just yet," I interrupted. "Your other choice is to say nothing. Unless you spoke to someone else about this, the only people who know what you've done are you, me, and Jordan. She's not going to tell. It doesn't do her any good. I have no reason to repeat this crap. So that leaves you. If you never speak of this again, no one will be the wiser. You'll still go to law school. You'll still become a lawyer and represent slimy clients and get rich and fat and happy and have a great life. The only downside is, I will, too. And I'll be with Jordan. You have to decide if that's something you can live with."

He shook his head as if that might change things. He was about to speak but I held up my hand to let him know I wasn't done yet.

"Now I realize you think you know what you saw that night. I could see how someone might misinterpret things. But I'm giving you the correct information now. I bear no grudges. You were trying to do right, Evan, and I respect you for that. But if you take this any further you won't be doing right. I'm telling you now, man to man, that whatever you did or didn't see, I did not sleep with Kelly Stone that night. I am not the father of that baby.

"You can choose to believe me or not. It's your call. The rest of your life is in your hands. Not everybody can say that, buddy. There are lots of people who's whole lives are determined by others. There are people out there who never get a chance to choose their path. Kelly never got a chance. Her future was snuffed out. One minute we were talking in a diner and the next she was gone. All her hopes and all her dreams disappeared in a matter of seconds. She never got a choice. Dan made it for her.

"I've thought about that a lot in the last few weeks—how most of us are the victims of circumstance. Maybe you happen to be on the road at the same time as that drunk driver or maybe your soul mate was. Maybe you have a weak heart or happen to get pricked by a dirty needle. There's no way to know what the future has in store for us, Evan. But you are in a position to determine your own future, at least part of it, at least for a while."

He sat down on the bed. When I first began talking he had looked like he wanted to interrupt me a few times. But by the time I finished, the urge was gone. He was lost. He stared at the bland area rug on his floor as if it could offer him suggestions. I said nothing. Finally he looked up at me.

"I know what I saw. I know," he said, as if trying to convince himself. "If you're lying about that, then how do I know you're not lying about the rest of it?"

He seemed to actually expect an answer from me.

"I don't know what to tell you. You know where I stand on this."

"I saw you," he repeated.

"I know you did, buddy," I said in my most reassuring voice. "Listen, this is what I'm going to do. I'm *not* going to tell you that you have to get back to me by this day or that day. I don't expect you to come to my place with your decision. I'm going to pretend as if our talk this afternoon and our talk just now never happened. It was in our imaginations. So I'll go about my business as if we're brothers and classmates and you know, acquaintances. I guess if you decide to pursue this, I'll find out about it eventually. I leave it up to you. Take care, buddy."

He still didn't respond. After a few seconds he looked up at me as if he expected me to say something more. I just shrugged and walked out. I took the stairs down two at a time and almost skipped out of the house. The air outside was clean and crisp. I inhaled deeply, letting the cold sweep into my lungs. It felt good.

CHAPTER TWENTY

The following day, I walked around much of the time in a kind of haze. I knew that it was unlikely that Evan would do anything this quickly. If he did go to the cops, it would probably take him a few days. The guy needed time to sort out his options. Still, I knew that my life wasn't really my own now. I hadn't been kidding when I told him that the future was in his hands. Until I knew what he planned, everything was up in the air. It was all a bit unreal.

I felt a little like I did after I had my wisdom teeth taken out in high school and I was loaded up with Vicodin to numb the pain. In addition to the numbness, the drug also had the effect of making me feel disconnected from everything. It was as if I was hovering over my own body, watching it interact with other bodies but not fully engaged. Only today, I got that feeling without chemical assistance.

I had called Jordan the night before to fill her in (mostly) on what had happened at Evan's. She seemed to be reassured by my description of the encounter. As an afterthought, I mentioned that I had gotten the New York internship. I wasn't really surprised by the lack of enthusiasm in her congratulations. It didn't seem that important to me either at that moment.

After classes Tuesday, I stopped by the biology library. I wanted to find out what Evan's pill was but I had reservations about searching the net on my own computer. If the police ever checked up on me, they might draw conclusions, especially in light of how Dan died. I waited until there was a big line at the librarian's desk. Everyone who uses the library has to sign a check-in sheet. But having my name on it would be more overtly incriminating than anything on my PC. I couldn't have a record of my being in the library at the same time someone was doing computer searches on likely illegal drugs.

As people signed in and asked questions I gravitated over to a bookshelf opposite the check-in desk. When I saw the librarian put her head down to check a student's ID, I quickly and quietly stepped to the other side of the bookshelf, out of sight. I wandered through the stacks until I was at the far end of the library, then made my way over to the computer stations. They were all in use. I decided to try going about my investigation the old-fashioned way.

I actually went to the section with books on drugs. There were several rows dedicated to illegal substances. I found one book that was basically an encyclopedia of various pills. It had pictures of each one and a description of its effects. The thing was thick. Because the book was in alphabetical order and I didn't want to miss anything, the search moved slowly. Every time I came across a pill that looked like Evan's, I put a Post-it on the corner of that page. After two hours and sixteen Post-its, I saw something interesting. I pulled Evan's pill out of my pocket and unobtrusively put it on the page next to the picture. They matched.

It was Flunitrazepam, more commonly referred to as Ro-hypnol, or roofies. I realized why it had looked so familiar. My entire freshman year, every time I opened the door to my dorm floor, I saw a poster on the corkboard in the hall. It warned of the dangers facing women on campus. Among them was a pill that could cause memory impairment, drowsiness, visual disturbances, dizziness, confusion, and a host of other problems. Guys sometimes slipped it into girls' drinks. It was, as the poster called it, the date-rape drug. Right next to the description was a picture of the pill. In retrospect, it looked exactly like the little whitish tablet in front of me now. I could have kept going through the book but somehow I knew my search was over.

For the first time all day, the numb haze that had surrounded me began to burn off. Evan had a stash of roofies in his sock drawer. I felt like cheering. It was more than I could possibly have hoped for. As I was relishing the moment, a girl walked by me. She didn't look down but it made me remember the pill was still sitting out in open view. I shoved it in my pocket, peeled off all the Post-its, then quickly shut the book, wiped the cover with my shirt to get rid of possible fingerprints and put it back on the shelf. I grabbed my bag and started for the exit when I noticed Lindsay heading in my direction. I tried to wipe the smile off my face as she got closer.

"Hey, I thought it was you," she said in a more friendly tone than I had expected. We hadn't had any unsupervised interaction since that night last week and I wasn't sure what she would do or say.

"Hi, Lindsay, what are you doing here?"

"I'm just working on a project, you?"

"Same thing. How's everything going?" I asked tentatively.

"Everything's good, Jake. No hard feelings, okay? You don't have to walk around on eggshells with me. I made a move and it didn't work out. I was pissed at the time but I'm all right now. I actually respect what you did. You must really love Jordan to have backed out when you did. It must have been hard. I haven't met many guys who could resist my charms in a situation like that."

"I'm glad to see that your confidence is still intact. I must admit that your charms are . . . numerous, but I do love Jordan and I appreciate you understanding that and not holding a grudge."

"Don't worry about it," she said, waving her hand dismissively. "Speaking of that, I heard a rumor that you're engaged. Is it true?"

"Wow, you have sources everywhere, don't you? Unofficially, yes. It's not formalized yet but we are planning on getting married."

"That's great, Jake, really."

"Thanks, but could you not spread it around? Like I said, it's unofficial and I don't want the whole campus talking about it before it's set in stone, you know what I mean?"

"Of course. So I guess that's why you had that goofy grin on your face before."

"Huh?"

"When I saw you before, you had a huge smile."

"Oh right," I said, "I guess I am pretty happy."

"Well, if there's anything I can do to help, let me know. Like I said, no hard feelings."

"Thanks," I said as we headed for the exit. I could not believe that this girl was the same witch-woman who had struck fear into my heart less than a week ago. I couldn't peg her down. Obviously, she was smart, tough, and capable. She (to coin her phrase) oozed those qualities. But every time she was nice to me, it set me on edge. I got the distinct impression that she was never nice without a reason. I had only known Lindsay for a short time but felt like nominating her as the spokesperson for multiple personality disorder. I decided not to share that idea with her.

But as we walked out of the library, I thought of another idea that I might want to share. It probably would have been more prudent to think it out before asking her but I was still on a high from my discovery about Evan. So I went for it.

"Lindsay, now that I think about it, there is a way you can help me out."

"Name it."

"Well, this is kind of sensitive, so I'd appreciate it if you kept it quiet. Can you do that?"

"I'd rather know what this is about before I make any promises," she said, hesitating.

"All right. Do you know Evan Grunier?"

"I know who he is, but I don't really know him," she said.

"Well, Evan is one of my fraternity brothers and I always thought he was just a regular guy, you know? But in the last few months, he's been acting a little strangely."

"What do you mean?"

"He's always asking about Jordan or talking about Jordan. He seems really enamored with her and whenever she's at the house with me, he makes a point of being very friendly to her. I mean unusually friendly."

"So?"

"So, at first I didn't make much of it. I mean, she's a great girl and pretty friendly herself. I figured he probably had a crush on her. No big deal, right? But lately, it's gotten weird. Jordan told me that when he sees her on campus, he always talks to her, that he'll sometimes walk with her all the way to her next class. He always seems to pop up wherever she is. It's like he knows her schedule. She said it makes her a little uncomfortable. And a couple of times, I thought I've seen him following us. I remember one night, I was walking her back to her suite and I swear I saw him hiding behind a tree."

"Are you sure?"

"Not a hundred percent, but pretty sure."

"So what do you want me to do? If you think I'm gonna go out with the guy to take his mind off Jordan, you are sadly mistaken."

"No, no. Nothing like that. But I remember you said you work in the admissions office, right?"

"Right."

"Well, they have the admission records of current students there, don't they?"

"Yes."

"Okay. So I was hoping that you could peek at his record for me."

"That's against the rules. I could be expelled for doing something like that," she said indignantly. Then she added, "Why do you want me to do it?"

"I just want to know if he's dangerous. Can you see if there's anything in his record? Any complaints about him from female students here or at his high school? Any disciplinary problems? Anything that might make me have reason to worry."

"How am I supposed to tell that sort of thing?"

"I don't know. If he's done something inappropriate, I'd imagine it would be in there."

"Why would they let him in here if he'd done something like that?" she demanded.

"Maybe it didn't seem like a big deal in the grand scheme of things. Maybe he explained his behavior away. Maybe his dad is super rich and offered the school a huge grant. Maybe the admissions officer just missed it. Lots of kids apply here and sometimes things get missed."

"I think you're overreacting. It's probably just what you said, a really intense crush."

"Fine, if that's what it is, then I'll stand corrected. Look, Lindsay, if you really don't want to do this, I'll understand. I just want to set my mind at ease. I want to make sure that I shouldn't be worrying about this guy. If there's nothing, then I'll let it go. But if there's something in there, I need to know. The guy is seriously creeping Jordan out and he's getting to me, too." I stopped. Anything more and I would be crossing the line from requesting into pressuring. I needed to maintain the image of concerned boyfriend, not desperate schemer. Lindsay was obviously conflicted.

"Listen, here's what I'm going to do. I will check his record for you. I don't expect to find anything, but if I do you have to make me a promise. You can't let the administration know where you got your information."

"Fair enough."

"I'm serious, even if I find that he has ten restraining orders out against him, you can't make any reference to that. You have to pretend like you don't know anything about his past. Let them check up on him themselves. If you say you know he has a reputation, they are going to be suspicious. Everything in those files is supposed to be confidential. These people are not stupid. They will put two and two together."

"I promise I won't say anything. I hope you don't find anything. I just need to be sure. Please let me know soon," I urged her.

She said she would. Realizing we had nothing else to say, we went our separate ways. I was a little concerned about even mentioning Evan to someone outside our little threesome, but I had to know. There was probably some other way to get the information and maybe I had let the excitement of my discovery get the better of me, but I figured I might actually be able to make this work for me.

If for some reason, I had to make a move against Evan, I now had it on record with an impartial person that I was concerned about his behavior. If he spoke to the police, Lindsay could tell them how I'd expressed concern about Evan's proclivity for doing odd things to get close to Jordan. Blackmail fit snugly into the "odd" profile. Blackmail, roofies, stalking, and, God willing, a record of some illicit behavior in his record—all these elements were nice hedges against any action Evan might take. I wasn't out of the woods yet, but I could see the clearing in the distance.

CHAPTER TWENTY-ONE

The fraternity decided to throw a party that Friday night. It was intended to be the biggest blowout since the orgie just before winter break. Some brothers worried it would be in bad taste considering Dan's recent suicide, but most agreed that, like Jordan's party in the wake of Kelly's attack, it would help everyone move on and prove that life, and fun, could continue, even after such terrible tragedies.

Jeff, who was one of the guys who thought the party was a mistake, decided this would be a good weekend to drive to Chicago to check for apartments. He'd gotten a job offer from a consulting firm there and wanted to see if it was the sort of place he could make home. He offered me the use of his room Friday night if Jordan and I chose not to make the long walk back to my place or to South Campus.

On Thursday night we sat in his room, having a drink as he packed for the long weekend. He was leaving first thing in the morning, skipping his Friday classes so he could get in a tour of the firm during business hours. I was officially here to pick up his extra key but my visit included an ulterior motive as well. I looked at my watch as he shoved underwear into the corner of his duffel bag.

It was 9:15. Lindsay had called me earlier to say she'd done what I asked. She wanted me to come over at ten to discuss what she'd found. I still had some time to spare, but I thought I better get down to business, so it didn't seem like I was raising my concerns at the last second. That might appear planned.

"So can I ask you a weird question, Jeff?"

"How could I possibly say no when you phrase it like that?" he answered, chuckling.

"What do you think of Evan?"

"Grunier?" he asked.

"Uh-huh."

"Are we on the record here?"

"What do you mean?" I asked.

"I mean, are we talking now as fraternity brothers who have a deep and abiding respect for all our fellow members or are we talking as friends who have known each other for four years?"

"What do you think?"

"Just checking. I don't think much of him. He's petty, self-involved, ambitious to the point of being cutthroat. He's also cruel when it comes to pledges. He's a jerk. I don't consider him a friend and I wouldn't want him as my lawyer. I know you guys are supposed to be vicious, but I should be able to trust my own attorney, right? I get the feeling he'd screw me as happily as anyone else."

"So you haven't really formed a strong opinion about the guy either way then," I said sarcastically.

"Why do you ask?" he wondered, ignoring my crack.

"Well, it's just that in the last few weeks I've noticed him acting a little strangely."

"In what way?"

"Mostly in how he acts toward Jordan. It's been obvious to me for some time now that he has a crush on her. It never bothered me before. I actually felt bad for him for a little while. But in the last month or so he's gone from giving her longing stares and talking to her all the time to other stuff. He follows her everywhere. He knows her class schedule and is always waiting when she's done. A few times I think I've seen him following us when we're walking around campus. It's getting a little weird."

"I know he's a pretty intense guy," Jeff offered, "I mean, we all know that. I've never seen him act in the ways you describe but it doesn't seem like something alien to his character. Intensity and obsessiveness aren't all that far apart on the behavioral spectrum."

"That's what I'm afraid of. I don't want to embarrass the guy but I don't know how far he'll go with this and I feel like maybe I should talk to him. I think if he knew I knew, he'd back off."

"I guess it's possible. What if he denies doing any of that stuff?"

"It doesn't really matter what he says. I'd expect him to deny it to save face. I just want him to know that *we* know. I'll tell him as politely as possible that Jordan only thinks of him as a friend and that she's uncomfortable with all his attention. I think that should be more than enough to cool him off."

"Probably. I know if the boyfriend of some girl I was hot for said that to me, I would steer well clear of the girl for the rest of my college life."

"Let's hope that Evan has your sense of shame."

I got to Lindsay's a little early. Two of her suitemates were watching TV in the living room. I asked if she was in and one of them waved me straight back to her room. I knocked on her door.

"Come in," she said. I opened the door. She was sitting cross-legged on her bed with a psychology text in front her. Seeing it made me realize I had no clue what this girl's major was. It'd never occurred to me to ask. A glance at her book-shelf, which held about a dozen other psych books, gave me a hint.

When she saw me, she closed the book and told me to sit down. I joined her on the bed (but at a safe distance). As she reached into the drawer in her nightstand, she smiled at my reticence to get too close. I amused her. She pulled a sheet of paper out of the drawer and handed it to me.

"I copied this from his high school record. I almost got caught," she added.

"Thanks," I said. It was part of his transcript. It looked like the last page. There was seemingly nothing out of the ordinary. I looked up at Lindsay. She could tell I was confused.

"Look at the bottom," she said. I did. At the end of the page, after a comprehensive list of his extra-curricular activities, was a handwritten note. It read: *grades transferred from St. Barnards upon request.*

"What does that mean, he went to another high school for a while?"

"Uh-huh," she said, "only the full records from the previous school weren't in his file. All it had was a list of the classes he took there and his cumulative GPA at the time of transfer."

"Is that unusual?" I asked.

"A little. Most of the time when a student transfers, the new school requires complete records from the original school. But in this case, the new school seemed to be satisfied with what St. Barnards gave them. And generally, if the school a student transferred to is willing to accept just a basic record, then Jefferson will do the same. Especially when the referring school has the reputation of St. Barnards."

"It's pretty good?" I guessed.

"It's one of the most respected, exclusive private schools back east, which got me thinking . . ."

"Why would he transfer from a fancy private school to an average run-of-the-mill public school?" I interrupted.

"Exactly."

"Why?" I asked, certain she knew the answer.

"I called St. Barnards to find out. I said I was Misty from the Jefferson admissions office and had a records problem with a former student. They gave me a nice secretary named Jen who'd only been working there for a few weeks. Apparently, Jen wasn't yet familiar with the procedure at St. Barnards."

"What procedure is that?"

"As someone who attended a school like this on scholarship I know that no records of students, past or present, can be given to anyone without a written request and written permission from both a school administrator and either the student or one of his parents."

"But . . ." I said, then stopped, fighting the urge to get her to cut to the chase. This was her moment and she clearly intended to enjoy it.

"But, Jen, or Jenny, as I called her, hadn't been filled in on that messy detail. Also, Jenny, like Misty coincidentally, is a huge fan of the group Poison, and like Misty, is really pumped to check out their reunion tour this summer. Jenny and Misty really hit it off, so Jenny didn't mind when Misty asked her to fax over the complete file of a former student named Evan Grunier. Jenny even said she and Misty should get together if Misty ever came to town. Of course, that'll be hard, since Misty doesn't exist."

I waited, knowing the payoff was about to come. Lindsay gave a coquettish little smile and said nothing, enjoying the moment. Then she reached back into the drawer, pulled out another file and tossed it to me. I went through each page carefully, trying to pick out what had her so self-satisfied.

Evan had gone to St. Barnards for his freshman and sophomore years. His grades were excellent. Every course he took was honors or advanced placement and he got mostly A's with a small smattering of B's. He was on the debate team and vice-president of the French club. He even volunteered for the city's legal-aid department, doing office work. He got extra credit for it.

I finally got to the end. The very last page (listing his courses and his GPA) was the one that had made its way into his public-school record. It was the second to last page that was interesting. The top of the paper was a continuation of guidance counselor notes from the previous page. They were nondescript. Below them was a handwritten section titled "additional notes." The first note was from 1992, his freshman year, and read as follows:

10/17/92—Student Grunier turned in four students for a cheating scheme that included three classes of Ms. Jape's American History course. All four were suspended for one week.

The next note was also from his freshman year:

11/4/92—Student Grunier treated for minor cuts/abrasions after incident in which he was attacked. Claimed it was in retaliation for his actions in regard to cheating scheme uncovered in October. He identified assailants as Geoffrey Winter, Kevin Close and Andy Devereaux. Devereaux was one of the students suspended for cheating. Winter and Close put on one week's suspension. Devereaux given two-week suspension/informed that any other incidents during the school year would result in expulsion.

The next note wasn't until his sophomore year:

9/12/93—Student Grunier alleges repeated verbal abuse by several students, among them, Devereaux, Close, Jason Steadener and Lenny Canazares. No proof of such abuse was found but a note was made in each student's record.

Then, later in that school year:

2/16/94—Student Grunier treated in nurse's office for facial cuts/abrasions/bruising to abdomen. Grunier denied he had been attacked by other students and claimed that he had been assaulted by unknown assailants while returning from a lunch break. No action taken.

The next note came two months later:

4/8/94—Student Grunier treated in nurse's office for facial cuts / abrasions / bruising to abdomen and back. He was then sent to St. Elizabeth's Community Hospital to treat a broken rib. Grunier denied he had been attacked by other students, claiming he fell down a flight of stairs. He refused questioning by authorities. Several students were questioned by Vice-Principal Mandenhaus. No action taken.

The last note came the following month. There was very little room at the bottom of the page so the writing was incredibly small and difficult to read:

5/10/94—Student Grunier agreed today to take a permanent leave of absence from St. Barnards Academy for the remainder of this school year and in the future as the result of an incident on 5/6/94 at the Downtown Grand Harbor Hotel on the occasion of the school prom. Grunier will accept this leave unconditionally. In exchange, no further punitive action will be taken against him. Student Melissa Devereaux attests that she will take no civil or other action against either Grunier, St. Barnards Academy or Downtown Grand Harbor Hotel as a result of any events occurring on 5/6/94. All details of this matter will be sealed at the request of parties Grunier, Devereaux, St. Barnards Academy, and Downtown Grand Harbor Hotel.

That was all of it. I looked up at Lindsay. She had an expectant grin on her face.

"Does this mean what I think it means?" I asked her.

"What do you think it means?" she shot back.

"I think Evan got very naughty at that prom with Andy

Devereaux's sister, maybe even did something illegal. I also think it couldn't be proven beyond a shadow of a doubt and everybody, including the school, tried to cover it up."

"I think you are thinking pretty clearly. Just to make sure, I called up a friend of mine at Brown who went to St. Barnard's at the same time. You'll never guess what she said."

"Tell me."

"She said that word around the school was that on prom night, Evan slipped some roofies in Melissa's punch and got her up to her brother's hotel room while everyone else was downstairs. The general consensus was that he raped her. But she couldn't remember anything, not even having sex with him. Apparently, Evan claimed that she came onto him, much to his surprise, and took *him* to the room. He said it was totally consensual and that he never put anything in her drink. Since Melissa's parents didn't want any of it to make the papers, they came to an arrangement where no one would go to the police. Evan would transfer, Melissa's parents wouldn't pursue legal action, and everyone would get to keep their good name.

"Of course, word got out. My friend said Andy spent the next year trying to find out where Evan transferred to. When he finally did, he was all set to kick Evan's ass but Evan said he had a restraining order out against Andy, that if Andy touched him he'd go to jail. He also supposedly told Andy that his baby sister was the best fuck he'd ever had and that he bet she was even better when she was awake."

"Wow."

"I know. So it looks like your loyal fraternity brother may be worth worrying about after all. Maybe you should file a complaint with Campus Police and the administration, just to be safe."

"I was thinking about it. The only problem is that none of this stuff is general knowledge. How could I make them take me seriously if they don't have access to this stuff? None of it's in his Jefferson record. I can't tell them to call St. Barnard's Academy in New England because I heard a rumor."

"No," she agreed, "but are you sure there's nothing in his Jefferson record? Maybe you should ask them to check his file to see if he has any history of threatening behavior, just in case. I have a feeling they might find something."

"Like what?" I asked.

"Like the original copy of the entire packet you're holding in your hands, with date of transmission gone and relevant pages and passages marked."

"You did that for me?"

"I did that for you." Her eyes were blazing. Lindsay looked far more turned on now than when we'd been going at it. She seemed to get off on this whole thing. To be honest, the intensity of her gaze while flattering, was also a little scary. But that wasn't all.

She looked impressed. She'd said she knew I was smart but she appeared to actually believe it now. In the most primal terms, I was a guy who'd seen a threat to his woman and done whatever was necessary to stop that threat, legal or not. She clearly admired that. Without sounding too arrogant, I think she found my questionable tactics not just sensible, but sexy. She'd made a good impression on me, too.

"You are amazing, Lindsay. Thank you so much. I thank you, Jordan thanks you, or she would if she knew about this, which she doesn't. I really owe you big time."

"I know you do," she agreed, "and I intend to collect."

"What do you mean?"

"I mean that at some point in the not too distant future I'm going to call this chit in and I expect you to pay up promptly, in full, without hesitation or argument."

"That sounds ominous. What exactly do you have in mind?" I asked, afraid of the answer.

"Don't worry about it."

"You promised me you were cool with that night. You said you wouldn't pursue it," I reminded her.

"You may be the most self-involved person I've ever met. Did I say anything about you and me? Maybe I want you to wash my car or give me a ride to the airport. Just chill out a little."

"Sorry."

"You're forgiven. So what's your next move?" she asked.

"I'm not sure. I have to decide whether to take this to the authorities or just deal with him myself."

"All I ask is that you keep me out of it."

"Of course." I hadn't even wanted to involve her this much. Having someone else know so much made me uncomfortable. But I had to admit that I never would have been able to get all that dirt on Evan without Lindsay's help. I admired her savvy, even if she did make me nervous.

As I drove home that night, I tried to put everything in perspective. I had escaped suspicion in two deaths. I had managed to convince my semi-fiancée not to pursue a paternity test that could renew suspicion, and I had enough shit on the one guy who could hurt me to make him keep his mouth shut until he was on Medicare. If I played my cards right, I could skate on through the rest of this nightmare without any scars to show for it. I tried to fight the giddy feeling in my stomach. I forced myself to remember that every time luck seemed to be going my way, something happened to complicate the situation.

I reminded myself that Evan could still make the dumb move and go to the cops. Jordan could still get cold feet about marrying me. And I still hadn't heard from Harvard. Really, my life was only good in that it hadn't been destroyed. The giddiness faded fast.

CHAPTER TWENTY-TWO

I considered approaching Evan after Ethics class on Friday but thought better of it. He had dark circles under his eyes and looked like he hadn't had a lot of sleep lately. Besides, I wasn't sure exactly what I would say to him. He'd had almost the whole school week to ponder his course of action. I knew he wouldn't decide anything right away, but we were getting to the point where he would have to do something. If he didn't go to the cops by the end of the weekend, I doubted he ever would.

My only reservation about playing it safe was the gnawing sense that I could assure his silence by letting him know I was aware of the St. Barnards situation. I considered mentioning that I knew someone who went there. I could let it slip in a conversation at the party tonight. My concern with that was that he would view it as blackmail and wonder why I was so intent on keeping him quiet.

I also worried that if I pushed too hard, he might decide screwing me was more important to him than his own future.

I didn't know what he was capable of. I'd spent the whole week convincing others that Evan was an obsessive who'd do anything to be with Jordan. I was starting to believe it myself.

He could have gone to the cops. Instead he blackmailed me, essentially committing a crime, just to break us up. He obviously wanted her badly. And I was only half-lying to Lindsay and Jeff. Evan *did* try to talk to her all the time. Jordan told me that he *did* wait outside her classes often. And while I'd never actually seen him following us on campus, he was always staring at her. Anytime someone is willing to blackmail a guy to get his girlfriend, I'd say things have progressed beyond the crush point.

I was still pondering all the possibilities when I walked into the deli to meet Jordan for lunch. I saw her leaving the pick-up window. She had already grabbed our sandwiches and was heading my way.

"Let's eat outside today," she said, leading me back out the door.

"Don't you think it's a little chilly for that?" I asked, as I followed her. Most of the snow from the last storm had melted but it was still in the low forties, even on a sunny day like this.

"I want to have a little privacy," she said, leading me to an empty bench outside the main library. We sat down and I unwrapped the sandwiches as she put straws in our drinks. It was brisk but I was starting to warm up to the privacy thing. I thought we might get cozy.

"This is nice," I said. She looked up and I could see from her expression that she wanted privacy for a very different reason than I had assumed.

"Jake, I've changed my mind."

"About what?"

"About the test. I've tried not to think about it, but I can't get it out of my head. I'm sorry. I know it's an issue of trust and I could be risking a lot by pushing this, but I want you to take it."

"What changed your mind?" I asked. I was amazed at how

level and calm my voice sounded. As I waited for her answer, I was sure she could hear the blood pumping in my ears.

"I know it's wrong but all week I've been having dreams, nightmares really."

"What kind of nightmares?"

"Mostly of you and Kelly going at it against the house wall or going back to your place and fucking in the same bed we sleep in and share secrets in. I can't get it out of my head, no matter how hard I try."

"I guess Evan's little plan worked. If he can't have you, at least he can make sure we're not happy."

"I know I'm just playing into what he wants, but I can't help it. I almost wish you hadn't told me the details of what he said happened."

"I didn't want to, but I thought if I didn't and he did, you'd think I was trying to hide something from you. I was trying to be honest. I thought that was the best way to make sure we got past this."

"I'm not blaming you, Jake. It was the right thing to do. I would have been upset if I heard it somewhere else. But I can't help how I feel. It keeps eating at me."

"So you want me to take the test?"

"I know it's a gamble, that it might get out, but I don't think I can marry you unless this is resolved for good. I'm sure we can convince the police to keep it quiet. They'll understand if you explain it to them. You're great at that. Make them understand how important it is that they keep it confidential."

"Jordan, I can't make the police do anything. Cardinal already thinks I'm a rich punk. I know he's pissed that his boss won't let him touch me. He'll make sure it gets out, just to embarrass me. And he'll do it so it can't be traced to him."

"After seeing him at Kelly's funeral, I don't believe that. Besides, couldn't you go over his head?"

"I doubt it. Even if I could, it would leak somehow. The truth is, if I take this test, we have to accept the inevitability that it's going to get out. There's no way around it." I didn't want to give her anything to grasp on to. My hope was that putting the situation in such stark terms would make her pull back.

"I think we have to take that risk. If we don't do this, it'll always hang over us. I don't care what leaks at this point, Jake. I need this behind me. I swear, no matter what people say, I'll stand by you."

"What about law school . . . and jobs?"

"I don't think it'll be as bad as you think. It's not realistic to think some half-assed rumor from your college days is going to ruin your entire legal career." She was using her most reassuring voice.

"I think you'd be surprised."

"Listen, Jake. I'll make you a promise, right now. You take that test and I'll accept your proposal. Screw the two-month thing. We'll announce it to the world—the future Mr. and Mrs. Jake Conason."

"As soon as you get the test results," I reminded her. There was no way around that little tidbit. No one would be accepting any proposals until the test came back negative. She didn't say anything, only nodded slightly. This was a no-win situation. Unable to think of any escape, I tried one more time.

"You know that just because this test comes back negative, that doesn't prove anything. Like I told you the other night, I could have still slept with her."

"It'll be enough for me," she promised. I knew she meant it.

"Okay. I'll take the test. I'll call them on Monday to set it up."

"Thank you. I know this isn't pleasant but I promise it will all be over soon. In a few weeks our life will be back to normal."

"I don't think it will ever be back to normal. But if this is what it takes to make you believe in me, this is what I'll do. I love you, Jordan. I'd do anything for you." She smiled at that and leaned over to give me a kiss. She tasted like chicken salad but I didn't mind.

I remember the exact moment that I fell in love with Jordan Lansing. It was Friday, April 24, 1998 at 8:30 P.M. Every year before spring finals, the school held an outdoor concert in the main quad. That year, they chose a popular local group that specialized in straight-ahead rock. Unfortunately, I missed most of the show because of a lecture by a well-known attorney my father said I'd be a fool to skip. Of course, the speech was boring and by the time I got to the concert, I was in a foul mood.

Everyone was already drunk and partying so I felt like a total outsider. I decided to just go home and went to tell Jeff and Kevie (who were in the front row) I was leaving. That's when I saw her. Jordan and I were the same year in school so I'd seen her around. But she existed in the art school world and I took real classes so our paths rarely crossed. But that night, she was impossible not to notice.

The band was doing a rendition of Bad Company's "Feel Like Makin' Love" and she was screaming the lyrics right along with them. She was very drunk. The lead singer was amused, so he pulled her up onstage to join him. Unashamed, she grabbed the mic out of his hand and began wailing away. Her voice was terrible but she had such confidence and charisma that she managed to get the whole crowd cheering and singing along. I'd never seen anyone so sure of herself. She was fearless.

She was also careless. As she leaned forward, she stepped on a cable, lost her balance, and fell off the stage. A few of us helped her up and led her out of the crowd. Even though she was limping, she told everyone she was fine and, not wanting to miss the fun, they all returned to the pit. I told her I was leaving anyway and would take her to health services to get her ankle checked out.

The health services people took her to the hospital (a good

move since the ankle turned out to be broken) and I went along. While she waited for doctors and test results, we spent hours talking. She ended up with crutches and a cast, so I spent the next week helping her get around. Two weeks later, we were officially a couple. But it was that first moment when she jumped onstage that hooked me. This woman considered the world an adventure, not an obstacle, and when I was with her I got a taste of that.

Of course, sometimes that wild, risk-taking nature made her willful and stubborn, which complicated the whole paternity test issue. But I could hardly get upset with her when it was that same "take on the world" quality that drew me to her in the first place. Besides, it was pointless to argue with her. Once Jordan made up her mind she rarely changed it. I'd have to think of something else.

I'd been debating whether to file a formal complaint against Evan with the school. After talking to Jordan, the decision got much simpler. I turned it in that afternoon before going home. It was pretty basic. I said Evan had been harassing Jordan and that she felt uncomfortable around him. I said that I'd seen him following us. I asked if an investigation could be started and whether he had any history of inappropriate behavior in his background. I left it at that (not wanting to overdo it) and made sure to drop it off after four, when I knew the office would be empty. No one would read it until Monday.

When I got home, I found that Rick had already arrived. The mail was on the kitchen table. I noticed one envelope had been placed off to the side, away from the rest of the letters. It was from Harvard. The postmark said Wednesday. That meant it had been sent before they received proof of my acceptance into the internship program. Apparently that had not factored into the decision. The envelope was thin.

I ended the torture and ripped the thing open. The letter was short and to the point, stating that I had been admitted for the 2000–2001 school year. I was going to Harvard Law School. I didn't think it was possible, considering the events of the last few months, but I felt genuine excitement.

A tingling sensation came over me. It was just like the moment after Kelly's head hit the ground and I saw the asphalt chunks jammed into her skull. Everything went black. I thought I was going to faint and managed to grab a chair and sit down before I fell. After a moment the tingling stopped and I could see again. I looked down at my pants and was surprised to discover that I had come.

There was a noise from the living room. Rick was puttering around with his guitar and amp. I went to my room, changed pants, and walked out to join him. He heard my footsteps on the creaky hardwood floor and turned around before I spoke.

"So, good news or bad?" he asked.

"Good," I told him, breaking into a goofy grin. He put down the guitar and jumped up to give me a huge bear hug, almost lifting me off the ground.

"Congratulations, man. I knew you'd get in."

"You knew more than I did," I said, sitting down in the easy chair. I still wasn't sure of my balance.

"Are you kidding? I think you could have willed your way into that place. If there's anything I've learned about you Jake, it's that you'll do whatever it takes to get what you want." His voice had the same happy, supportive tone as always but something about the way he said that last sentence sent a little chill down my spine. I looked at him closely. He wore a casual grin and looked exactly the same. But to me, it seemed off, like he had a wink in his voice.

"What do you mean?" I heard myself asking him even though my brain was shouting that I should just let it go, pretend that I hadn't picked up on it.

"You know what I mean, buddy. I don't think you would deny that when you want something, you go after it pretty hardcore," he said, sitting back down and strumming absently on his guitar.

"That makes me like ninety percent of the students at this school," I pointed out.

"Yeah, but we both know that you'd do a hell of a lot more than any of them to get to the top, don't we?" When he looked up from his guitar, something in my face made him stop playing.

"What are you saying?" I demanded.

"Jesus, Jake, don't get upset. I meant it as a compliment. If I worked half as hard on learning Clapton as you did on getting into Harvard, I'd be playing Busch Stadium right now."

"It didn't sound very complimentary," I said.

"Well, I'm sorry man. I tell you what. Let's dispense with the complimentary words and move on to the complimentary drinks." With that, he pulled out a bottle of scotch and two full glasses that he'd been hiding behind the couch. I accepted his apology by taking a glass and a seat.

"Are you coming to the party at the house tonight?" I asked. "I put you on the list."

"Thanks, but I doubt it. I think I'm gonna stay here and write. I'm finishing up a song," he said. "Hey, I heard something today that I wanted to ask you about."

"What's that?" I asked, ignoring the sudden leap in my stomach.

"Did you propose to Jordan?"

I leaned back in my chair, took a sip of scotch, and smiled.

CHAPTER TWENTY-THREE

By the time I headed out to the party around nine, Rick and I had finished the entire bottle. The walk was nice. There was no wind and the snow had melted enough that I didn't have to worry about negotiating tricky sidewalks or slipping and cracking my head. I took my time. Jordan wasn't supposed to show up until ten so I would have all the time I needed once I arrived.

I got to the house just before 9:30 and took the fire escape I was so intimately familiar with up to the third floor. I poked my head into Kevie Poo's room and, as expected, found it to be empty. I walked over to his bed and took a key off the nail on his bedframe. Kevie was the house manager and as such, had a master key that could get him into any room in the house. Unfortunately for Evan, Kevie was not especially concerned about security and it was common knowledge that he kept the master key on that nail. It was helpful to know that detail when Kevie was out of the house (very common) or passed out (extremely common). It was also helpful when someone wanted to get into a locked room without permission. I shoved the key in my pocket and left.

As I walked down the hall to Evan's room, I realized that it was almost directly across from Dan's, which still had police tape across the doorway. I don't know why I had never noticed their proximity before. Maybe it was because, until recently, Evan had not been anything more than an annoyance. I just never thought about the guy unless he was right in front of me, being a pain in the ass. I was thinking about him a lot these days.

I knocked on his door but got no answer. I'd expected him to be downstairs at this hour so I wasn't really surprised but I knocked again just to be safe. It was always possible that the guy was so bummed about his dilemma that he'd decided to skip the party and crash early. Still no answer, so I turned the knob. Locked. Also not a surprise, considering we were dealing with Evan, an anal and overly self-protective individual even if he didn't have illegal substances in his sock drawer. I glanced around to make sure I was still alone in the hall, then pulled out the key, unlocked the door, and stepped inside.

I relocked the door and got started, moving with business-like speed. I went straight for the sock drawer and found the bottle of pills exactly where I had left them. After popping the top, removing four of the five remaining pills, and wiping the bottle of any fingerprints, I returned it to the drawer. Only this time I dropped it front and center so that it would be immediately visible to anyone who slid it open. I put the four other pills in a small sandwich baggy along with the one I'd already stolen and put them back in my pocket. Then I slowly opened the door, checking for wandering partiers. Seeing none, I left his room, making sure the door was now unlocked.

I hurried over to Dan's room and used the master key to unlock it. The light was off. I turned it on and shut the door. As I mentioned before, I'd been coming here occasionally after Dan's death to get away from the hustle and bustle. The place looked just as it did the last time I was here. I had heard that the police now wanted to leave it in its current condition until Kelly's case was officially closed. No one had objected. It's not like any of the other brothers were clamoring to get his bunk bed or his computer. His parents had been too distraught when they came into town to worry about anything as trivial as selling the furniture in his room.

I walked over to the mini-fridge and opened it. I was a little surprised to see that the bottle of Vodka and the orange juice container were still there. I didn't think Dan would mind if I took advantage of his hospitality so I grabbed a cup from the shelf and poured myself a drink, heavy on the vodka. It only took a few gulps to finish the beverage and mere seconds to refill the cup. After a few more sips, I pulled the baggy out of my pocket, put it on the top of the fridge, grabbed the vodka and carefully used the base of the bottle to grind the pills into a fine powder. Then I put the baggy back in my pocket.

I moved over to the bed, cup in hand, and lay down on the bottom bunk. Looking up at the springs of the top, unused bunk, I noticed a few of them had popped. I wondered if Dan had ever caught the same thing. This had been his room for almost five months. He must have noticed. In fact, maybe the reason he slept on the bottom bunk was *because* the springs had popped. Maybe the top bunk was unsafe.

The alcohol was having an obvious impact. Half a bottle of scotch had already sent me well into the land of good buzz. The screwdriver was pushing me toward full-on inebriation. I took another gulp. It occurred to me that I might be able to more effectively put my plan into action if I was sober and that getting drunk could lead to serious mistakes. But I knew myself pretty well and I doubted if I could complete all the elements of this plan unless I was at least a little numb.

It had been different with Dan. There were so many tiny things to remember on that night that I couldn't take any risks. And of course, with Kelly, everything happened so fast that anesthetizing myself to what had to be done wasn't even a consideration. Tonight's events required some forethought and discipline but not the same level of concentration. In fact, being a little looped might help in the larger scheme of things.

It took a moment before I realized I was drifting off. My eyes were opening and closing just as Dan's had that night. I sat up straight. For some reason, it didn't hit me until right then that I was lying in the same place where Dan had died—where I had killed him. It was in this exact spot where I had watched his last conscious moments. I recalled the last thing he said to me before he drifted off—"it doesn't seem worth it."

I remembered the guy sitting on the chair across from me, talking about how confused he was—how he couldn't understand what was happening to him. He was pouring out his soul to me, to the one person who was least likely to help him. I had used every word he said to me against him. I had manipulated him into making himself seem like a suspect.

And it had been easy. You can't imagine how easy it is to destroy a person if you really make it your purpose. But it was simple. No reasonable person would conceive of the possibility that one human being would do such things to another. People stole. People maimed. People even killed. But this was so elaborate, so intentional, so instinctual.

Where did I get the ability to do these things? I was not a perfect person, but until that night in late January with Kelly, I'd never done anything unquestionably wrong. I'd done things that were wrong, of course. I had shoplifted. I'd bought alcohol using a fake ID when I was underage. I had cheated on a few tests and copied homework. Sleeping with Kelly was wrong. But none of that stuff would have gotten me disqualified from running for office or reasonably judging myself to be a good person.

There was a newly born or perhaps long-dormant darkness in me that felt as comfortable as any old pair of shoes. I don't know where it came from, but it was real and it was strong. It was almost cozy, the two of us here together.

If, a few months ago, someone had described for me the things I'd done lately, I would have said that no decent man was capable of such behavior. Just thinking of the crimes I'd committed would have made me ill. But I had somehow done all these things, willfully, easily, naturally. If Kelly had never slipped on the ground that night, what would I have done? The options seemed endless to me now. Threats, bribery, blackmail, violence—they were all possibilities to the Jake Conason sitting on Dan's bed at this moment.

I suspect that the Jake before that night would have agreed to stand by Kelly, whatever her decision. He would have admitted his infidelity to Jordan. He would have agreed to marry Kelly. He might or might not have still gotten into law school. Whether or not he could attend was up for debate. He would have accepted the ridicule and disappointment of friends, professors, and even his parents. He would have continued to slog along and make the best of things, letting fate deal its cards and playing them as best he could.

But the second Kelly's head hit that frozen asphalt, I became the dealer. I wondered now if I had grabbed her arm a little harder than I needed to that evening, knowing she might pull away, might slip, might fall. Was that possible? If I closed my eyes, I could still picture that night in the park, standing almost naked over her limp body, lying bloody in the snow. I remember the little chunks of brain and skull flying in the air as if it were a slow-motion replay in a Sunday afternoon football game. I remember how easily her head had given way when faced with the force of that crowbar.

I beat her over and over. I left her in a frozen snowbank, where she lay for hours, half-dead, half-alive, with my unborn baby in her belly, my daughter, unprotected, crying out for her mommy. I murdered an innocent man. I murdered an innocent woman. I murdered my own child. And for what? I had done these things to make my life easier and it still wasn't over.

I was still planning and scheming and predicting every possible permutation. From the night of that first attack, I'd had a constant headache, one that throbbed with such regularity that I'd forgotten it was there. I felt it now. All my conniving and trickery had twisted my brain into a pretzel. All I cared about now was solving the puzzle. To that end, I had done wrong and in a few minutes I intended to do more wrong.

What would happen if I stopped? What if I aborted my plan and just let events from this point forward follow their natural course? If I had learned anything from all this, it was that no matter what I did, I couldn't control everything. I'd always forget something minor or someone would behave in an unexpected manner. I was at the mercy of circumstance, no matter how hard I fought.

But not completely. I could be engaged to a girl I didn't know right now, with a baby I didn't want on the way. I could be in jail for negligent homicide or murder or triple murder. I could be in any number of very bad places. But instead, I was at a fraternity party, with my gorgeous fiancée-to-be waiting downstairs and an admission letter to Harvard Law School on my kitchen table. Strictly speaking, the way I had played this game so far had me ahead.

There were still a few cards to play. Evan was one, although I had learned how to read him pretty well of late. The real wildcard was Jordan. It was ironic that one of the things I loved about her—her unpredictability, her unwillingness to follow the rules laid down for her, had set this evening in motion. Jordan was always the wildcard.

I stood up and chugged the last of my screwdriver. I noticed my shirt was wet. At first I thought some condensation had dripped from my cup, but my cheeks were wet, too. I realized I'd been crying. I wasn't anymore. I put the empty cup back on the shelf, locked Dan's door from the inside, and turned out the light. Darkness returned.

CHAPTER TWENTY-FOUR

After I returned the master key to Kevie's room, I used the fire escape to get back downstairs and circled around behind the house so it looked like I had come straight from my place. I walked up the stairs from the back entrance to the main room. The party was in full swing. I looked around to see if I could spot either Jordan or Evan but the room was just too crowded to distinguish anyone in the limited light. I glanced at my watch. It was 10:15. I had been upstairs longer than I realized.

Someone near the back window waved at me. It was so dark, I couldn't tell who it was but I headed over anyway. It wasn't until I was a few feet away and had pushed through the crowd that I saw it was Lindsay. She was smiling broadly and had the same glazed eyes I'm sure I did, proof that she'd been drinking for some time. I couldn't be absolutely sure, but the sweater she wore looked suspiciously like the one she'd had on the night of our encounter. It was V-necked and because it was too small, it rode up, exposing her stomach above the belly button. I thought the jeans she had on may even have been the same as that night.

"Hey, Jake," she said, greeting me with a hug and a quick peck on the lips, "happy Friday to you."

"Happy Friday to you, too," I said cautiously, unsure if her friendly affection had crossed any lines.

"Please don't take offense, but it appears that you've been consuming a significant amount of adult beverage."

"What makes you say that?" I asked, making certain that I didn't slur my words.

"Your eyes are bloodshot and you're swaying a little."

"Oh."

"What?"

"I just said oh," I repeated.

"It's so loud in here, I can barely hear you. Let's go downstairs for a minute. I need to ask you something." She grabbed my hand and led me through the throng to the stairwell I'd just come from. I looked around, unable to contain the mix of apprehension and guilt I felt as I followed her. Neither Jordan nor Evan were anywhere to be found. Lindsay took the stairs to the basement two at a time but rather than going down to the slop room, she stepped outside at the same back exit I had entered from five minutes before.

The area behind the back of the house was an eyesore. Apart from one huge tree that hung over the entire back portion of the house, the rest of the area was covered in asphalt. A big, ugly metal Dumpster (the one I hid behind the night Dan died) took up much of the space right next to the exit. Lindsay led me behind it so that we weren't visible to anyone in the house or walking by. When we were out of sight, she turned to me and giggled, leaning against the Dumpster for support. Had I not been so drunk, I'm sure I would have been bothered by the disgusting scent that always emanated from the monstrosity. But apparently the alcohol had numbed my sense of smell as well as my sense of couth.

"Did you file that complaint?" she asked, closing the giggle spout as quickly as she had turned it on. She was all business now. I tried to think of some reason why I shouldn't tell her, but came up empty. After all, she was the one who'd discovered the smoking gun in Evan's past. She already knew all the details of the "harassment" he'd engaged in. There was no good excuse not to be straight with her.

"Yeah, I dropped it off this afternoon," I told her, "there was no one in the office, but they'll find it first thing Monday morning. I debated whether or not to do it. But ultimately, I figured it was better to err on the side of caution. I'd feel awful if he did something and I had this information and just sat on it."

"I think you did the right thing, Jake. I don't think they'll expel him for this. It's not like he lied about his record. He just didn't volunteer incriminating information. They'll probably just put him on some kind of probation. If he's serious about his future, Evan will take it as a warning to shape up. It may actually help him and it will definitely help Jordan."

"I hope you're right," I said, knowing that it would never play out that way.

"So when do I get my reward?"

"What reward?"

"Don't you remember my chit? I want my reward for helping ensure the safety of your girlfriend and getting a creepy stalker off your back."

"What did you have in mind?" I asked, on guard.

"Well, I figure that since she gets you for the rest of her life, I should get you for the next ten minutes." She didn't make any kind of move toward me. She just stood there, leaning against the Dumpster, letting her comment hang in the air.

"Listen, Lindsay, I'm really grateful for everything you've done, but I thought we established that day at the library that nothing more was going to happen between us. You said it yourself, she's the one I love. It would be a little weird if I turned that off for ten minutes, wouldn't it?"

"Ten minutes for a lifetime. It seems like I'm getting the short end of this deal."

"I don't get this. A month ago we barely knew each other. We still don't know each other very well. We went through a traumatic event together and made some kind of connection, I guess. But despite your claims to know me better than I know myself, I don't think you do. You'd be very surprised if you knew what I was really like. I'm not this super guy. I'm self-involved, I'm a control freak, and I'm kind of neurotic, at least lately."

"I find those qualities attractive," she said, a smile playing at her lips.

"That's cute. Listen, you're a very sexy girl. I mean that in the best sense. That sweater does you enormous justice. For the life of me, I don't even know why you're interested in me. To be honest, you'd get bored with me in a few weeks. I'm only mediocre in bed. You could do a lot better. I've seen you do a lot better. Whatever happened to that football player you were going out with last year?"

"I didn't think you kept tabs on my relationships," she said, still smiling. "The truth is, he had no edge. I could predict his every word, his every move. He was way too safe."

"You think he was safe, I'm walking milquetoast." I don't know why I was so desperate to keep her at bay. In light of the course of this evening's planned activities, it wasn't really that big a deal. But something about the way this girl looked at me made me squirm. Even my deadened central nervous system couldn't numb that.

"We both know you're not milquetoast, Jake. Now all I'm asking for is ten minutes of your time. I think I've earned it." She wasn't really asking anymore.

I shook my head, trying to clear it. She interpreted that as me saying no and responded by nodding hers. There was a job to do tonight and I was being sidetracked. I tried to focus on the things I had to get accomplished in the next hour. If I didn't

do them tonight, I doubted I'd get another opportunity in time
to salvage my sinking ship.

But Lindsay didn't care about that. Before I was fully aware
of what was happening, she had me pressed up against the side
of the Dumpster. I could feel the cold metal through my jacket,
my sweater, my shirt, all the way to my skin. Her mouth was
everywhere. She kissed my lips, my cheeks, licked at my ear-
lobes. I felt her hot breath on my neck and heard her quick,
shallow panting. Her hands were under my shirt, rubbing my
chest. I closed my eyes as she fumbled with the zipper of my
jeans.

Despite myself, my hand moved to the top of her head,
fondling the soft, curly locks of her hair. I could tell she liked
it because she took one of her hands and placed it on top of
mine, clasping fingers with me. Then she was kissing my stomach, letting her tongue run in and around my navel. I opened
my eyes and looked up at the dark night. There were no stars
in the sky tonight.

All at once, I felt incredibly sober. I looked down at Lindsay,
doing her best to get me all hot and bothered, without success.
I didn't want to hurt her feelings but I had to end this, so I
took her softly by the shoulders and pulled her up so we were
face-to-face. She assumed I wanted to kiss her and leaned in
but I put up my hand for her to stop. She gulped as she tried
to register what was going on.

"I can't do this," I said with a conviction that impressed
even me, "I love Jordan. I can't betray her like this. I appreciate
everything you've done for me, but we aren't going to be
together the way you want. I'm meant to be with someone
else."

She started to say something, then stopped herself. I looked
at her with genuine sympathy. I felt guilty, but I knew this was
the right thing to do. She still hadn't spoken.

"I've got to get inside," I said.

"You're meant to be with her?" she repeated, still in dis-
belief.

I nodded, gave her a kiss on the forehead, and started in.

"Jake," she called out after me, "nothing is meant to be. You should know that."

I knew she was hurting but I couldn't turn around. I walked back into the house.

Twenty minutes later, I saw Lindsay leave the party. I had found Jordan and was talking to her at the time, but I wouldn't have said good-bye, even if I was by myself. My girl had done a little prepartying, too. She and some of her suitemates were loaded up on wine coolers. I spent a few minutes making fun of her for that before telling her about the Harvard acceptance. She was ecstatic and jumped up and down, screaming and whooping in joy. What was left of her beer spilled on the floor, splattering on my shoes.

"Oh my god, I'm sorry, sweetie," she said, leaning down to try to dry them off with her jacket. I pulled her up.

"Don't do that to your coat," I told her, "it's just beer."

"I know," she said with a goofy grin, "I just wanted to take care of you."

I laughed at her misguided attempt at caregiving. Out of the corner of my eye, I saw Evan over near the bar. As usual, he was pushing some pledge out of the way to get closer to the keg. I turned back to Jordan.

"Let *me* take care of *you*. I'm going to get you another beer. Stay here and don't go wiping off anyone else's shoes, okay?"

"I promise," she said, crossing her heart and giving me a kiss. I headed to the bar, fighting my way through the bodies bouncing rhythmically on the dance floor. I wasn't surprised by Jordan's behavior. She probably wouldn't admit it, but I knew the reason she was so giddy was directly related to my agreeing to the paternity test. Just saying I would take it had eliminated most of her gnawing doubts. In her mind, I wouldn't have said yes if I thought I could be the father, which meant I couldn't have slept with Kelly. Case closed.

And I knew that she was also thinking about her promise to accept the marriage proposal if I took the test. As far as Jordan was concerned, she was now engaged. She was going to get married and her fiancé was battling through drunken college students to get her a beer. Life was good. Of course, she couldn't talk to anyone about the contingencies associated with the engagement, so she was acting out by being incredibly goofy and affectionate and sweetly silly. It was cute.

I finally managed to get to the bar where I ended up directly facing Evan. I remained cool but he was startled. He had a beer in each hand and almost dropped one of them. I gave him my most nonthreatening smile and spoke to him for the first time in almost a week.

"Hey, Evan, how are you doing?" I made sure that my voice didn't have any arrogance or cockiness in it. He studied me closely. I could tell that he'd had his fair share to drink tonight also but he was doing his best to evaluate my intentions.

"What do you want, Jake?" he asked, unable to contain his bitterness.

"Why don't we go over there for a minute?" I said, pointing to one of the few unpopulated corners of the room and leading him there. He hesitated, then followed me over, still holding both full beers.

"What?" he asked again.

"Listen, I'm just going to say this. You can take it for what it's worth. You can ignore it. You can tell me to fuck off. That's your call." I had to shout to be heard over the pulsing beats of "Ray of Light." "Just let me say what I need to say and then I'll be on my way, okay?"

He looked a little less skeptical than he had seconds before but I still made sure to tread lightly.

"Jordan and I talked," I continued, glancing in her direction so he could see where she was, "and we agreed that we may have overreacted a little. I understand how someone can have a crush and let it go a little too far. So does she. You do whatever you need to do, but I wanted to tell you that as long as things stay the way they are right now, that is as long as things are cool among the three of us, we don't have any hard feelings."

"What are you saying?" he asked, clearly wanting me to spell it out for him.

"I'm saying that this last week never happened. If you can accept that, then so can we. I've spoken to Jordan. She's not as creeped out as she was before. I mean, four days ago she was talking about restraining orders. Now look at her."

Evan did. She was immersed in a conversation with Kevie Poo and his lady of the moment. She seemed to be telling some story that required elaborate hand gestures. She was having fun.

"She seems okay," Evan admitted.

"She is. I don't think she holds any grudge. In fact, tell you what. I was about to get her a beer. You have two. Why don't you take one over to her and I'll grab one for myself and another so you can double fist it?" I said all this in my most robust, friendly drunken tone possible. I was in "all is well with the world and you and me" mode.

He still appeared hesitant.

"Are you sure she's cool with it?" he asked. I was a little surprised at how easy this was. It occurred to me that Evan must have given up on the idea of talking to the cops some time ago. There was none of his usual aggressiveness. He seemed more interested in patching things up than I did. His week of soul-searching must have led him to the conclusion that rocking the boat would likely do him more harm than good. It became apparent that I was going to be able to play him. He wasn't going to call my bluff. Jordan was the only wildcard left.

"Well, she's not gonna make out with you if you bring her a beer, Evan. But I think she'll be okay with it. She might even say thank you."

That did the trick. Evan steeled himself for the obstacle course that was the dance floor and started to wend his way through. I made straight for the bar, pushed past some pledges, and began to quickly fill up two plastic cups of my own. I was just topping off the second one when Evan reached Jordan.

He tapped her on the shoulder with a free finger. When she turned to face him, the surprise on her face was obvious, even from this distance. Before she could speak, I saw him say something and hand her one of the beers. She took it without thinking. He spoke again and pointed with his free hand in the general direction of where we stood earlier. Jordan looked over but I was not where Evan had indicated.

I saw the expression on her face change quickly from surprise to anger. She said something to him that made him take a step back. Kevie and his date both looked a little shocked by her words, too. Evan tried to say something else, but she interrupted him. I still couldn't hear a word over the throbbing sounds of Moby's "Bodyrock," but I could tell that she was yelling. The people around them were staring. Evan took another step back. He was stunned. Jordan didn't wait for him to say anything else. She pushed past him and plowed into the crowd.

I could see her looking around desperately for me. I blew the foam off the second beer and carefully maneuvered through the revelers to meet her. I saw Evan in the distance. He was talking to Kevie and the other girl. They still looked confused, but I could tell he was now more embarrassed than anything else. I called out to Jordan. She saw me and hurried over.

"What's wrong?" I asked. "You look really upset."

"Evan came over just now. He was acting like everything was normal and even offered me a beer. He said you were cool with him now and that he hoped I was, too. He was acting like nothing had happened. I couldn't believe he would say that bullshit to my face after everything he did."

"He said I was cool with him?" I repeated, dumbfounded by the assertion. "I cannot believe the gall of that motherfucker."

"He really upset me, Jake. I thought all that crap was over and then he just walks up to me like that." She was on the verge of tears. I knew the confrontation wouldn't have gotten her so riled up if she'd been sober. Jordan tended to get emotional when she drank.

"Listen," I said, adopting my most reassuring voice, "I want you to go upstairs. Wait for me outside Jeff's room. I'm going to have a word with Evan and I'll be right up."

"Okay. You promise you'll come right away?"

"I'm just going to let him know what's what. I'll be up in two minutes." I gave her a kiss on the cheek and sent her on her way. As she headed for the stairwell, I moved toward Evan. He looked very apprehensive, but to his credit he didn't try to leave. Kevie and his date were still standing next to him.

"Kevie," I said, once I got close enough to be heard, "could you excuse us? I need to talk to Evan alone for a minute."

Kevie nodded and left with his date. I looked at Evan. He seemed scared.

"What the hell did you say to her?" I demanded, not quite angry, but almost.

"I just said what we talked about. I told her that if she could let everything go, I could, too. And she freaked. She started yelling that I had some nerve to come near her. She was screaming at me."

"That's crazy, Evan. When she and I talked earlier tonight, I mentioned that I was going to try to smooth things over with you and she was cool with it. You must have said something to set her off."

"I swear I didn't. You can ask Kevie. She just spazzed out." He was genuinely confused.

"Well, I know she's had a few drinks. Maybe she misunderstood what you were trying to say. I don't know. But she was really upset just now. She would barely talk to *me*. I'm going to go see if I can find her and calm her down. Do me a favor. Just steer clear of her for the rest of the night, okay?"

"I would never have gone near her if you hadn't told me to," he said, finally showing some of the smart-aleck backtalk that had been missing the rest of the evening. I gave him a stern glance. There was no way I was going to put up with that. He saw the look in my eyes and immediately backed down again.

"Just steer clear," I repeated, making sure the disgust in my voice was transparent. Without waiting for an answer, I headed for the stairs. When I went into the main restroom on the second floor, there were a few people milling about at the sinks but the stall at the far end was open. There were no doors on any of the stalls so I had to face the toilet to make it look like I was pissing. I rested one of the cups of beer on the back of the commode. With my free hand, I took out the baggy of roofies and dumped the five powdered pills in the second cup. I used my index finger to mix it up until the solution looked normal again. There was a little residue at the bottom of the cup but it was barely noticeable.

I flushed the toilet, grabbed both beers, and went to wash my hands, taking extra care to completely clean the finger I had used. Before I left the bathroom, I looked at the three brothers who were checking themselves in the mirror. They were all underclassmen and I didn't know any of them well.

"Hey guys," I asked, as I opened the door to leave, "have any of you seen my girlfriend, Jordan? I can't find her anywhere."

They all shook their heads no.

"If you do, will you tell her I'm looking for her?"

They nodded, more than willing to help out a respected older brother. I thanked them and left, taking the last flight of stairs to Jeff's room, where I knew Jordan was waiting.

CHAPTER TWENTY-FIVE

She was leaning against Jeff's door, clearly struggling not to let the effects of her alcohol consumption get the better of her. When she saw me walking in her direction, she broke out into a big grin and ran to meet me. Apparently, she was over the altercation with Evan.

"Wait, don't hug me. I've got full cups," I said just in time. She was still holding the drink Evan had given her. I put the spoiled beer in her free hand and reached into my pocket for Jeff's key. I opened the door and we stepped in. No one saw us enter.

"Here's your drink," Jordan said, handing the second beer back to me.

"No, I got that for you, so we wouldn't have to go back downstairs for constant refills."

"That was sweet of you," she said, "you're always thinking of me, aren't you?"

"You better believe it. Here, let's sit. I'd hate for this fine Corinthian leather to go to waste," I said, nodding at Jeff's ratty couch. Jordan settled in and rubbed the spot next to her seductively.

"Take a seat, sailor," she said, doing her best to emulate the Demi Moore–style throaty voice she knew I found so sexy. I did as I was told. She took a last big chug from the nearly empty cup Evan had given her, threw it to the floor, then let out a monstrous burp.

"That's attractive," I said.

"It's my mating call. I can't tell you how many men have heard me belch and come a-runnin' with love in their eyes."

"That wasn't what got me a-runnin' your way," I said.

"Oh no? What was it for you?" she asked.

"Your singing, of course," I reminded her.

"Oh yeah, you thought it was sexy."

"Something like that."

"Would you like me to sing for you now?" she asked.

"I'm thinking . . . no."

"How rude! You should be punished for your insolence," she said. Then, deciding she would do the punishing, she grabbed my sweater and pulled me to her. I prepared myself for a violent kiss but just before our mouths met, she stopped. Our eyes locked. She cupped my face in her hands and stared at me for a long time. I was uncomfortable for a few seconds, thinking she'd noticed something. Eventually, I realized that she was just caught up in a romantic reverie. She was staring into the eyes of her future husband, appreciating the beauty of the moment.

She may have been drunk and clumsy but her lips were not. We began to kiss. For twenty minutes I forgot about everything. Our bodies intertwined perfectly. It got to the point where I couldn't tell where I ended and she began. After what seemed like forever, she began to pull my pants down. Then she leaned back and began to unzip her own jeans.

I used the break in the action as an opportunity to take a drink. She did the same. It took a moment for what had just happened to register. It was her first sip of the spoiled beer. She wiped her mouth and resumed the undressing process. And just like that, my brain snapped out of one mode and into another. Events had been set in motion now and I had to do my part if I wanted them to go as I planned.

"I just realized I don't have any protection," I told her as I patted my front and back pockets. She frowned.

"Are you sure?" she asked.

"I'm positive. Hold on. We're in a fraternity house. I'm sure I can find something. You stay here. I'm going to go see what I can do," I said as I pulled my jeans back on.

"Hurry up," she demanded, pretending to be angry but failing to pull it off.

"I will. I bet you I can find a rubber and be back here before you finish your beer," I challenged.

"Are you kidding me? I'll empty this cup before you get to the stairs."

"If you do, then you can start on mine. Just don't leave this room. And don't change outfits while I'm gone," I ordered. "You know how I love those panties." She giggled at that. I started for the door and was about to open it when she stopped me.

"Hold on, if this is a contest, we have to make it official. We've got to start at the same time," she said as she picked up the cup. "Ready, set, go!"

As I hurried out the door, I saw her begin chugging. Bets worked every time.

I took my time going down to the party. I already had the condom in my pocket so that wasn't a concern. Priority one was making sure I exhibited the proper demeanor when I reached the main room. When I got there, the party was raging even harder than when I left. I glanced at my watch. It was almost 11:30. It had been almost a half hour since Jordan had last been seen by anyone other than me.

I wandered over to the bar, swiveling my head left and right as if I was looking intently for someone. One of the pledges on drink duty (I could never remember their names) poured me a cup and handed it over with a smile. He saw my frown and asked what was wrong.

"I can't seem to find my girlfriend anywhere. Evan said something that pissed her off a while back and she ran up the stairs. I haven't seen her since. Have you noticed her around?"

"No, Jake, sorry," he said, then asked his fellow bartenders the same question. They all shook their heads no.

"If you see her, will you tell her I'm looking for her?" I asked them all. "I'm a little worried."

They all said yes. I thanked them, took my beer, and continued to wander among the frenzy of dancers, a troubled look on my face. I "accidentally" banged into a few people, then absently apologized. I made my way outside to where some guys were attaching a funnel to a tree in the courtyard. It was almost time for the obligatory cannonballing contest.

I asked a few people in the courtyard if they'd seen Jordan. No one had. Kevie, with a different girl than before, said he hadn't seen her since the argument with Evan. I thanked him and walked around some more. I noticed Evan was outside, too. He was at the edge of the courtyard, engaged in a shot-gunning contest with three pledges. He was taking it very seriously.

I looked at my watch again—11:45. Jordan would be getting anxious. I ambled casually around the side of the house, making sure that no one noticed me. It wasn't hard. Everybody was fascinated by the engineering feat of suspending a six-foot funnel from a tree branch. I used my favorite fire escape to get back to the third floor. This time I had the key to get in, but as usual, it wasn't needed. The door was unlocked. I made sure the hall was empty before scurrying to Jeff's room.

When I returned, condom in hand, Jordan was still conscious but the drug had plainly started to take effect. She was lying on the couch in her underwear, sprawled out as if she didn't have a care in the world. She tried to sit up when I entered and I noticed that her limbs had a sloppy rag-doll looseness that doesn't come from just too much beer. It was a struggle for her to get completely upright.

"Where you been?" she demanded, her voice lacking the force and clarity she obviously wanted to convey, "I been waiting here, for like, forever."

"Sorry, I got sidetracked, but I'm here now," I said, sliding into the spot next to her. I wasn't all that familiar with how long it took for this drug to work its magic, so I hesitated to go to the next step in the plan. Jordan leaned over as if she wanted to hug me, but missed and ended up resting her forehead on my shoulder instead.

"So toasted," she announced.

"Are you okay?" I asked. "You seem really out of it. Maybe you should give it a rest on the drinks for a while, huh?"

She tried to say "okay," but had difficulty getting the word out correctly, so she tried instead to say "uh-huh," but still, the proper sounds would not come. Finally, she just gave me a half-hearted nod that indicated she agreed. It was time. I told her what I wanted to do in a very loud, slow, methodical voice, as if I was explaining to a three-year-old how to color inside the lines.

"I've got a funny idea. Do you want to play a joke on Evan to get him for how mean he was to you earlier?"

At the mention of his name, Jordan scrunched up her face in displeasure. She made some sound that wasn't an actual word but indicated she had no desire to do anything with Evan. I tried a little harder.

"This is going to be great. We'll get him for being mean, okay," I said, grabbing her face so that her eyes fixed on mine. "I want you to say exactly what I say, all right Jordan?"

She swallowed hard. I was pretty sure she understood me but I wanted actual verbal confirmation so I pushed a little harder.

"Sweetie, do you love me? Because if you love me you'll

do this for me. All I want you to do is say what I say into the phone. Do you love me enough to do that?"

She nodded but didn't speak. I could tell she was frustrated. She didn't want to disappoint me.

"Then let's try. Repeat after me. Evan, you are mean."

"Evan mean," she said after gathering herself for a few seconds.

"That's pretty good, baby, but you have to say every word I say, all right? Every word. Let's do it again. Evan, I want you."

She giggled at that. No matter how drugged up she was, Jordan Lansing still found that suggestion preposterous. But she spoke anyway.

"Evan," she said, "I want you."

"That was awesome, baby. So great. Okay, I'm going to get him on the phone now and I want you to say what I say, like you just did. You were so great just now."

Her head rolled around atop her neck as if it were only half connected. As I prepared to call the house phone downstairs, I pulled her in so that her cheek was pressed against mine. That way we could both hear and I didn't have to look at her. I dialed the number of the phone on the wall in the main room downstairs. It took ten rings before anyone picked up.

"I need to talk to Evan Grunier," I said in what I hoped was a convincingly high-pitched girly voice.

"I don't know where he is exactly. There's a party going on here," the guy downstairs said.

"I know there's a party, but I have to talk to Evan. It's important. Check outside. He's probably outside."

The guy told me to hold on while he checked. I hurried to Jeff's window, which overlooked the courtyard. Evan was there, all right. The cannonballing had begun and he was waiting his turn. Cannonballing, for the uninitiated, is like shotgunning, except that instead of downing a can of beer rapidly, a long funnel is used. The funnel is filled with beer and placed above the contestant's head. In this case it was suspended from a tree branch. The contestant blocks the mouth of the hose until the funnel is completely full. Then he removes his hand and chugs. The force of gravity combined with the narrow beer passageway means that the liquid barely has time to be swallowed. Instead, it shoots straight down the esophagus with such force that swallowing is an afterthought. Very few people can actually consume the entire contents of the funnel without choking or spitting up. For the guys of Kappa Omega, it was a true test of mettle. And as a result, a huge crowd of spectators had formed around the tree.

The phone guy found Evan and reluctantly tapped him on the shoulder. It looked for a moment like Evan was going to blow him off, but the kid was persistent. Evan gave the funnel a last, longing stare, then wandered inside.

"Okay, this is it," I said, shaking Jordan a little harder than I intended. "You say exactly what I say, okay baby?"

"What you say," she repeated.

"That's great, just like that."

Evan picked up the phone.

"Who is it?" he demanded brusquely.

"It's Jordan," I whispered, putting the phone to her mouth.

"It's Jordan."

I grabbed the phone back so I could hear him.

"Jordan? What do you want? I thought you never wanted to speak to me again."

"I'm sorry," I ordered.

"I'm sorry."

"Sorry for what?" he asked, suspicious.

"I was mean."

"He was mean."

"What?" he asked.

"No," I hissed, pulling the phone away, "say the words 'I was mean.' "

"I was mean. I was mean," she almost shouted.

"Fine," Evan said. "So what do you want, Jordan? Why are you calling me?"

"Come over," I told her. She looked up at me and shook her head vigorously. She didn't want him to come over. There was a long pause on the other end as Evan waited for an answer. I pulled Jordan's face close to mine. We were almost touching noses.

"If you love me, you will say the words, 'come over.' "

She tried to say something, but not the words I wanted. She was trying to tell me something but she couldn't get the right sounds to come out of her mouth. Tears started to stream down her cheeks.

"Say come over," I repeated calmly, pointing at the phone. Slowly, she leaned in to the receiver.

"Come over."

"You want me to come over? Are you sure? What about all the shit you said before?"

"Say come over now," I said.

"Come over now." She wasn't fighting me anymore.

"Where are you?" he asked.

"Say my place. Say the words 'my place.' "

"My place," she said. The tears were coming fast now and I had to wipe them away because they were getting the phone wet.

"If that's what you want," I heard Evan say as I clicked the off button, "I'll come over right . . ."

I didn't need to hear him to know what he would do. The man was an idiot. With his past and my warnings, he should have known better. He should have politely said "no thanks" and returned to cannonballing. But as I suspected, all it took was a hint of interest from Jordan to get the boy all lathered up. True, he was pretty drunk and not in the best of decision-making modes. But even so, his brain was on vacation.

I peeked out the window again. Evan was moving fast. He

walked around the crowd and headed in the direction of South Campus and Jordan's suite. Someone else had started cannon-balling and everyone's attention was focused on that. No one gave the guy scurrying up the path a second glance.

CHAPTER TWENTY-SIX

had to move fast if this was going to work. Unless he ran (something I doubted even Evan would do), it would take him at least thirty minutes to get to Jordan's suite, figure out that she wasn't there, and return to the party. If he dawdled at her place, it might take upward of forty, but that was at the outside. I let Jordan slump back onto Jeff's couch and picked up the phone again. I called her number and waited for her machine to pick up.

"Jordan, where the hell are you? I've been looking for you everywhere. I know Evan was bugging you and that you wanted to get away from the guy. Sure, he's creepy but come on, don't disappear on *me*. If you're there, please pick up. I've looked all over the house for you. I don't know where else to check. Listen, sweetie, you've had too much to drink tonight and I am seriously worried. Please call me when you get this message. I love you."

I hung up. Jordan, who had been listening, looked confused. I didn't blame her. That would be a weird message to figure out even if she was stone-cold sober. In her condition, it must have been beyond comprehension.

"I love you, too," she said. I realized my last words had stuck in her brain.

"You are the best," I said, scooping her into my arms and hugging her tight. I knew I had to get to work but this would likely be my last chance to be with my girlfriend while she was conscious and I thought I deserved to take a moment, schedule be damned.

She didn't have much muscle control left but managed to grip the sleeve of my sweater and grasp it tightly in her fist. She was like a little newborn with the involuntary ability to reach out and clutch something. A baby that age may not be able to open its eyes but it can hold on to something for dear life if it gets a good grip.

"You are so beautiful," I whispered in her ear, "I have never met a better person than you. I'm going to miss you so much. I love you baby, you know that, right? You forgive me, right?"

She could only half hear me now. There was a smile on her face but I wasn't sure exactly what was causing it. I grabbed her jeans and tried to put them back on but gave up after getting to the knees. It was too difficult without her help. Hooking my arms under her body, I braced myself, stood up, and walked to the door. She stirred at the movement.

"Gonna be big wedding," she muttered.

"You bet it is," I cooed back. "Now I need you to be quiet for a few seconds, honey. No talking."

I opened the door and peeked out. The hall was empty, not a surprise with the craziness going on downstairs. I moved swiftly, cutting across the corridor to Evan's room, trying not to jar Jordan as I moved her. I tried to open his door but with Jordan in my arms, it was hard to get a good grip on the handle. I tried again—no luck. My hand was sweaty and kept slipping off the metal knob.

I was about to put her down when I heard voices coming up the stairs. They were getting close fast. I looked back at

Jeff's door but it was closed, too. I'd have the same problem with it. The voices were at the top of the stairs now. As soon as they rounded the corner, I'd be seen with Jordan and everything would be ruined. I turned back to Evan's door. There were only seconds left. I shifted Jordan in my arms so I could wipe my sweaty hand on my jeans, then grabbed the doorknob tightly and turned. The door opened. I stepped inside quickly, just as the voices rounded the corner to an empty hallway. They didn't come any closer.

Once inside, I shut the door, locked it, and lay my fiancée down on the floor with her back against the closet door. I checked the sock drawer to make sure the pill bottle was still there. It was. I decided not to take any chances and opened the drawer halfway so that it jutted out conspicuously farther than the others. I returned to Jordan.

First I opened the closet door and slowly laid her back so that her upper body was inside the closet and her lower half was in the room. Then I pulled off one of her shoes. Now that she was flat on her back, I was able to slide her jeans up her legs a little more so that they reached mid-thigh. I took a deep breath. Now for the hard part.

I grabbed her panties along her left hip and ripped them so that they split halfway. She was still covered but it looked like someone had struggled with her to get her undressed. Then I lifted her sweater up part of the way so that her face was covered and her arms were above her head. Her bra had shoulder straps so I yanked at the left one. It broke easily. I briefly considered pulling the bra down a little so that one of her breasts would be exposed. But the thought of her being found like that made me uncomfortable. Jordan would have been embarrassed if she knew a bunch of strangers had seen her naked.

I stood up to take stock of the situation. I wasn't experienced in this sort of thing, but if I walked into this room, unsuspecting, it definitely would appear to me that a girl had been physically assaulted, maybe even while she was unconscious. It occurred to me that it might be more realistic if she had bruises or scratches but there was no way I could do that. This would have to do.

I was about to walk out the door when I heard her groan. I tried not to panic. Were the pills wearing off? Had they not been as potent as I thought? Was she waking up? That could not happen. I waited breathlessly for twenty seconds to see if it was a fluke. She groaned again.

I thought she might be in pain, but after a moment I realized that she was wanly struggling to hug herself. It was cold in the room, especially now that most of her body was exposed. I could see goosebumps on her tummy. But she couldn't figure out how to get her hands free of the sweater. I heard a muffled word through the material covering her face.

"Freezing."

Hearing that made me want to throw a blanket over her, but of course, that wasn't possible. I debated turning off the light but decided to leave it on, as Evan had. I did lock the door from the inside before venturing out into the hall again. I could hear the cheers from the courtyard outside below. Someone had successfully cannonballed.

I returned to Jeff's room to collect all the plastic beer cups we had used, making sure to grab the one with whatever Rohypnol residue remained. After locking the door, the fire escape was once again my exit of choice. Outside, I walked around the back of the house and threw the cups in the Dumpster. Then I walked through the back entrance, up the stairs to the main room and out to the courtyard, where I joined the rest of the crowd.

I wasn't sure how long I should wait before I resumed asking if anyone had seen Jordan. I glanced at my watch. It was 12:15—fifteen minutes since Evan had left and at least fifteen before he would return. It was also a little more than forty-five minutes since Jordan had taken five powerful sedatives, mixed with a large amount of alcohol. It had taken less than twenty minutes for her to get sluggish and nonresponsive. I guessed that another half hour would put her near death.

While I waited, I took a seat on one of the courtyard benches. In fact, it was the same one I was sitting on last December when I saw Kelly leaning against the wall of the house, crying. I tuned out the cheers of the besotted revelers all around me and focused on more important things. I know it seems strange that I would poison my own fiancée, the girl I loved more than any other person in the world. It probably seems hypocritical that I talked about how close we were and all the great times we had but was still willing to kill her. But it's not as simple as that.

I did love Jordan. I still do. But that's not the point. The truth hit me hard earlier that afternoon at the library, as she was asking me to take the paternity test. The reality of the situation was that Jordan was not going to be comfortable with "us" until I successfully passed that test. She acknowledged as much to me. But of course, that was a test I couldn't pass. And when she found out that I was the father of that child, it would be over between us.

The whole point of everything I had done was to keep the two of us together. Or at least that was a big part of it. If I had told her about my one-nighter with Kelly or if I had actually taken Kelly to the hospital instead of the park, Jordan would have eventually dumped me. She did not suffer infidelity lightly. And I couldn't blame her. If she ever cheated on me, I would end it in a second. What I'm saying is, the purpose of this whole mess was to keep me and Jordan together, and taking that paternity test would tear us apart.

Even worse, once I was discovered to be Daddy, the door to all those other possibilities would crack open just a bit. It occurred to me now that, while I had planned everything else out so carefully, I had somehow blinded myself on this issue. I'd spent so much time trying to prevent the paternity of that baby from being determined that I had never realistically considered what I would do if it was.

Yes, I might be able to make the authorities believe that Dan had killed Kelly out of jealousy over our rendezvous and the pregnancy. But I hadn't been honest with them in the first place that there was a rendezvous. And if I had lied to the police about that, it wasn't that much of a stretch to wonder if I'd lied about other stuff. And why would I lie? It was awfully risky. Despite his orders to the contrary, eventually Detective Cardinal or someone else would get industrious and pursue those questions. Once the questions started, the answers would follow.

I wasn't foolish enough to delude myself into thinking that I had left no clues. I'm sure I screwed up a dozen different ways. The only thing that was keeping anyone from noticing was that no one had any reason to look at me. Even Cardinal thought that, at worst, I had covered for Dan. That test could give them a reason to start looking again. Not even my father's name could prevent that.

And Jordan was the only person who could make that test happen. She was the wildcard. I should have known she wouldn't just let it go. It wasn't in her nature. That was why this was necessary. It was during our lunchtime library conversation that I recognized that this was the only way out. It was inevitable. Otherwise the dominoes would fall. I take the test, I'm found to be the father, I'm humiliated in front of everyone, I lose credibility, and likely my law school admission. I potentially lose my freedom and even my life. And in the end I lose the girl anyway.

Sometimes I think Jordan might have understood. She knew how important Harvard was to me. She knew what it meant to my dad. And she knew that my professional future was dependent on my good name. I'm not saying that justifies my actions. I'm just saying it's not always so black-and-white.

A collective moan emerged from the crowd. The most recent cannonball contestant had failed. I could see that interest in the competition was waning. People were starting to return to the dance floor. It was time to get back to work. I was worried about Jordan's whereabouts. Had anyone seen her? I made concern my mantra and walked inside, troubled once more.

I must have asked about ten people if they'd seen her. All her suitemates were at the party, dancing in a circle. I spent about two minutes with them, all of us throwing out places she might be. I mentioned that someone had told me they'd seen her in the second-floor bathroom about an hour ago and that she didn't look good. I couldn't remember who said it, but it had me concerned.

The conversation was very effective and a few of the girls, including Joanie, stopped dancing and started asking around themselves. I ran into Kevie Poo, who had switched girls again. He still hadn't seen Jordan since the blowup with Evan. That reminded me. I hadn't even seen Evan in a while either. I really hoped he wasn't bothering her. He'd already upset her enough for one night. Kevie was sure I was overreacting, but said he'd keep his eyes peeled.

It was now 12:30. Evan could return at any moment. I was worried that if he came back too soon and went straight to his room, he might find her and call for an ambulance. It was unlikely, but at this point, I wasn't dismissing any scenario. I made sure to keep one eye on the pathway at all times, even when I stepped outside for a second to get some air. The bartender pledge from before whom I'd asked to be on the lookout saw me and wandered over.

"Hey, Jake, how's it going? Did you ever find Jordan?"

"No," I told him, "and I'm starting to get worried. She was so upset because Evan was freaking her out that she just ran up the stairs. I've been looking all over. She's had a lot to drink tonight and I have a bad feeling."

"If you want, I can help you look for her," he offered.

"Do you know what she looks like?"

"Oh yeah. I actually know her a little," he said, then seeing my quizzical look, continued, "I'm in the Fine Arts Depart-

ment and she's kind of a legend over there. Her project is amazing. And she's always helping the underclassmen. She's like a
T.A., only she doesn't get any credit. I would have been
screwed more than once without her."

"I'll bet."

"I hope you don't think I'm out of line saying this, but you
really did well for yourself. That girl rocks. She's just got a
thing, you know?"

"Believe me, I know."

"Yeah, of course you do. You know, she was actually one
of the reasons I pledged Kappa Omega. I was having a real
problem with an assignment and just with school in general.
Anyway she sat me down and we just talked, for like twenty
minutes. She helped me with my work and convinced me that
this place could be fun. She told me about you and how you
managed to work hard and have a good time. She's the one
who suggested I check the house out."

"I'm surprised she never mentioned any of that to me," I
said.

"Oh, I asked her not to. I thought it would make me look
pretty lame if I was being recommended to a fraternity by a
brother's girlfriend, even one as awesome as Jordan."

"She is pretty awesome," I agreed.

"Then maybe we ought to find this awesome girl," he said,
clearly pleased that I was taking any kind of interest in him.

"Yeah, let's. Why don't you come with me? I want to check
the whole house, from top to bottom. We'll start in the basement."

The pledge was a bundle of energy. He hurried down the stairs
and into the pool room, calling out Jordan's name and even
checking in a storage closet. Since I was so loaded, I took my
time. I walked through the slop room to the kitchen. I wandered around the island in the center of the room and moved

over to the pantry. I don't know why I pushed open the door. After all, she wasn't in there.

When the door opened, I was hit with the pantry's mix of scents. It had a powerful effect. The combination of pickle relish, flour, and peanut butter reminded me immediately of that night back in December when the two of us had made this our personal playground. It was in this room that we had the argument that set everything else in motion.

I had a brief flash of that evening, of the two of us rolling around on the flour-strewn floor, oblivious to everything around us. It was one of those perfect moments where two separate individuals connect so deeply that they could be one person. I hadn't appreciated it at the time, but in retrospect, I realized it was magic.

There was a bag of flour sitting restlessly on one of the shelves. For some reason, I walked over, grabbed it, lifted it above my head, and slammed it to the ground with all the force I could muster. There was an explosion as white dust rose all the way to the ceiling, bathing me in grainy powder. All of a sudden I felt very dizzy. My knees buckled and I reached out awkwardly to a shelf for some support. My hand accidentally knocked a huge jar of mayonnaise to the floor. The sound of shattering glass coupled with the thud of thick goop made me sick to my stomach. It reminded me of the sound of brain and skull being crushed.

Jordan was upstairs, less than two hundred feet from me, dying. She might be dead already. I was overcome by fear and anxiety. The girl I had asked to spend the rest of her life with me, the most perfect girl in the world, had trusted me. I handed her a cup and she drank from it, never suspecting for a second that I had given it to her with malice. I had harmed the woman I loved, and suddenly I couldn't remember why.

The pledge appeared behind me from nowhere.

"Are you okay, Jake?" he asked, seeing me doubled over and sweating. I wasn't.

"We've got to get Jordan. She's in trouble."

"Are you sure?"

"I'm sure."

I pushed past him and rushed out the kitchen door. I was panicked. Jordan was in danger and I was the only one who knew it, the only one who could stop it. I had made a terrible mistake. I'd ignored something very important when I was putting my plan together. It's a lot harder to kill someone you love than it is to kill someone you've only fucked.

I took the stairs two at a time. Every second counted. Unfortunately, I didn't see the puddle of water on one of the rubber-coated stairs. When I stepped on it, my foot slipped out from under me, sending me flying toward the ground headfirst. I tried to throw my arms out in front of me to block the fall but I was moving too fast. I hit the step. There was a sharp pain at the front of my skull as I landed. Then nothing.

CHAPTER TWENTY-SEVEN

When I came to, there was a crowd around me. I tried to sit up but the splitting pain in my head made it impossible. I glanced around and saw that I was lying on one of the dinner tables in the slop room. My face was wet and I realized someone had just thrown cold water on me. Something was terribly wrong. I knew it but I couldn't remember what it was.

Somebody told me to relax, not to get up, but I couldn't see who was talking. I looked up at the faces surrounding me. I could hear the pulsing bass from the music upstairs but I couldn't identify it. My mouth was dry and salty. I could taste blood. I forced my brain to kickstart. What had happened? Why was I here? There was something gravely important going on and I had to deal with it if only I could remember. It was just out of reach. I couldn't quite bring it front and center.

"What happened?" I asked. Kevie stepped into my line of sight.

"You slipped running up the stairs. Jerry ran up to get help."

"Who's Jerry?" I asked.

"He's the pledge who was with you when you fell. He said you were freaked because you couldn't find Jordan."

It all washed over me in a fraction of a second—too fast. I couldn't process everything. I wanted to scream and run at the same time but I couldn't do either. How long had I been out? Had they found her? Had they even been looking? Was she alive?

"Where . . . ?" I started, unable to complete the question. Kevie thought I was asking where Jerry was.

"After he got us, he grabbed a few guys to keep searching the house for Jordan. He said you thought she might have passed out. They're looking now."

I checked my watch. It took a second for the numbers to unfuzz. 12:42. I couldn't have been out for more than a few minutes. The throbbing pain in my head was unbearable. Every beat from the music above felt like an anvil being dropped on my head. I tried to ignore it and pushed myself up. A wave of nausea hit me and I vomited on the floor, just managing to turn my head enough to miss hitting anyone. The crowd around me jumped back to avoid the splatter.

"Don't move, Jake. You should stay lying down," the girl standing next to Kevie said, then turning to him, added, "I think we should take him to the hospital."

I swung my feet off the table and started to stand up. The people around me protested but I ignored them. My legs were unsteady and I motioned to Kevie to help me. He came over and hooked my arm around his neck.

"Take me upstairs," I ordered. Despite my weakened state, he could tell I meant business and led me to the stairwell. We had only made it to the midpoint between the first and second floors when Jerry the pledge met us. He looked frazzled.

"Is he okay?" he asked Kevie. I interrupted before he could answer.

"Did you find her?"

"No," Jerry said, "we checked all the bathrooms and every unlocked room. She wasn't anywhere."

"Only unlocked rooms?" I shouted. The nausea came again and I had to put my head down to stop from puking. I couldn't see Jerry but I could tell from his voice that he was surprised.

"I knocked on every door," he swore, "I didn't know what else to do."

I took a deep breath, trying to gather the strength to tell him where to look and what to do. Kevie beat me to the punch.

"Go to my room. It's unlocked. Grab the key from my bedpost. It's the master for the whole house. Open every door, locked or not. She could have wandered into some room, locked the door, and passed out or tripped or anything. Obviously, Jake thinks she drank way too much, so hurry."

Jerry immediately ran back upstairs. I wanted to shout for him to start in Evan's room but he was gone before I lifted my head up and I was having trouble getting the words out anyway. Kevie started to sit me down on the steps but I grabbed at his sleeve and shook my head vigorously, causing a sharp stabbing pain that made me gasp.

"You need to rest for a second," he pleaded.

"No," I managed to mumble as I pointed upstairs. He sighed, got a good grip, and led me up again. We went one step at a time. It was excruciatingly slow. I listened intently for a shout of discovery from upstairs. There was nothing. When we finally reached the third floor, I realized why. Almost everyone had locked their doors because of the party and Jerry had started opening the rooms closest to the stairwell. Evan's room was at the other end of the hall.

Jerry had just looked in the room next to Evan's but instead of going there next, he crossed the corridor to Dan's room. He looked at it for a long second before putting the key in the lock. He was wasting valuable time. I swallowed hard and shouted at him.

"She's not in there." I was about to yell at him to unlock Evan's room but I needed a second to regroup. It felt like my brain was dripping out of my skull. Every word was a challenge. Jerry turned to look at me. He was confused. Kevie had said to check every room. Jordan was less than ten feet from him and he was standing dumbly in the middle of the hall, doing nothing. If I had the strength I would have throttled him. A voice behind us made that unnecessary.

"What the fuck is going on?" I didn't need to turn around to know it was Evan. Kevie spoke before I could.

"Evan, we're looking for Jordan. We can't find her anywhere and Jake's really worried. Can you unlock your room?"

"Why would you think she's in there?" he asked, with a suspicious lack of self-righteousness. I couldn't turn around to face him, but I could tell from the expression on Jerry's face that he thought that response was inappropriate. I could see the wheels turning in the kid's brain. He remembered our conversation about an argument between Jordan and Evan and how I'd said she found the guy creepy. Jerry was making connections fast and furious and I saw that he was now very worried, too.

"We're checking all the locked rooms," Kevie said, "in case she accidentally wandered in somewhere and passed out."

"But I locked my door before the party started," Evan argued. Even without seeing him, I could hear that the guy was still very drunk. He was probably also confused, still trying to figure out the weird phone call he had received and couldn't mention. He should have recognized that protesting only made him look bad. But confusion, guilt, and inebriation were not a constructive combination, as I was painfully aware. Jerry had had enough of Evan's stalling and moved to the door.

"I'll open it," he said.

"Don't go near my door, you fucking pledge," Evan yelled and rushed over to stop him. "I'll open it myself if this is such a big deal."

As he put his key in the door, he looked down the hall. I glanced around and saw that a crowd of about ten people had gathered behind us. We had an audience. Evan noticed, too, and I saw a flash of alarm in his eyes. As he opened the door, I could almost read his thoughts. They were clear. He was asking—what if she *is* in here?

As soon as the door was open, Jerry pushed past Evan to get inside. Kevie helped me quickly down the corridor. We were just arriving at the door when I heard the gasp. Jerry was staring at the closet.

"What the fuck?" he said. Kevie and I stepped inside to see what he was gaping at. There was Jordan, just as I had left her a little more than an hour ago. The ripped panties and bra, the sweater over the head, the jeans pulled down to the thighs, they were all the same. I couldn't tell if she was alive or not. Jerry bent down and pulled the sweater off her face. He put his ear to her mouth, then her chest.

"Is she breathing?" Kevie whispered.

"I can't tell."

The room was starting to fill up. People were peeking around the corner to get a look at the commotion in the closet.

"Call an ambulance," I managed to squeak out as I dropped to the floor and crawled over to my fiancée. That snapped Kevie into action.

"Call an ambulance," he said, pointing at one of the girls in the room. "Call quick."

She looked around Evan's room and saw the phone on the nightstand by his bed. She pushed past him and picked it up. The minor collision seemed to snap him out of his daze. Until that point, he'd just been staring at the half-naked girl in his closet like everyone else.

"How did she get in here?" he asked, almost to himself. "The door was locked."

"That's what I was wondering," Jerry said accusingly. "How *did* she get in here?"

I slid next to him and put my own ear to her lips, trying to find any hint of breath. I touched her skin. She was still warm. I leaned forward and put my head to her chest, trying to find a heartbeat. The sharp movement made my skull throb.

"She must have meant my place, not her place," Evan said absently. He did not work well under pressure.

"What the fuck do you mean, your place?" Jerry demanded. He stood up angrily.

"She called me earlier. She said she wanted me to come to her place. She sounded drunk. She must have meant my place." He was trying to figure it out even as he said it. Jerry was incredulous.

"She wanted to meet with you? I find that hard to believe. She thought you were a fucking freak. I doubt she'd want to be anywhere near you."

"She did. She called me. I swear she did."

I tried to concentrate. There was Jerry yelling and Evan protesting and the panicked girl on the phone pleading with 911 to get here now and Lenny Kravitz downstairs, singing about flying away and my own loudly pulsating head. I put all of them out of my thoughts and listened. I could hear a beat. It was faint and slow but I was sure it was there. I held my breath so even that noise wouldn't interfere. There was an endless silence. Then a beat . . . another measureless pause . . . a beat.

"She's alive," I croaked, "I hear her heart beating."

Everyone stopped. Then Kevie turned to the girl on the phone.

"Tell them to get that ambulance here now," he ordered.

"It's already on its way," she replied. "They said to try to wake her. If she's passed out, we need to try to help her regain consciousness." She put the phone down and hurried over to help me do just that. I was relieved that someone else was taking over. Another girl pushed through the crowd at the door and joined us. She lay Jordan flat on her back and started mouth-to-mouth. I moved out of the way.

Everyone watched the two girls work. No one spoke. I sat silently, my back leaning against Evan's chest of drawers. Jordan might live. Despite whatever consequences I might face, I prayed that she would. And then I thought of something. I looked up at Evan's shocked face. I saw the anger brimming in Jerry. I saw Kevie stuck somewhere between confusion and hostility himself. I wondered if there might still be some way out of this for me.

If Jordan survived, I was probably screwed. She would know what really occurred that night and Evan would be vindicated. If that happened, I would face the consequences of my action fully. But if she didn't make it, the table was set for me to conceivably extricate myself from this nightmare. If I acted quickly.

"What was that you said about a phone call?" I asked Evan. He hesitated, then answered me.

"I know you'll find this hard to believe, Jake, but Jordan called me a little while ago and asked me to come over. But I guess she was waiting for me here." He was trying to solve the puzzle aloud, never a good move.

"But how did she get in here if you locked the door?" I asked.

"I don't know."

"And why," I demanded, my voice rising, "is she half-naked? It looks like someone tried to rip her clothes off."

"Maybe she tried to take them off herself while she was waiting for me." He was digging a hole. Suggesting that Jordan Lansing had voluntarily stripped and waited for Evan in his room clearly didn't wash with anyone. Even Evan didn't look convinced. What he didn't realize was that the idea was offensive, especially to Jerry.

"Why would a girl who ran away from you earlier tonight strip for you later?" It was a good question and Evan wasn't quick with an answer. Jerry was doing much of the heavy lifting for me but there was one topic I needed brought up and it didn't look like it was going to get mentioned if I didn't address it myself.

"Are you fucking kidding me Evan?" I shouted angrily. "My girlfriend decided to strip for *you*? Look at her. She's totally fucked up. This is the worst case of alcohol poisoning I've ever seen and she didn't drink *that* much. Jesus, it almost looks like she's been drugged." And it worked. The word "drugged" hung in the air, curling through the minds of the now twenty-odd people in earshot.

Evan stepped back when I said it, as if he'd been punched. I watched him closely. Everyone did. If he was sober or had even a second to think about it, he likely could have stopped himself. But he wasn't sober and he didn't have a second. His eyes darted to the sock drawer. He looked away too quickly. I looked at the drawer myself, as did Jerry and Kevie and everyone else in the room. I didn't want to be the one to find the bottle but I had to make sure the moment didn't sneak away.

"What were you looking at, Evan?" I demanded, still yelling. "What's in the drawer?"

"Nothing," he said, too fast.

Kevie moved over to the drawer and looked in. He picked up the waiting bottle and shook it. The rattle was deafening. He popped open the top and dropped the pill into his open palm.

"This doesn't look like Advil," he said, "what is it?"

"It's nothing," Evan told him, "it's headache medicine."

I didn't want to get caught up in a debate about drug identification. We were so close. I decided to push us over the edge.

"Did you drug my girlfriend?" I asked, disbelieving. He didn't answer. What good would it have done him? Apart from the two girls working to revive Jordan, the room was silent. I let it last as long as I could, then went for it.

"You son of a bitch," I screamed as I struggled to my feet. My head pounded but I lunged at him anyway. If I'd been healthy I would have gotten to him easily. But in my weakened state, I was too slow and Kevie managed to grab me before I got to Evan. My former blackmailer stepped back even farther. He was an aspiring lawyer and while he would never be a great one, he did have a natural facility for attempting to explain away the seemingly unexplainable. He should have known that a good lawyer also knows when to keep his mouth shut.

"She must have found them while she was waiting for me. She must have been curious and taken a few. That's the only explanation." The call I had Jordan make was still confusing him. Evan was so consumed with making it fit in with the current state of events that he refused to consider any other theories. He just couldn't break out of the box.

The problem was that his outlandish claims had made Jerry as angry as I pretended to be. He turned to face the guy and I could tell that he was furious.

"You motherfucker," he shouted as he swung his fist in Evan's direction. His punch landed squarely on the jaw and sent the motherfucker sprawling back against the wall. Not satisfied, Jerry jumped on the older but smaller man and began pummeling him in the stomach. It took three brothers to pull him off. Two of them yanked Jerry out of the room. The third sat Evan down at his desk and told him to stay there and shut up.

The ambulance arrived about three minutes later. The technicians had her inside the vehicle with the doors closed in less than ninety seconds. I rode along and watched as they worked on her all the way to the hospital. Someone gave me a towel and told me to hold it to my head until we got to the emergency room. The whole trip from door to door lasted less than eight minutes. It was incredibly impressive. As I followed the stretcher through the swinging doors, I couldn't help but wonder: If I had called 911 that night with Kelly, could they have saved her? It was an intriguing question, but of course, it was moot now.

CHAPTER TWENTY-EIGHT

The doctor had me stay overnight, just to be safe. They did a CT scan and told me I'd suffered a mild concussion but that there was no intracranial bleeding and that I'd be all right. I woke up the next morning with a terrible headache and an ugly gash but nothing more. The nurse said several people had come by to see me during the night, but that no one was allowed in until I woke up and the doctors had seen me again.

I asked about Jordan and was told that she was recovering nicely. Last night, the medical staff were still working on her when I was taken away to be examined myself. The cops arrived and asked me some questions while I was being checked out. I gave them the bare bones. Not sure how things would turn out, I didn't want to paint myself into a corner so I acknowledged that I had been drinking and that I was still fuzzy from the head injury. I said they should talk to Kevie and Jerry, knowing that they'd be able to provide details I couldn't. Then I was taken for more tests, still unaware of Jordan's status.

So it wasn't until this morning that the nurse told me that

despite a few anxious moments, she was doing much better now. She was unconscious, but was expected to wake up any time in the next couple of hours. I could see her as soon as the doctors and the police were done with her. For some reason, it hadn't occurred to me that the cops would want to question her. Of course they would. The thought made my head pound worse.

I asked what had happened to Evan. The nurse didn't know all the details but said he was under arrest for attempted sexual assault and some drug-related offense. I wanted to press for more but figured that might appear unseemly under the circumstances. Besides, the nurse clearly only knew the basics.

After the doctor checked me out, they let Rick visit. He filled me in on the rest. Evan was being held without bail. Rumor had it that he'd confessed to having roofies, to having an argument with Jordan earlier in the evening, and to having a crush on her. But he was still sticking to his claim that she had called him that night and asked him to come to her place.

Rick said a bunch of people wanted to see me, including Kevie, Jerry, and Jeff, who had driven back from Chicago late last night when he heard the news, but since only one person could visit for now, he was the selectee. He said television vans were parked at all the hospital exits and that the series of incidents at Jefferson University had led all the morning newscasts. It was too much to process.

The nurse came back in and told me that Jordan was starting to regain consciousness and that the doctors thought it would help if I was there when she woke up if I could promise not to get too upset. I said I would stay calm and she led me down the hall to her room. When I walked in, a doctor and two nurses were hovering over her bed. Standing quietly in the corner were Cardinal and a uniformed cop.

The nurses checked various monitors as the doctor poked around, apparently doing some tests. One of the nurses saw me and waved me over. She pointed to a seat by the bed. I sat down and she took my hand and put it in Jordan's, squeezing them together. The nurse leaned over so only I could hear her.

"Be supportive and be strong," she whispered, and gave me a reassuring smile. I sat quietly while the doctor finished his tests. He explained to Jordan where she was and asked a series of questions about how she felt. Her eyes were closed. Initially, she sounded groggy and her answers were hard to understand. She kept swallowing. I could tell she had terrible dry mouth. But as the doctor asked more questions she became clearer, both verbally and mentally. Finally, she opened her eyes and blinked a few times.

Her eyes were glassy but I could tell she was scared, bordering on freaked out. I remembered how panicky I was when I first came to after hitting my head on the stairs last night. And I was only out for a few minutes. She studied everyone in the room, trying to find a familiar face. Then she saw me.

Now let me start by saying that from the second I saw Cardinal in there, I'd been preparing for the worst. The moment last night when I changed my mind and decided to try to save Jordan, I accepted that I'd probably get nailed. She was a witness to all parts of my crime and the witness had survived.

As I sat next to her, holding her hand, I didn't regret what I had done. It would have been a sin to take her from this world. She was needed. But there was a price to pay. I was afraid to look her in the eye. I was ready to accept whatever came my way but I couldn't bear to see the hatred, the disappointment on her face. So I kept my head down and my mouth shut.

Cardinal stepped forward with a small notepad, apologized for having to do this so soon, and began to ask questions. He asked her to walk him through the whole night, from the start of the evening until she lost consciousness. There was silence. He rephrased his question. Either it was too overwhelming or she must still be having trouble getting words out. Still nothing from her.

I looked up. Jordan didn't appear particularly upset and she didn't look like it was too hard to speak. Most important, she didn't seem angry. She glanced around the room at everyone and let her eyes fall on me again. I recognized the expression immediately. She was genuinely confused.

"I don't remember anything," she finally said. "I know I had dinner with my suitemates before we headed to the Kappa Omega party. I remember having spaghetti and some red wine. After that, we went to the row. And then I woke up here. That's pretty much it. What happened?"

Cardinal asked if she remembered the party? If she remembered speaking to Evan Grunier? Or an argument? Or going upstairs in the house? She shook her head at each of these questions but each one made her more agitated. It was clear something terrible had happened whether she could recall it or not.

Cardinal turned to the doctor and asked what was going on. He said that this was not that surprising. Many victims of Flunitrazepam (I assume he didn't say roofies for fear of freaking Jordan out) had memory impairment. In some cases, it returned. In many more, the victim never recalled the incident. That was one reason why the drug was so popular. He said that Cardinal could give it a few days but that the likelihood was that if she couldn't remember anything now, she probably never would.

Jordan was still giving me that questioning stare so I was careful not to show any reaction. That was partly because I didn't want to upset her. The doctors would have to be the ones to tell her that someone allegedly drugged her and tried to rape her. I was also afraid that if I allowed myself any quarter, my face might betray my current emotion, which was relief.

She didn't remember anything. Not the drugging, not the phone call to Evan, not the undressing and the ripping of the clothes. It was all a blank to her. The power of that moment was so great that I felt myself begin to cry.

"What's wrong, baby?" Jordan asked, putting aside her own worries for the time being. I couldn't speak. Instead I stood up and leaned over to hug her. I put my face in her chest and let the hot tears pour down my cheeks and soak her blanket. I listened as the doctor told her what had happened to her. Every now and then, Detective Cardinal would add something.

They made it clear that she had not actually been raped, that she'd been found before that happened. The doctor assured her that, apart from her apparent memory loss, she shouldn't have any long-term effects as a result of the drugging. Cardinal promised that Evan would be aggressively prosecuted, that even without her recollection, there was enough physical evidence to convict on various charges. He said Evan had even foolishly confessed to having the pills, thinking that his admission might help him.

I could tell she was angry, but Jordan dealt with it all surprisingly well. She asked a few questions, mostly ensuring that Evan wouldn't get away with it. She wanted to know the likely sentence for what he'd done. As she spoke, her voice rose a little and she tightened her grip on my fingers. She was under control but I had a feeling that if Evan were to walk in right now, she'd rip his throat out.

Cardinal was very reassuring, personally promising to bring "that bastard," as he called him, to justice. He never even looked at me. Eventually, Jordan asked if she could have a little time alone with me. The room emptied immediately and we were left by ourselves.

I waited for her to speak. There was some small part of me that still worried that even though she had said she remembered nothing, she was covering. Why, I had no idea. But, the thought bounced around in my head as I waited for her to talk.

"What happened to you?" she asked, pointing at the huge bandage covering my head.

"Nothing," I said, then relented. "I tripped running around trying to find you and landed hard. I knocked myself out." She giggled slightly at that, then stopped because of the pain in her raw throat.

"I wanted to talk to you about something," she said, "but I couldn't do it in front of everyone."

I nodded and squeezed her hand tight. I was prepared.

"It's about the paternity test."

I had put that out of my mind. I knew it was out there, waiting to rear its head, but that was one variable I just couldn't deal with, with everything else going on. Now it was back, front and center. It was the very reason the two of us were in the hospital right now. And despite all my machinations, it was still my albatross. My baby would get her father's name, even if she hadn't lived to use it.

"What about it?" I asked.

"Let's forget about it," she said.

"What?"

"I should have never asked you to take it. I let that psycho Evan get in my head. He made me doubt you, even though I knew it was wrong. I just couldn't stop thinking about that image of you and Kelly against the wall. I made it real in my head. And why? Because a sick fuck like Evan couldn't have me, so he made it his mission to mess us up. I should have known. That little shit tried to screw with us and it almost worked. And now I'm ashamed of myself. I'm ashamed that I asked you to take the test and I'm embarrassed that you said yes. I'm sorry."

I didn't know what to do. In my wildest fantasies, I couldn't have imagined her saying the words I just heard. If my head weren't still throbbing, I would have thought I was dreaming.

"Are you sure?" I asked, pressing my luck but needing to hear it again.

"Yes, I'm sure. I don't need any tests to prove you love me. I want to marry you. And I want to do it as soon as possible."

I kissed her. Not long or hard because I could see that her mouth was still sore and swollen from all the manipulation it had undergone last night. But I kissed her. And she kissed me back. Less than twelve hours ago I had resigned myself to that never happening again. It was like a miracle.

CHAPTER TWENTY-NINE

Detective Cardinal was waiting for me when I left Jordan's room. I was a little apprehensive when I first saw him but it turned out he only wanted to offer me his condolences. He said that whatever differences we'd had in the past, he would do everything in his power to make sure Evan was punished for what he had done. As best I could tell, he was being sincere. I thanked him. It was nice.

As he walked down the hall to the elevator, I saw a few familiar faces waiting in the chairs along the wall. Rick, Kevie, Jeff, Jerry, along with a few other brothers and several of Jordan's suitemates were milling about. I was touched but didn't feel up to talking to them right then. So I returned to my room. The doctors had cleared me to leave at noon. It was 11:30 now and I thought I could use a little private time before facing the certain chaos of the next few hours.

I walked in, shut the heavy door, and sat down on the bed. My whole body was sore and my eyes felt heavy and dry. I closed them and sighed.

"Tired?" I heard a voice say. My eyes snapped open. Lindsay was sitting unobtrusively in a small chair in the corner of the room. I fought the urge to ask her to get the hell out.

"You would not believe," I said.

"I can imagine," she assured me, "you had quite a night. It sounds like all the excitement started right around the time I left."

"Be glad you missed it."

"I am. I'm also glad it wasn't me Evan had his eye on. Amazing how well you pegged him, huh?"

"I guess not so amazing considering the stuff you found in his file," I reminded her.

"Oh yeah, I've been meaning to talk to you about that," she said.

"What?"

"I didn't put anything in his file yet."

"Why not? I already filed a complaint against him yesterday." I knew I sounded shrill, but I couldn't help myself. "They're going to be going through his stuff on Monday. If you don't get that information in his record, it could hurt the investigation on him. He tried to rape Jordan. They have to know about the other incident. Without those records, they might not find out about it." I doubted she realized the significance of her laziness. I hadn't asked much of her and she still couldn't get it done.

"I know."

"Then why didn't you do it?" I demanded. Lindsay stood up. She had a peculiar smile.

"You better get comfortable, Jake. Maybe you should lean back in bed there. I've got to tell you something and I need your full attention. I'm only going to say this once, so don't interrupt."

"What are you talking about?" I asked impatiently.

"Jake, don't talk. Listen. It's only Saturday. There's lots of time for me to get that information into Evan's file. And I will do that—under certain conditions."

"What conditions?"

"Do you want this thing resolved properly? If you do then you'll shut the fuck up." Something in her tone made me do just that. She sounded too confident for my taste. When she was sure I wasn't going to speak, she began.

"If you meet my conditions, I will go down to the admissions office this afternoon and put the information in his file. But if you don't, I'll simply burn Evan's records. Then it'll be much more difficult for the police to learn about his past. I know you don't want to deal with the awkwardness of bringing his history to their attention yourself. How could you possibly know about his high school days? You couldn't. It would raise unwanted questions and I know you don't like those."

As she spoke, the pain in my head started to get more intense. She didn't seem to notice, because she went on, undeterred.

"See Jake, you're not quite as clever as you think you are. I know that you and Kelly weren't friends. Kelly was my roommate. We slept five feet apart. I knew her very well and I know you and I know that you couldn't talk to that girl for more than ten minutes. You two wouldn't be friends in a million years. I kept thinking how strange it was that she'd confide in you about her personal life. It just didn't make sense, no matter what connection you claimed to have with her.

"And I just didn't buy how distraught you were at the hospital that night or in the days after. I never once saw you with Kelly. It's quite a stretch to believe you had some special kinship and I never even knew you knew each other. But it made a lot more sense after I found out she was pregnant. You may not have had an intellectual relationship with her, but that's not the only kind of relationship a man and a woman can have, is it?"

I started to speak but she just shook her head. She wasn't done.

"Anyway, you don't need me to walk you through all the details of how I reached certain conclusions. You already know the specifics. All I'll say is that I've noticed a lot of coincidences in recent weeks. My roommate is upset, but won't say why. She goes to meet 'someone' and ends up viciously beaten. It turns out she's pregnant. Everyone suspects her boyfriend, who kills himself. My roommate dies along with her baby. Then a guy with a history of sexual misconduct attacks another girl. And smack dab in the middle of the whole thing is one person. How weird is that?"

It was a good thing Lindsay had told me to lean back in the bed. Otherwise I would have fallen off it. All I could do was sit there and let her lead me where she wanted to go.

"Of course, not everyone's connecting these coincidences. Maybe they don't seem that odd unless you're looking at them a certain way. But I *do* find them odd and if you don't mind, Jake, at this point I'm going to stop referring to them as co-incidences and just talk to you straight. You don't have a problem with that, do you? It's okay, you can answer me."

"Please, don't let me stop you while you're on a roll," I said, going for an air of amused indifference because I didn't know what else to do.

"That's sweet of you. So I'm guessing that a guy as smart as you planned these things out very carefully and probably has alibis and explanations and all manner of inventive tricks at your disposal. But I'm also guessing that all it would take is for some-one like me to make an accusation or two. All of a sudden, those alibis that seem so sturdy on the surface might start to fall apart when poked and prodded.

"Why, just a few days ago, Detective Cardinal came by my place. He had a few additional questions for me. Mind you, he was there in a strictly unofficial capacity. He wanted to make that clear. Apparently they've hamstrung his investigation quite a bit of late. But he seemed awfully curious. I told him I didn't have any new information for him. Of course, that could change.

"All of that might not matter if you covered your tracks, but even if you escaped charges for murder or whatever they threw at you, I'm thinking you'd be ruined. Your reputation would be shit. You'd have to take that paternity test and Jordan would discover that you fucked another girl, got her pregnant, and lied about it to everyone, even after the girl died. Harvard might want to reconsider your acceptance. That's right, I heard about Harvard. Congrats on that by the way.

"And if you're thinking there's a remote shot that you're not the daddy and can keep Jordan as a result, you can let that one go because it doesn't matter. After all, you fucked me and that's enough to make her drop you."

I was about to correct her on that point, but she didn't even allow me that, moving on before I could interrupt.

"Even though you didn't fuck me Jake, you fucked me. I'll say you did and that's all it'll take. That and the video I have of our night at my place, which conveniently cuts off just before you backed out. By the way, that night you were shoving your hand down my jeans, I believe your girlfriend was getting ready for a memorial service in honor of a girl you butchered. Not classy."

As I listened to her lay it all out so meticulously, the general bad feeling I had grew more intense. It was around the time she made the butchering reference that the nausea overwhelmed me. I leaned to the side of the bed and hovered over the little plastic trash can, waiting to vomit. But I could only dry heave. Lindsay stopped talking and waited patiently until I was done. I sat back up and wiped the dribble from my chin.

"Shall we continue?" she asked, "because here's the kicker, the part you've been waiting for, kiddo. It doesn't have to be that way. As you're painfully aware, I'm telling all this to you instead of Detective Cardinal down the hall, who, from what I could tell based on our little visit and despite recent events, isn't your biggest fan. I'm sure you've been wondering for the last five minutes why he's not in on this conversation. Here's why: because I'm very fond of you, Jake."

"What?"

"I like you a lot. And I think you like me. Hell, your dick

gets hard every time I enter the room so I know *he* likes me. I understand you and although you've woefully underestimated me, I think you get what I'm about, too. We connect. We're perfect for each other. I know how much you hate awkward moments and I'm offering you a way out of the most awkward moment you'll ever have in your life."

"I'm not sure I understand exactly what you're asking?" I said.

"I'm not asking anything. I'm telling. I'm calling in my chit, Jake. And not for a few minutes of groping behind a Dumpster. I don't know if I'm in love with you but I feel something. I like how you're willing to go to the mat. I like that you don't give up. I like that you're unpredictable. I find those things serious turn-ons. It may sound weird, but I think if you channeled your energy in more constructive directions, you could do great things. I can help you with that. We'd make a great team, if you got off your high horse."

"You're crazy," I told her. "You are truly whacked out of your brain."

"That's not fair," she said, clearly hurt, "especially coming from you. Now let me tell you what's going to happen because time is short. You're trapped. I've got you. You don't know it yet, but we are going to be together. If you don't agree, you'll be going to jail for a very long time. You might even get some sort of injection. Here's what you're going to do. You will go back into Jordan's room and break up with her. Give her whatever reason you want, but make it quick and clean. You also need to make it clear that you won't be talking to her anymore after today."

"Listen Lindsay, I admire your balls, but this is ridiculous. I'm not breaking up with Jordan. We were just talking about our wedding."

"You might as well forget about that because it's not happening. I'm trying to be matter-of-fact about this to make it easier on you. I didn't want to get all dramatic. I didn't want to bore you with threats and flourishes. But I will if I have to.

You're not marrying Jordan. You're dumping her and you're doing it in five minutes. You *will* be getting married, but I'm your bride. You can refuse. I can't make you do it, of course. But if you don't do what I say, I'm going to tell Jordan and the police everything I've told you."

"You're full of shit," I said, not as convincingly as I would have liked.

"Oh, I just realized why you're fighting me on this. I haven't told you about my insurance. Let me fill you in. This morning I sent out a letter. I won't bore you with the details but the gist of it is—my family attorney will soon have documents outlining all the stuff I've just gone over with you. He doesn't know what's in them, but he has instructions to open them if anything happens to me. Anything. If I die, whether by accident or suicide or whatever, he opens them. If I'm in a coma, he opens them. If I disappear, he opens them. One can never be too careful when you're involved.

"The instructions specify that these procedures are to be followed if anything happens to me before I turn seventy-five. And I assure you, if I'm still around when I'm seventy-four I'll revise those instructions. It'll probably be moot because by then we'll have been in love for so long that you won't be tempted to try anything, but I've decided to err on the side of caution.

"Now, there's divorce, too. Of course, you won't be able to get one or I'll tell. If by some chance, you disappoint me and *I* decide to divorce you, I'll tell. I'll say that you told me the whole sordid thing in a moment of weakness. I'll say you threatened to kill me, too, if I said a word, but that I had to do the right thing. That should give you a real incentive to keep me happy, lover. Happy and healthy, that is.

"So you understand the situation. Marry me and let me be the best damn wife you could ever have, or refuse and face the long arm of the law. It's your call, pardner, but you have to decide quick. See, I spoke to my lawyer a little while ago and told him that unless he hears from me at noon our time, he's to open the letters as soon as they arrive, which I FedExed by the way. The clock's ticking, sweetheart."

"You barely know me. Why would you want to marry me, especially if you think I'm a murderer?" I asked, hoping that logic would snap her out of this madness.

"I'm a good judge of character. Besides, that's not really your concern. There'll be lots of time for these little spats and discussions once we're man and wife, but for now, you're just going to have to trust that I know best. Now, I made the deadline noon because I figured this might be hard for you to digest and you might have a bit of trouble walking in and telling your fiancée to take a hike, but it's 11:45. You've got to get in gear."

I looked at her. It might have been an act, but she was behaving as if this was the most normal thing in the world. It was like I was making her late for a movie and she had to nag me to hurry so we could get there before it sold out. She'd made up her mind. I put my head in my hands and tried to think. There had to be a way out of this. But my skull hurt and I was feeling sick and I just didn't have the time. I suppose I could have just walked out and called her bluff.

But like she said, I did get her and I knew in my bones that if I didn't do what she wanted, she would walk straight up to Cardinal and tell him everything. *She* hadn't done anything illegal. She was just a citizen with information to offer. I sensed that she wanted it to work out between us but if I made it difficult she would cut me loose and move on. I wracked my brain for something to make her reconsider. What could mess up her plan? Then, out of the cloud of that addled brain, a thought emerged. Jordan. Jordan was the wildcard.

"Lindsay, what if I break up with Jordan and she gets upset? She asked me to take that paternity test yesterday and backed down today. If I dump her, she might make noise about it again, maybe to the cops. Then the plan falls apart."

"I can help you with that. Detective Cardinal should probably know that Kelly told me that when she was home for winter break, she was mad at Dan because of his cheating and she got together with a guy from high school. I didn't think it mattered before, but now that I hear Dan wasn't the father, I thought I should come forward. After all, she's dead now. What good would it do to look for the real father? Kelly never told me his name and it would be terrible to go around her hometown asking every guy if they nailed her last Christmas. Do you think our friends in the department would drop the issue if it was presented to them like that?"

"Is that true? Did she really sleep with someone over break?" I asked.

"Does it matter? The point is it would end the investigation, just like it would break wide open if I also remembered Kelly telling me that she hooked up with you."

"What if Jordan wanted me to take the test even after you mentioned another guy?"

"What can I tell you, Jake? That's your problem. There are risks involved in anything worth doing. I don't want to be cold but if she demands a test and it ruins your reputation and your life, oh well. It's no skin off my nose. It's your responsibility to make this work. Your ass is on the line, not mine, so *make* her not ask for that test. You can be a pretty convincing guy if you want."

"I can't just do this out of the blue," I protested, "she just woke up. It's not fair."

"Once again, Jake, not my problem. Now I hate to press, but you've only got twelve minutes. And I don't want you pulling any tricks. If you try to tell her it's only temporary or try to get back with her or sneak around to see her, I'll find out and I'll tell. Remember Jake, she still loves you and thinks you're a decent person. You can keep that lie alive for her if you do this right. I'm giving you a chance to keep your dignity, here."

"I don't know if I can do this," I said as I stood up. She took my hand gingerly and led me to the door.

"Sure you can, sweetie. Think of it this way. If you look at it objectively, she's better off without you." She opened the door for me and nodded in the direction of Jordan's room.

"What time is it?" I asked.

"Eleven-fifty. I'll be waiting by the phones. Come see me as soon as you're done." She turned and started down the hall. I hesitated. Then against my better judgment, I called after her.

"Lindsay, were you serious about Kelly and that other guy?"

"Oh Jake, don't torture yourself with that. After all, there's only one way to find out for sure. Besides, you'll be a daddy soon enough. I promise you that."

She smiled warmly, then headed down the corridor again. I watched her go. When she was out of sight, I shuffled the short distance to Jordan's room. I stood in front of the closed door for as long as I dared. Time was running short, after all. I felt an enormous lump at the base of my throat as I lifted my hand and knocked.

"Come in," I heard my favorite voice in the world say.

I opened the door and stepped inside.

CHAPTER THIRTY

It was mid–March and even though the weather was generally mild these days, this morning was unseasonably cold. All the snow from the last storm had melted weeks ago but the wind whipped through the air vengefully. It was especially bad at the cemetery because the whole area was exposed with nothing to block the vicious gusts.

I bundled up tight to protect myself against the elements. As I walked the grounds, every part of me was covered with the exception of a small opening in my hood for my eyes and nose. It might have been overkill. It wasn't *that* cold. But the wind was a good excuse. No one would ever be able to identify me with my huge parka and hidden face. That was important.

It took a while to find the spot. The headstones were surprisingly simple, quietly resting beside each other. The first read: KELLY ELIZABETH STONE, BELOVED DAUGHTER, 1977–2000. The second said only: JESSICA LILY STONE. I hadn't known Kelly's parents named the baby. A name made it more personal.

I reached in my jeans pocket and fumbled around a bit. With the cold and my heavy gloves, it took a second. Even though the sun offered little warmth, it was bright today and the tiny necklace I pulled out glimmered when the light hit it. I placed it on Jessica's grave, where it rested modestly among all the flowers. I stood there for a moment, not sure what to do next. I stared at the headstone, wondering if my baby girl really had her own special grave or if the separate marker was just a gesture. The wind stopped. It was awfully quiet. I wanted to say a little prayer but somehow, after everything that had happened, it didn't seem right.

EPILOGUE

It's late September and things have changed a lot. I've been attending classes at Harvard for a month now and they are hard. I can't skate through like I did as an undergraduate. It's been an especially rough transition because Jefferson gave me a pass for my final semester and I've been out of studying mode. With all the chaos that happened, the school gave both Jordan and I across the board A's in all our classes. Even Sheridan, never a pushover, didn't begrudge me an A in Legal Ethics. The truth is, I was on my way to at least a B+ so it wasn't that much of a stretch for her.

Lindsay and I announced our engagement to my family over Labor Day weekend when we went down to Texas to visit. With our search for a good Boston apartment and my New York internship, that was the first extended time my family got to spend with her. I think they felt it was all a bit sudden and I might be reacting a bit capriciously, because of everything I'd been through. But no one said anything critical and my father seemed to really like Lindsay, just as she promised he would.

He'd always referred to Jordan as "the artsy-fartsy girl." That wasn't a concern with Lindsay.

Evan was still in prison in Missouri. He plea-bargained his way down to ten months. I didn't follow the details of his case because Lindsay thought it would look vindictive for me to keep up with it. I told her reading a story in the newspaper isn't vindictive but she wouldn't hear of it. I do know he's supposed to get out in February. I don't know what he plans to do then.

Rick moved to L.A. after school. I don't know if he learned every Clapton song by the time we graduated, but he got damn close. Last time we talked, he was trying to start a band and supporting himself as a waiter.

Jordan never asked me to take the paternity test. I should have known she wouldn't. It wasn't her style to be petty. I won't go into the boring details of the actual breakup except to say that I blamed it on her. I said that I was upset that she put herself in a compromising situation with Evan that night. I also said I was hurt that she had asked me to take the paternity test, even if she had ultimately changed her mind. It showed a lack of trust and I couldn't be with someone who didn't offer me unconditional trust.

As you might imagine, she took it hard. For a while, she tried to contact me, but eventually she got the hint. It helped that I never spoke to her again, refusing to even look at her when we passed each other on campus. I pretended she didn't exist. I would have preferred to at least offer a friendly smile, but Lindsay said no contact, no communication of any kind, and I didn't think it would be prudent to test the limits of that.

Lindsay wasn't totally unreasonable. We didn't "officially" start dating until a month after the attempted rape because she thought it would look tacky if I started up with a new girl right after my ex had been assaulted. It would raise questions. The practical effect was that it made things a little less painful for Jordan. I didn't want her to think I'd had a chippy on the side all along. Lindsay floated the story that we'd become close after

Kelly's attack, that she'd also consoled me after my breakup with Jordan and that one thing led to another. No one thought less of me. They knew I'd had it rough.

I heard that Jordan was back in Florida now, doing some work for some Miami arts center. She was supposedly also working on her master's. Every now and then I get the urge to call her. Sometimes the ache of her absence is too much to bear. But I don't dare risk it. If Lindsay found out, I'd be screwed.

Besides, knowing Jordan, she's probably started to move on. She's a trooper. We were supposed to get married and be together forever but that didn't happen and Jordan isn't the type to pine away over a lost love. She has things to do. There's a glow about her and nothing I've done has snuffed that out. She'll be fine without me.

I don't know exactly what happened to Detective Cardinal. A friend back in St. Louis mentioned that he'd been passed over for promotion as a result of the way he handled the case in general and me in particular. Supposedly, some of the higher-ups thought he'd put the department at risk. I don't know if that's true and to be honest, I don't want to risk trying to find out. I know it's silly, but on my way to class one day, I could have sworn I saw him in a crowd across the street. But when I looked closer, he was gone. I'm pretty sure it was my imagination.

It might sound odd, but Lindsay's been great. She never lords any of it over me. In fact, since that day at the hospital, she never mentioned our little bargain again. When I disagree with her, she doesn't give me the "are you sure you want to argue with me?" look that I thought would be omnipresent. I haven't disagreed with her on any huge issues yet, so the jury's still out. But for all intents and purposes, we have a normal, totally equal relationship.

Since I'm in school, she's the breadwinner. She works as a junior high school guidance counselor. It's not a ton of money but my parents help a little. She's amazingly attentive. When I get home from class, she's always giving me back rubs and foot massages. She's also a great cook. The truth is she pampers me.

And I have to admit she was right about one thing. We do connect, especially in bed. Lindsay's the most voracious woman I've ever known. She's insatiable. And she seems able to read my mind. I know that doesn't come as a surprise, considering how we hooked up. But half the time, she knows what I'm going to say before I say it. And I'm starting to figure her out, too. I can already predict her moods and her gestures. Sometimes I can sense when she's about to walk through a door.

She says that we're well on our way. Sometimes when we've had a little too much to drink at dinner, she'll start talking about our future. She says that I'm going to be a great attorney and that after we move to New York, I'll be the Manhattan DA by the time I'm thirty. She says I'll be governor by thirty-five and president by forty. I've warned her that her timetable might be a tad optimistic but she won't hear any of it. She says I have the talent, the smarts, and the guile to get there. And she says that I have her. She says she's my secret weapon. I can't disagree with that.

Do you ever stop for a moment to take stock of your life? I figured I would know where my life was headed by now, that I would know my future profession, the person I would be with, and who I was.

As it turns out, I do know all of those things. Of course, the answers to some of those questions are much different than I thought they'd be just nine months ago. But the answers I'd have given back then would have been wishes more than truths. I know now that my future is set. There's a course I must follow and it's mapped out in greater intricacy than I could have ever imagined as a child.

There are things I know about myself that most people never have to face. Sometimes I'm ashamed to know what I'm capable of. But the fact is, that knowledge gives me an extra edge. It gives me a permanent advantage. It gives me power.

Things look a certain way right now. But life is long and

things can change. Five years from now, or maybe ten, Kelly Stone and Dan Curson will be distant memories and I'll be a man of respect and honor. A time will come when the past loses its power. And that's when I'll make my move.